THE RAVEN'S
WARRIOR

DRAGON

Seal Script Calligraphy from the time of the First Emperor
QIN SHI HUANG DI

THE RAVEN'S WARRIR

A NOVEL

VINCENT PRATCHETT

YMAA Publication Center, Inc.
Wolfeboro NH USA

YMAA Publication Center, Inc.
PO Box 480
Wolfeboro, NH 03894
1-800-669-8892 • www.ymaa.com • info@ymaa.com

Paperback edition	Ebook edition
978-1-59439-258-0	978-1-59439-259-7

Editor: Leslie Takao
Cover Design: Axie Breen

POD0613

Publisher's Cataloging in Publication

Pratchett, Vincent.

The raven's warrior : a novel / Vincent Pratchett. -- Wolfeboro, NH : YMAA Publication Center, c2013.

p. ; cm.

ISBN: 978-1-59439-258-0 (pbk.) ; 978-1-59439-259-7 (ebk.)

Summary: Wounded in battle (900 A.D.), a near dead Celtic warrior is taken by Viken raiders and sold into a Baghdad slave market. He is dragged further East, through the desert, into the 'Middle Kingdom' where he is bought by a warrior priest and his beautiful daughter. Hazy images of silk, herbs, needles, potions and steel, can only lead to one thing, he has been purchased by a wizard and his witch. Arkthar fears for his soul.--Publisher.

1. Celts--China--Tenth century--Fiction. 2. Magic, Chinese--Tenth century--Fiction. 3. China--History--Tenth century--Fiction. 4. Taoist priests--China--Tenth century--Fiction. 5. Adventure fiction. 6. Historical fiction. I. Title.

PR9199.4.P73 R38 2013	2012954198
813.6--dc23	1301

Editor's note: Viken is the historical name of a region in southeastern Norway, believed to derive from the Old Norse word vík, meaning cove or inlet. Etymologists have suggested that the modern word "viking" may be derived from this place name, simply meaning "a person from Viken".

Disclaimer: This is a work of fiction. Names, characters, places, and incidents either are the product of the author's imagination or are used fictitiously, and any resemblance to actual persons, living or dead, businesses, companies, events, or locales is entirely coincidental.

Dedicated to my ancestors with respect,
and to my descendants with love.

Every man's life story begins at first breath, but this is not my story alone, and so it begins much closer to my last.

THE BEGINNING

I soar in effortless circles around the plodding caravan far below me, gently riding the desert winds. It is not the glitter of sunlight on jewels that attracts me, for I do not covet the spoils of war, but crave only my humble share of war's terrible outcome. The hot rising air is cradled beneath the feathers of my outstretched wings, and carries with it the tantalizing odor of sand and blood. I fly on, driven by primordial hunger and beckoned by the smell of death. Drawn closer now, I am intrigued, for I have found its source.

I can see him clearly. He is chained behind the cart laden with plunder and pulled by great horned oxen. He jerks and stumbles forward at every tug of the cattle's methodical steps. Blood is the clothing that covers his body. Wounded and tortured, decay did not wait politely for death's cue, and the flies have already joined the feast.

My spirit knows that this cruelty is the work of men, nature is much more merciful. I can see that the dying captive is mad. He raves with agony and fever at every near fall. Nature mercifully has removed mind from body, so his mind knows nothing of its body's plight or pain, and by nature's mercy I sense his journey will soon be over.

But that time has not yet come, and I fly upwards towards the heavens to banish my gloom. As clouds part and early stars move slowly before my eyes, I bite and savor simple concepts, tasting the timeless comfort of universal truths. With pain and blood they are born, they live, create life and take life, and then with blood and pain they leave through Death's cold gateway. It is Death's black finger that puts the final punctuation at the end of every man's life sentence.

It was then that I heard Death laughing, and when he had finished his chuckle he began to speak. "I have heard the delirious ramblings of countless dying minds. I am amused by yours. Heavy philosophy to hapless metaphor, '*my* black finger puts the final punctuation at the end of every man's life sentence?' That is very funny given your circumstance. Fly down with me to see the wretch again." As we flew lower Death continued to speak.

"Many times in many battles I came to take him, but he was elusive and agile. Even though I couldn't reach him, he did my work well and sent me many. Did you know I have whispered to him every step of his journey and still he will not come? Yet even if he does not die along the way, he knows I wait to embrace him at the executioner's block. Why does he resist?"

We angled closer to the man as he continued. "I know this unreasonable tenacity is testimony to the power of life and creation, and to feel life's pulsing strength is a new experience for me, an experience for which I will always be grateful." We flew closer still, and hovered. The stench was intoxicating. I saw the war prisoner's wild eyes, and in a heartbeat ravenous euphoria was replaced by terror.

I saw and understood that this smell of what was once a man was me, and in panic I began falling from the sky.

Death steadied me, "Do not be afraid," he said as I plummeted towards myself. "I came once more to take you, but I am in your debt. You have challenged me, aided me, helped me hear life's song, and finally you have even made me laugh.

'*My* black finger puts the final punctuation at the end of every man's life sentence,'" and his laughter began all over again.

We had begun the final dive of a bird of prey. There was no turning back. We were very close and flew very fast, faster than the speed of reflex. For me there could and would be no stopping. A wing tip away from impact, he flashed his final words. "No punctuation, Vincent, your life sentence has just begun."

Instantly my world blazed white. Like the coals of a forge it cooled, sinking steadily through a sea of red and orange. Finally it settled into the black cold depths of the night, from where I emerged and moved as a man once more.

The fever had broken. The heat and redness around the wound still remained, but my arm no longer ached at every passing heartbeat. The blood that had seemed unstoppable had slowed to a trickle and had cleaned the wound as best it could. Dead flesh was gone, and the children of the flies had also vanished. A mind forced away by the body's anguish has returned to its temple to worship at its altar of bearable suffering once again.

I had survived, I had begun to heal, and I had forgotten everything that Death had said to me.

THE ARRIVAL

My downcast eyes had measured both my journey and my life, but not in length or duration, for me time and distance no longer existed. No, they measured simply by what they had seen. They saw my body, wounded, starved, and ill, wither to the bone. They saw rivers turn to ocean, fields turn into forest, and forest turn to sea. They saw seas become mountains, and the mountains turn to desert.

In the desert they saw the sun paint my body with a color it had never worn, the color of the shifting sands. When they had seen my mummification process complete, they saw more. They saw desert become dusty road, and dust become cobblestone. They told me we had entered the kingdom of my enemy. When they saw the ground before me stop moving, they stopped measuring and told me I had arrived at a far flung outpost. It was here that they struggled to finally look up. I saw the multitude of strange people that surrounded me stretch to the horizon, and I felt only pain.

This was not an ocean of blue and green water, but a sea of brown, and shades of brown like an ocean of sand. It was a vast sea of human waves. It was a desert of the drifting dunes of humanity, and it made my eyes thirst. My eyes did not thirst for water like the flesh does, the endless shades of desert brown made them thirst for color. They had not seen bright colors since the blood had ceased its flow, and now they craved them.

On the distant horizon they saw sunlight split to rainbow, the answer to their prayer. It was like the sparkle of the setting sun on water or a shaft of light shining through jewels. My thirst was quenched, and my pain had faded. My eyes once again saw the people around me, and I felt something stronger than pain. I could feel their fear, their wonder, and their pity, and I wept.

The once distant flash of rainbow drew closer now. The desert of humanity parted before it, and it passed unimpeded. I saw that it was not a cruel mirage of deprivation, but a rider wearing the dazzling cloth colors of red, blue, green, and gold on a background of silver white, and they shimmered magically with his every movement. He was real, and followed closely by a horse-drawn wagon led by a female servant clad in the ordinary brown colors of the desert's caress. My eyes followed their progress.

As they entered the square the servant and cart hovered back, while the man of color approached. His strong graceful movement told me that this one was skilled in the arts of war, and the long straight blade sheathed on his back hinted that my execution was at hand. Beside me now, he spoke in my language but in a tone and rhythm all his own. I had to listen carefully and closely as he asked only my name. Then I had to fight hard to remember it; it had been so long since I had answered to it. "Vincent," I replied as strongly as my voice would allow.

He began to laugh. "Latin, meaning one who conquers," he said. "That is funny given your circumstance." My blood ran cold, for in my world, the one from which I had been so violently taken, being questioned by those that know Latin is almost always followed by a slow and agonizing death. The reality of my present situation flooded in, and I began drowning once again in a dark and paralyzing emptiness.

His first words had plunged me under but his next seemed to grab my head and hold me up, allowing me to breathe again. "Do not despair," he said calmly. "Some believe that the one that endures has conquered." And then a movement faster than an arrow's flight, his hand was drawing up the bladed edge. I could hear it gather speed out of the sheath, and then silence as it cleared and swooped down. I stretched my skinny neck to give a clean target, but instead felt a jerk at my wrists, as his blade's arc bit the chain that had held my hands together for so long. The links fell at my feet like the pruned branches of an olive tree.

Since boyhood I had heard the warriors tell stories of reverence about a sword that could cut through iron like a cleaver through meat, but these were just stories. I had been a soldier my whole life and had never seen one. Now looking at the metal bonds that lay coldly at my feet, I felt strangely complete.

I braced for the next cut, but the sword had returned to sheath, and its wielder had turned to address the throng. Although I didn't understand his words, I clearly understood their meaning. "This man now belongs to me." He directed their attention towards the cart of plunder. He studied the horde and asked, "Are there any objections?" There was only silence as the crowd's interest had now shifted towards the rest of the spoils. His eyes met mine and in a low voice he said, "From today I am your owner. Vincent, your life sentence has just begun." His servant helped me to the wagon as the crowd pushed closer to the treasure-laden cart.

My eyes caught the flash of shadow moving across the ground where a high-flying carrion bird had come between us and the sun, and I knew then that Death would wait.

REBIRTH

The wagon that I fell into was lined with pillows and overlaid with a beautifully patterned carpet. I lay on my side, unmoving, like an egg in its nest, or an unborn baby in a wondrously colored womb. I heard the one who had claimed ownership of me say, "the road home is long and arduous; whether my daughter tends or buries, is not for me to say." I felt the wagon begin to move, and I felt the one who I thought a servant climb in beside me. Clouds above and road below, my eyes closed, and I hovered between two worlds.

The first leg of the journey was difficult. She began her work immediately. I felt the skill of healer in her hands. She massaged me firmly but gently, leaving no damaged areas neglected. Her fingers dug deep enough to draw moans from my broken frame, and then her palms smoothly reassured its bone and tissue. I could feel both strength and confidence in her attention, and I marveled at her dexterity.

This went on day after day, but at week's end I felt I could take no more, and I fell into the fearless sleep of the nearly dead. Through the depths of my slumber I smelled the fire, and as night descended she brought me a soup of bitter herb and beast unknown. After the meal I remember nothing until morning came, and I awoke to the sound and motion of wheel on road once again.

The next week's travel brought more of the same, but was less strenuous. Now I grew used to the pungent aroma of plant and potion. I could feel the infused oils rubbed into my skin surface and beyond. I didn't know if this was to cover my smell or to heal my wounds, and I didn't care. We pulled on, and slowly I began to come back to myself.

My limbs were drawn and stretched, and joints almost immobile began to loosen. Some treatments brought heat, some cold, others I could taste when applied. My body drank this attention like a sponge, and paused occasionally to sip strange teas from the cup she held for me. With each new nightfall I was happy to hear the fire built again, and ate ravenously the stew she served.

Our last full week upon the grinding road began routinely with the rising sun, and her work continued. I watched her slip needles from a pouch and insert them deeply into my arm, chest, and shoulder. I braced for pain, but I felt none, even as she rotated them one after another. The feeling of having nothing and being nothing was beginning to lift, I was no longer burdened by this emptiness, but liberated by it. The insipid smell of desert sand had been replaced by the lush aroma of plant and blossom. My world was turning green, as if spring had come to me at last.

I ate well that evening, and I left the confines of my traveling nest. By firelight I saw their faces, and for the first time I saw how beautiful she really was. I was a man well starved, but I did not hunger openly. I watched her from the cool darkness and was nourished by her presence. The moonlight played on her thick black hair. Its rich luster was like the coat of a wild fresh-run stallion. Her skin was soft even to the touch of my eyes. It had the color of amber spring honey, and the echoed fragrance of jasmine. Honey and jasmine, like the mead of my homeland, I felt strangely light headed as I drank her in.

Their eyes were different than any I had ever seen, black like the richest and darkest wood and shaped like the knots that give it character. Hers picked up the reflection of the bright flames, and banished any trace of the night's chill from my bones. I listened without understanding as they spoke in the language of their world. As I lay down, it washed over me like a wandering brook, and for the first time in a long time I began to dream again. There were the sounds of sword biting metal, the lightness of my arms, the flashing of silver edge, and the feeling of flight. I was both weapon and wielder in an ethereal battle that raged far beyond my waking senses.

By mid-morning well into the fourth week, I was sitting in the wagon. Light still played on the clothing of the rider, and his darkly clad daughter rode with him on the back of his powerful mount. There was life all around us; songbirds were in full form, small creatures scrambled from our approach. Tall trees waved young leaves that caught the soft winds. A movement of his arm spoke that this land was his. We climbed higher and could soon see all around us. Almost hidden in the center of this view, I saw a dwelling.

As we came closer, the grazing animals stopped and looked up at us. Birds swooped closer as if to spy, a raven cried from a branch overhead, and wild deer and game stepped out from foliage just to show themselves to him. We entered the walled courtyard protected by a huge wooden door that closed behind us. We stopped first at the barns, and I was shocked by how well I felt as I stepped onto the ground.

The horses were fed and tended, and the young girl took the sword from her father as if he were himself a horse being stripped of brass, blanket, and bridle. As we walked towards the large house, we passed a deep pond of lilies. I could see fish thrash and surge to hold orange heads above the surface. Their wagging tails reminded me of my wolfhounds, which once jostled happily to greet their returning master.

We entered the house through a great hall. Weapons and armor from all over the world lay scattered from far wall to near. I recognized some, but most looked foreign, from a different place or a different time perhaps. Many pieces were just strewn and dust covered, others seemed waiting to be picked up and handled again. There were spears, clubs, short swords, scimitars, slings, projectiles, helmets, shields, and breastplates.

It brought from my memories tales about the dragon's lair, dark and cavernous, littered with the weapons, armor, and bones of brave souls previously dispatched.

I thought once more of the mythical serpent, childhood dreams and adult nightmares, of journeys ended and journeys begun.

MY MIND'S CONCLUSION

My body's passage over, my mind raced onward to catch and hold the truth. Days before, lying within the moving wagon, it had fought to grasp reality. It had moved in vision from event to event, and weighed each one heavily against the possible and the probable. It saw the one beneath the shimmering robes that could not hide the strength and power of the man who wore them. It fixed itself upon his flashing steel—a sword described in legend.

My mind saw again the creatures of his land, wild animals that at a glance were tamed by his authority. It seemed that every living thing knew its place, and that he was the keeper of this garden. From lofty sky to waters deep, all awaited and respected his command.

It turned from man to girl, and remembered her skillful touch and unworldly beauty. It reviewed the passing of recent events with care and accuracy to avoid all room for error. It saw again the mixing of the plants and potions and remembered the strength giving magic of her bitter teas. It remembered their pungent but not unpleasant smells, it wandered further and held experience up to reason's light.

The needles had been sunk deep beneath my mangled skin, and then rotated one by one, but as if by magic no pain did come. Surely this was not possible in any realm of man. Emotion screamed through my careful logic. This was powerful sorcery bound to witchcraft bold and unrepentant.

I arrived at the certainty that I was to be the object of their ungodly rituals, and sweat ran down my middle back. I thought about how to escape, but I knew I was still far too weak. I felt my blood drain instantly from my face, and as if by curse my limbs hung useless. I have never feared death, but now in every corner of my being I trembled, frail and pathetic. It was not my flesh I dreaded losing, it was my eternal soul.

As if on cue they entered the room and stared at me with concern, alarmed I think by my pallor. "Stand away from me," I shouted. "My enemies have delivered me into the hands of a wizard and his witch. In another time and another place, I would be the one lighting the fires of purification under your feet." I tried to run but tripped over some canes piled near the door. As I struggled to rise she was beside me helping me to my feet, laughing freely like a child. Then in a solemn tone, "I have heard about the burnings," she said.

Her father, too, had finished smiling. "Be at peace," he said, "this is not your time or your place, it is ours. My name is Mah Lin. I am a warrior monk, and the last of my Order. This is my daughter Selah, and in our time and our place she is a respected and skilled practitioner of Traditional Medicine."

"Merlin, Sea Lass," I repeated carefully, while they laughed at my butchered pronunciation. "Rest now and grow strong, and know that my sword has called your name," said the wizard. In my language but with the richness of her tone and meter, "I will show him where he sleeps," said the witch.

I fell asleep that first night thinking about the life that I had lost, and the life that I had found, and the dreams came back to me strongly.

THE NOVICE GATE

From first breath life had not been easy, for he had arrived at a difficult time. Natural disasters had become the norm rather than the exception. If there was no drought, there was flooding, if there was growth, there were locusts. The last two seasons had been the worst that the living could remember. The land was not forgiving. Seeds perished where they were sown. The heavens were not pleased, and for this the earth now suffered.

In the world of men the rich were now poor and the poor were now dead. Animals starved in fields and people starved in hovels. Human flesh was sold in markets, and this two-legged mutton was cheaper than the meat of dog. This was the world into which he was born.

He was a good child and toiled hard beside his parents, but in these times hard work was not enough to build a life or keep a family together. Side by side father and son scaled the mountain and spoke little. The sadness within his heart overpowered any joy that conversation might have brought. Abject poverty had dictated the decision made. When a young mouth can no longer be fed, an alternative must be found. They had told him about the monastery, and he had seen the orange clad monks on many occasions, but he had never wanted to become one.

Although he was only twelve years of age, he had already found his life's love, and it was her that he would miss the most. Her family had lived here in the shadow of the mountain temple, they had been neighbors all of his short life, and now he would see her no more. As the climb leveled and the temple loomed before him, so did fate. The tears that streamed down the haggard face of his father fed the hollow feeling in his gut. A hard embrace would be a son's last memory of the father that loved him but could not keep him. Pushed gently toward the temple's novice gate, the boy stared down to hide his pain.

He sat alone and empty before the massive wooden doors, and thought about his love. He gathered every detail of her within his mind. The night fell like the cold relentless rain, and as the boy shivered, he vowed in heart to hold her memory.

His solitude was shattered with the arrival of the dawn, for with it came another youth. This one had traveled far and was equipped with a comfortable bed roll and a generous supply of food. The new arrival was not pleased to find another, but with an arrogant look he surmised quickly that his predecessor would offer no competition. Both boys were the same age but very different in both appearance and demeanor.

The first to arrive was undernourished and filthy. His unkempt hair lay matted to his forehead, and the rags that draped his skinny body held the odor of the fields. He looked more a beggar's child than an aspiring monk. He stared blankly at his surroundings, downcast. Many in this time shared his look, much work and little food had taken their toll. Yet there was something different about him. Something intangible spoke that while everything about him was broken and weak, something within him was not. The boy was glad that although he had nothing, at least he was no longer alone.

The other was well fed and much bigger. Although he had traveled far from the capital, he still had the look of polish. Dirt did not stick to him. In manner he was confident and focused. He had prepared well for this moment. He had rehearsed answers for any questions, and knew what qualities these monks were looking for. Now all he had to do was wait quietly for the doors to open for him. He would not fidget or look impatient, but within the hour he did both. He thought perhaps he could intimidate his nemesis and saw quickly that any looks in that direction went unnoticed.

For five full days and nights the boys had sat and slept. One cold and hungry, one warm and well fed, one anxious to begin his life within the temple, and one who no longer cared for his life at all. The rains had lashed down until, late into the fifth night, the clouds cleared and the stars appeared. In the darkness that precedes the coming day, a meteor tore a bright swath across the glittering night sky and crashed far off in the distance. As if on cue, the gates opened and the abbot emerged to see what offerings the harsh seasons had brought his temple.

To the eyes of one, the abbot did not look like what he was expecting. For a temple that was supposed to have a vigorous training regime, this monk seemed small and unimposing. Where he had expected to see muscle he saw little definition at all. This abbot's appearance resembled more the beggar boy than any soldier he had ever seen. He tried hard to hide his disappointment. The eyes of the other saw something else, and this one, who had seemed so broken, now gazed boldly and directly into the eyes of the old priest.

Rice and tea were brought, and neither lad moved until the abbot took first bite. The youth that sat on the thick bedroll was now politely eating, but the other urchin did not move at all. The abbot pointed invitingly but realized immediately that this small boy cared no longer whether he lived or died.

The abbot focused on the bigger boy, the one that had purposely made the long journey to join the temple. This one answered all questions asked with studied precision. He made it abundantly clear that all his life he had worked toward joining this temple. When the conversation ended, he sat confidently waiting for the outcome he felt was inevitable.

The old one turned his attention to the other and asked only one question, "Why do you want to join our order?" The mind of the youth formed no thoughtful reply. Instead the boy's entire life flashed before his eyes. In less time than the beating of two hearts, it measured all he had suffered and all he had loved, and ended at the image of his only vow. He answered immediately and honestly, "I do not."

The abbot's laughter pealed out like bells upon the mountaintop, and his decision was as easy as it was immediate. This boy was probably trouble, but brought the gift of truth. The other youth watched in disbelief as the doors he had waited so long to enter were shut and bolted. Through the heavy oak he heard the abbot ask, "Your name, son?" and heard the soft reply, "Mah Lin." He clenched his fists, gathered his rage, and spat upon the closed entrance with all his might.

Without food the homeward journey became a long and bitter march, and with this pain came new direction.

WEAPONS AND WORDS

Four years would pass with only minor incidents, but this time the abbot had heard troubling rumors, and as he studied the face of the novice summoned before him, he knew that they were true. Discipline is the backbone of any sacred order, and the breaking of its trust could not go unnoticed. Mah Lin was still young and held much promise, but his surreptitious night foray must be addressed. The abbot was a kind man, and the monk before him had always reminded him very much of his younger self, headstrong and impetuous, and indeed a bit amorous. He smiled without explanation and thought carefully about the punishment that he would hand out.

"Mah Lin," the abbot began as the young monk moved uncomfortably from side to side, "it has been told that you left these grounds at night and sought the arms of a woman." Mah Lin looked at the floor, a look that was both an answer and a confession. He felt the silk tunic beneath his priestly robes and hoped the abbot did not know of this souvenir. The abbot continued, "This behavior is a bad example to those that look up to you. What could bring you to this reckless course of action?"

Without hesitation the young monk replied, "Love."

Mah Lin was startled by the laughter bursting suddenly from the venerable one. When the abbot had finally collected himself he spoke in serious tone. "Yes, Mah Lin, love is by nature a very strong force, a force that helps to shape and bind the universe, and it is a force that heals and transforms both the body and the soul." The old monk's eyes reflected a journey far back into his own past, and that memory seemed to bring him joy. The eyes of the abbot caught Mah Lin and held him motionless with their intensity.

"From now you will concentrate on your physical training, perhaps if you are tired enough, desire and temptation will be lessened." The abbot seemed satisfied with his own decision, and then said to Mah Lin, "Report back to me in one month. I need time to consider your permanent reprimand, and I do not want to seem headstrong and impetuous." Once again the old one's eyes seemed bright with laughter, and Mah Lin bowing, took his leave.

Mah Lin was confused as he walked down the corridor; the punishment dealt out was no punishment at all, for it was well known that he had taken to the martial disciplines like a bird takes to the air. He would, of course, comply and worry what his permanent castigation would be. For the next month the young monk trained like one possessed, and although his mind still wandered outside the temple walls and to the home of the beautiful woman, he knew that his life's purpose remained within them.

Under the youthful eyes of the old abbot, Mah Lin set to task. The venerable one had seen potential beneath the outer rebellion of the young monk. Sometimes as it was now, a challenge can be a gift and a punishment merely a test.

For the young monk, the day began much sooner than the dawn. His regime now started well before the sounding of the rooster. Nourished only by a hasty breakfast of rice-gruel and vegetables, the vigorous training of mind and body began with stretching and stance. When the other monks were given time for rest and contemplation, the young Mah Lin was made to learn new and more demanding forms. Sweat rolled from his shaved head and over wiry shoulders, where it channeled down like a river guided by the muscles of his sturdy chest.

If this reprimand was designed to break body or spirit, it did neither, for as much as was thrown on the shoulders of the young monk, he took more. When all his brothers were settled for the night, Mah Lin was still practicing the physical lessons of his day. At its end he would descend to the temple library and sweep the dust from floor and shelf, from here he would move on to the polishing of the weapons within the armory and the shoveling of the coal dust from the temple forge. Only then, filthy and exhausted, would he close his eyes long enough to begin another day.

Time flew by; a month seemed like a week. Lately he had taken to looking openly at the sacred texts and brandishing the temple's finest swords. It was here in the lamp lit darkness of the temple cellar that both blade and imagination flew. The day arrived when that flight was cut short by the abbot's stern voice. Mah Lin jumped like a child with a hand caught in the honey jar.

The abbot's words boomed out, "It seems you are drawn to both weapon and word, but as novice you must drink milk before you eat meat, as child you must crawl before you can run. Sword and literature lie at the foundation of our order, but their proper study requires both time and guidance. Report tomorrow and accept your full and permanent retribution, your month has passed."

By morning the stark confines of the abbot's chamber were washed by the soft light of the new day. Mah Lin saw the scrolls hung upon its walls and the gathering of senior monks that sat cross legged where floor met wall. An ancient but exquisite blade had been brought from the temple vault and now lay prominently upon the patriarch's simple desk.

Mah Lin had never seen this sword, but knew by instinct what it was. Often in the quietness of the nights he had heard of its existence, whispered conversations always wrapped in tones of awe and reverence. As Mah Lin wondered if its purpose was to cut him swiftly from the Order, the abbot got straight to the matter at hand.

"Mah Lin, you have violated your sacred trust, and your position within these cloistered walls has been assessed. It has been decided that you are to continue your routine of punishment. Your seniors say that you learn well, but there is still much they have to offer. They will break you or they will build you—time will tell.

In addition, you are now the keeper of the forge and the protector of our sacred library. You will be taught the secrets of transforming earth into metal and study with the most venerable the sacred documents which you are now, with your life, sworn to protect." The abbot lifted the sword from the desk and walked towards the novice, passing it respectfully to the young monk he continued. "This weapon is named The Sword of Five Elements and is the soul of our dwelling. It is your blessing and perhaps your curse. May wisdom guide you in its purpose. Mah Lin, you are dismissed."

And so, as quickly as it began, it was over. Mah Lin walked from the old priest's chambers, still not sure what had just transpired. The abbot for his part smiled and conversed with the senior monks, feeling much younger than his many years. He had known all along that this punishment fit the talented offender well, and that Mah Lin was the only one with the qualities needed for the honor bestowed.

Still reeling from the morning's event, the young monk moved lightly along the hallway and down the stairs. Alone once more, he examined every detail of the sword within his hands, and with the eyes of his soul peered into its depth.

Steel and parchment were now his life's one purpose, and his spirit sailed upon the winds of destiny.

THE SACKING OF
THE TEMPLE

Selah had spent her first six years fatherless, but with no regrets. By age seven she was both strong and resilient, and the taunts of older children were quickly silenced with a small but well aimed fist. In the quiet shadows of night she had often seen her mother lovingly caress the orange robe by her bedside. Instinctively she knew it held a memory and therefore a bond. She did not know, however, that it brought her mother back to that night long ago when a young monk had climbed over the temple walls.

For her mother there would never be anyone else. From conception's first night she would dedicate herself completely to the study of traditional medicine. As she treated her steady stream of patients, Selah would be there helping prepare tonic, antidote, and cure, for ailments of all description. Mother and child would often forage like free animals for the rare and potent healing herbs that grew in the surrounding area. They would speak often of the time when as an adult she would meet the father she had never known, and he would meet the daughter he never knew existed.

She was surprised when the dark and distant plume from the temple summit had brought forth from her mother tears of sorrow. She did not understand the grief with which her mother prepared the cart and said, "We go now to meet your father." She knew only that this was not the joyous meeting that they had talked about so often and for so long. Following her mother's emotional cues, she prepared herself for whatever was to come, and at the age of seven found the strength of steel in her young and innocent soul.

The acrid black smoke that had billowed upward from the ruined temple had changed texture. It hung in the air like the oily black plumage of the crows watching from high places. As the small girl and her mother struggled to pull their cart from mountain path to entrance, the last remnants of a smoldering gate collapsed in what seemed an ominous gesture of welcome.

The open courtyard that had once pulsed with the sounds and routine of sacred monastic life now screamed silently from the faces of the many corpses that lay strewn and scattered about. The actions of the woman and child mirrored perfectly the actions of the scavenging crows; they began methodically to pick apart the dead. This, however, was no common pillage.

They had no interest in the valuable armor and weapons of the many dead soldiers. Instead they searched robe to saffron robe looking relentlessly for him. They sat defeated and still, until a raven cried out from a mountainous pile of armored bodies, awakening them from their despair. They both moved at the same time, and with one mighty push, the black bird flew up and the large body at the top went tumbling down, revealing the treasure that the woman and child had been seeking. They had found Mah Lin.

While the woman struggled with the task at hand, the small girl studied the large black bird. It stood calmly, framed by the open door before it, peering into the dark interior. 'What was it staring at?' she wondered, her childlike curiosity immediately banished fear. When the raven walked inside Selah quickly followed. With awkward hops it led her down the stone steps and disappeared into a cool square room. She stood still, listening for its whereabouts and letting her eyes adjust to the darkness.

Her vision cleared and the scrolls and parchments on the many shelves now became her focus. She scooped up an armful. By dust and smell she knew that they were old and that she must show them to her mother.

By sundown the body of the monk, his sword, and the ancient manuscripts he had died protecting were halfway down the mountain on the rickety wooden cart. The raven was never far away. By deep night they had reached her home and only then did it fly directly to the monk and begin picking, not at the flesh, but at the many arrow shafts protruding whole and broken from chest and torso.

She and her cub moved once more in unison. They pulled open the blood stained robes. Underneath was the silk tunic she had spun for him some eight years ago. It was his way of keeping his one night of transgression close to his heart. With a twist and a pull, the silk eased the many broad-heads out as faithfully as it had stopped their full penetration.

As the door closed behind them, the woman and child gathered all their healing skills, and the black bird flew up to join the darkness.

TRANSITIONS

The pale monk lay still but for the occasional cough and the shallow rising and falling of his powerful chest. Selah sat quietly and watched her mother work. In stoic concentration she went about the business of healing. Infection, blood loss, and trauma were the enemies she fought against, but it was the powerful love of a woman and her daughter that kept the monk on this earthly plain.

Over the next year Selah grew in loves complete embrace. Her father took well to life on the small farm. For him the work was joyous and productive. Even the most mundane tasks were undertaken with nurturing in mind. The love between her parents was as vast and solid as the temple's mighty mountainous foundation. Her father didn't talk much about his former temple life, but by moonlight he would look toward distant peak and remember.

The army that had ravished it did not pursue him. Perhaps they thought that all twenty-one monks had perished, perhaps they thought no surviving monk would continue to live in the temple's mountain shadow, or perhaps they were just smart enough to let sleeping dogs lie. The monk that knew the secrets of blade making, and the protector of the monastery's ancestral wisdom, was now just a simple family man.

For the next eleven years they thrived. Selah, her mother, and Mah Lin lived life with the hearts understanding how strong the bonds of love are, and how fleeting life is. They knew that even if a person lives a hundred years, it is still just a blink of an eye to the mountain. As a family every minute of every day was lived and loved to the fullest.

The rain was gently misting on the day father and daughter returned happily from their labor in the fields. They worked well together and shared a love for all that was nature. They spoke on this day about the changing weather and the coming of the new season. As they crested the last hill before their home, they both fell silent. Selah felt the blood drain from her face and her stomach shrivel.

At a glance they knew that their life had changed. As they neared the house their pace quickened to a run. From a distance they saw that the smoke that always rose up at cooking time was absent. They saw that in its place at the chimney's mouth perched the raven. Both knew even before they opened the door and saw her still form on the floor, their time here as three had ended.

She lay where she had fallen, pale to the eye, and cold like marble to the touch. Her beauty lingered long after her life force had departed. Even in death her features were calm, and serenity was her last expression. Mah Lin knelt beside his love, closed her eyes, and kissed her one last time. Selah opened the fingers of her mother's cool hand and lifted from them the leaves of a freshly picked plant. It was woad, the flowering shrub that boils down to the richest blue. Selah was surprised because her mother had said nothing about dyeing any silk, she looked sadly at the dark green leaves and bright yellow flowers, closed her eyes, and inhaled their gentle fragrance deeply.

Death had been kind and swift. She had not suffered or lingered. Instead she had crossed from the world of flesh in one seamless step. Selah's father said that her heart had just stopped beating, and her spirit had left in a single breath. Perhaps it was because she had put so much of her heart into the healing on that night twelve years ago. In less than a heartbeat, three had become two. For father and daughter their strength and their hope rested in the fact that they still had each other.

Together they buried her by the roots of a young oak tree. Despite Death's kindness, the pain of her passing cut into Mah Lin and Selah like a razor sharp knife.

That evening, they knelt by the earthen hearth of the cooking fire. The orange flames from aromatic wood leapt and licked up the sides of the metal cooking pot. The water boiled fiercely as it changed from liquid to vapor. For a long time there was only silence. Eventually Mah Lin asked Selah what she saw. "The elements, father," was her reply. "Yes, daughter," was his.

They stood up together and reached into the fire for a burning bough. They paused on the way out only long enough to toss it gently on the empty bed. The horse had already been hitched to the wagon and the temple library already loaded. Mah Lin had drawn his sword and sliced furiously at his long dark hair. The blade was soon cutting across scalp and the blood flowed freely but unnoticed. By the time his head was shorn and shaven, the flames had filled the house and poured out and upwards from every opening.

Both father and daughter moved wearily, weighed down by the pain of transition. As they turned together and began walking away, she adjusted the sword on his back, much like her mother would have done. In the dancing light of the raging fire she saw the pentagram on its hilt. On each of the star s five points, a character: fire, earth, metal, water, and wood.

By the time they reached the mountain their old house glowed like a tiny ember, and their previous life had been transformed into just a memory.

RENEWAL

Selah never questioned why or where they were going. This was not the time for talking; it was the time for her unwavering faith in her father's judgment. Dawn was breaking as they reached the base of the temple's mountain, and by mid-morning they had arrived at its blackened summit. She followed him closely with horse and cart, just as she had done with her mother many years before. Now, however, she was no longer a child, but a woman grown rich in both wisdom and beauty.

The brick and mortar that was this place lay scattered and moss covered, like the bones and armor of its dead. She held her trepidation in check and wondered if this is the only peace that war can bring. Their obedient mare had soon found water. It grazed happily in the over grass, content for now with the chance to rest. Both monk and soldier lay where they had fallen. Selah watched her father solemnly go about the business of gathering and piling the skeletal remains of his monastic brothers. Quietly she began to help him with his task.

From a respectable distance she saw her father kneel in silence beside the ragged robed bones of his abbot. To these he summoned life. With closed eyes he recalled time spent and lessons learned. Reaching into the mottled robes of the master, he removed the treasured relic he knew the abbot would have died defending. The metal shone brightly in the sunlight.

Placing the object safely beneath the folds of his tunic the priest said calmly, "The vajra, from the hands of Bodhidharma to the earliest monks of our order." This was the connection of past with present, the object that linked steel to scroll. Seeing the unspoken question in his daughter's eyes he offered more. "The vajra, the library, and the sword – The spirit, the mind, and the body." His role and responsibility within the temple had not ended with the destruction of its mighty walls, it had merely been transformed.

Together on this holy ground they built a crypt of blackened stone like a monument within a monument, and when they had finished Mah Lin began the prayers for the dead. The father and husband that she had known was a good and formidable man, but here at this destroyed temple she saw his strength gather to unearthly proportions. She remembered the monk that mother and child had found broken and lifeless, and now witnessed him emerging from the ashes of these sacred ruins like the phoenix of ancient tales.

Mah Lin continued his search of the mountaintop looking for something other than bone or fragment. He chose carefully from the armor parts and weapons strewn about, some still protecting a long perished body part and some still held tightly in the grip of the dead, as the load of humble cart steadily increased. On the eve of the third day, Mah Lin found what he had been seeking. It lay underneath a fallen shield, undisturbed by the passage of time. The monk picked it up and cleaned it off with the sleeve of his tunic.

He called to Selah to show her what he held in the palm of his outstretched hand. She gazed in wonder at the beautiful artifact, small but substantial, lovingly crafted, and timeless. On the dull bronze pentagon lay the raised metallic image of the imperial dragon. A round hollow lay clutched in its five-clawed talon, and within this circular well a delicate needle lay suspended and precisely balanced. As her father offered this dragon to the four corners of the world, the needle moved quickly around to keep its original place.

"Selah, we have new purpose, and now direction," were the words of the powerful monk, the action of a loving father was an embrace. Only then, within the safety of his protective arms, did her tears fall freely upon his dusty shirt. When the storm of her grief had passed, he stroked her shimmering hair and gently whispered as only a father could, "Selah, we will go now, it is complete."

So it was that they traveled on, their cart carrying the relics of this consecrated place, and their hearts carrying the remnants of their former peaceful lives. As they descended the path with the well-loaded carriage, the sharp-eyed raven took flight and followed, calling out their progress and championing their renewal. Mah Lin knew that the second pair of eyes that had been watching them secretly would also give voice to their actions.

He understood that information would flow upward from hidden sentry to high commander just as surely as the mountain stream flows down from savage peak to gentle lowland.

A NEW DIRECTION

By day and by night they traveled, stopping briefly to cook and eat what sustenance their route graciously provided. Moving relentlessly from north to southeast, Mah Lin would consult the spinning needle and study carefully one of the oldest parchment maps saved from the destroyed temple.

Over the course of their steady progress, Mah Lin explained that not all the manuscripts they carried were from his former monastery. Some, like the map they now followed, came from a much older place, and it was to this place, the place of all origins, that they were heading. It was this sanctuary that would provide them with the safety and protection that they needed, and within these walls of security they would once again build life.

Selah was very much like their dependable load-pulling horse. She never complained about the length or severity of their journey, or even questioned its nebulous purpose. She thought sometimes about the life they had left behind, but realized that they were not so much leaving something as moving towards something else. Her heart knew that the steady pace they had set had both direction from the delicately spinning needle, and purpose reflected in the calm and serious expression worn on the face of her father.

Mah Lin spoke of a world in a state of chaos, like the destruction from the heavens that brings the hail, the rain, and the winds. He spoke of it churning slowly and grinding steadily in its natural and unstoppable rotation. He explained that the place they now sought was a place of refuge from this tempest. The ancient of ancient temple site was the calm within this storm, the eye of this ever-expanding hurricane.

The star filled night sky covered the two travelers like a simple beggar's bowl. As Selah's eyes grew heavy her father's grew more vigilant. He had heard the diminutive sounds of snapping twigs and the slight rustle of leaves in the underbrush. Now he sat calmly waiting, while his skilled hands comfortably touched the familiar wooden sword handle.

From the darkness stepped the huddled and half-hidden figure of an old man. Like a moth attracted by the fire's light he sought to share a morsel, and perhaps some idle nighttime conversation. In truth he desired only the basic warmth of human contact. He was garbed in blackened tattered robes that cried out loudly of neglect, and his head moved coal black eyes from side to side to pierce the darkness. As a skinny arm reached carefully for the hot tea offered, Selah thought about the raven that followed them.

The monk and the beggar shared the fire's comfort and talked well into the quiet night and long after she had fallen asleep. Their tone was for the most part serious, punctuated in places by honest laughter. He was gone by the time she awoke, so she did not see his parting gesture. The beggar had solemnly dropped a large rock onto the skirt of the dying fire. Neither did she know that the dropping of the rock coincided perfectly with the falling head of a distant sentry who had just finished making his last report.

Within the moon's half cycle the end of their travels was in sight. They could see from the sparse lowland an oasis of lush green rising up before them in the distance. It stretched for miles untouched and unvisited by the few locals that lived nearby, for often a land long sacred carries within it the power to remain unmolested. The arrival of monk, woman, horse and cart, to holy ground attracted little attention, and needed no explanation.

To Selah this quiet protected area called to them, as if it had always belonged to them and them to it. As they arrived at its hub, she felt its welcoming nature. It hinted once again at security and family, even though her mother was painfully absent and terribly missed. They moved past the outer walls to the great hall, where they unloaded the weapons and armor from the cart of their tired horse.

The site was ancient, but not in tremendous disarray. It was simpler than most temple structures, more home than place of worship. She would start with a good cleaning. Within only a few months her work and womanly touch began to breathe vitality here once again. A small but adequate garden was soon planted and tended. Wild game was abundant, and before long there were cattle grazing and hens nesting or scratching and pecking as they roamed freely around the place.

Her father renewed his vows of priesthood. Martial training occurred daily, as did the study of the ancient manuscripts that had found their resting place within the structures simple library. All daily chores were done in a way that enhanced his strength and fighting skills, and by evening's lamplight he poured over the written mysteries of age-old documents.

Like her mother before her, it was not long before Selah was collecting and categorizing the medicinal plants growing in this serene location. Also, very much like her mother, she had begun to feed mulberry leaves to the worms, and spin, dye, and weave their silken bounty. Her father meanwhile seemed more focused than ever.

The destroyed ruins of his former monastery hovered high and silent on the distant mountaintop, but its essence lived on within his soul. Day by day he methodically prepared spirit, mind, and body, for a challenge he sensed inevitably drawing closer.

The oldest scrolls were painted more than a thousand years before, from the time of the First Emperor. One particular passage veiled in the prophetic tradition held his attention, and he meditated daily upon its words. He soared with wings of wisdom to places of light and darkness and ascended toward the serenity of understanding, duty, and acceptance.

> "From setting sun a man doth come, beaten by the rain,
> Drawing sword from stone, he will rise through blood and pain.
> From slave to king, to free the beast, that lies beneath the hill,
> Eternity the last embrace and Death must drink its fill."

Mah Lin listened to the raven's call, and within the echoes of its fading cry, the priest heard much more.

The day that she had finished making her father his richly colored full silk robes marked the creation of a new weaving, a cloth long ago finished and only now begun. "Selah," he said, "a man soon arrives. Since the beginning of time we three were woven together. Make ready the cart, and give the raven an extra tasty morsel. We must leave to collect him." Selah was surprised by the news, but obeyed without question.

She set to her tasks with a smile, intrigued by her father's enigmatic tone and amused that he had noticed she had taken to feeding the bird that had long claimed them as its own.

SLAUGHTER AND STEEL

By the glow of moonlight, the battalion quietly snaked its way up the temple mountain like a great mythical beast. Some of the old veterans felt that the young general's rise up through the ranks had been far too rapid. He was not well seasoned in battle, and the few he had fought had been little more than skirmish.

Although competent, to those that knew well the temper of war, disturbing traits had surfaced. This handsome general chose his opposition carefully. These lesser adversaries were dispatched cruelly. By taking as few risks as possible he had moved up in the military machine, for as the old ones often joked, "Ambition and avarice are easier to quietly promote than to loudly rectify."

The emperor had learned that this monastery held the secret of the world's finest blades. He had watched his young general test one recently acquired. The spring steel swords that were the standard issue of his troops snapped like twigs under its onslaught. Before an army of these, nothing could stand. He had given these monks the honor and opportunity of gifting their country, but citing religion, they had politely refused. Strong principle coupled with superior arms is a dangerous combination, and not one that could be allowed to survive.

The general's past had secured his first large assignment. He knew the layout of the temple grounds. Karma—this direction had not been the intended one, yet it brought him back to this place. He knew that these monks were not a simple collection of spiritual misfits. He knew that they practiced martial arts but that their way was one of peace.

His rejection by the soft weak abbot, and the smell of the dirty boy returned vividly to his mind and vengeance ruled his judgment. He hated this place and the monks within its walls. Their piety, wisdom, and peace had long ceased to hold a place within his world. They had been given the option of life but instead chose death, and now they would taste the bitterness that faith and devotion bring.

By dawn the general and his entire battalion had taken up their position on the mountaintop. The armor of horse and rider greedily drank in the new morning rays and reflected nothing. Not a single bird sang out as five hundred heavily armed and battle seasoned soldiers waited for the order. Surprise would not be necessary for they held the overwhelming strength of number. Although a mundane operation, it would not be joyless.

The general carefully reviewed his mission one last time. He alone knew what would be done. All the monks must die, and the great library would be carried back and handed triumphantly to the emperor; extermination and presentation. With his first gesture the heavy oak wood of the temple gate was set ablaze. He smiled as the fires were lit against doors that had once been closed in his face. The smoke from the wood stacked upon them curled frantically skyward, from black to white and whiter still, until angry flames burst forth to do their work. Within the hour the protective gateway was weakened and breeched, the soldiers poured in and the slaughter began.

Not even the most battle hardened expected the resistance they met. In an instant what the general thought their strength had become their weakness. They fell by the score, cut down by monk steel like wheat in a summer's field. They stepped and slipped on their fallen comrades pushed forward by the weight of their sheer numbers. The void left by absent birdsong was filled that morning by the nightmarish screams of the dying soldiers. Inevitably the gore robed monks began to fall, and of them, not one cried out.

He sat upon his horse and for most of the conflict stayed well back and out of harm's way. For him appearance was everything. In the eyes of his men he must seem to be strong when he knew he was weak, he must seem to be brave when he knew he was fearful, and must seem to be clear when all thought was confusion. The steed beneath him jostled without direction as, with sword in hand, the general shouted meaningless orders to his falling soldiers.

He wore his bravado like a loud and boastful cape; a cape that he hoped hid from his men the sum of all of his fears. He was prepared for softness, but instead faced hard warriors. These men did not die like lambs, but fought with a skill that the general had never been allowed to know. Victory had become a battle of attrition.

All the monks that fell that fateful morning fought and died like true warriors, but even in the company of these heroes one monk stood above the rest. With strength, skill, and courage, this singular monk inspired his brothers throughout the battle. He held his ground on a growing pile of bodies, while the remnants of his monastic order fell one by one. Eventually, only this one still lived, and the storm of battle raged solely around him. He was the last of his order.

His silver blade flashed through flesh and sunlight, its razor edge the border of life and death.

REVENGE

Recognition struck like a thunder clap. He knew this monk. His features had changed little—he could still smell the dirty little boy.

Even from horseback the general had to look up at the sole survivor. The monk fought like a wild animal high upon the hill of those who had fallen under his blade. Steel moved too fast around the monk to be seen, but on the slower moving hilt of the young monk's sword, the general glimpsed a pentagram within a circle.

The face of the monk was almost completely covered by the blood of those that had tried to take his life. The vivid colors, the smell of dying, the sounds of agony; these were memories seared into the mind of the general. But it was the eyes of the monk, eyes that spoke of true power that branded the general's very soul.

Amid the chaos of war and destruction the general saw a man at peace. In the chilling heart of combat he witnessed monks inspired and emboldened by this man's true courage. He saw men follow without question. No amount of blood could obscure the terrible truth: this monk was everything that he was not, and everything that he had wanted, all his life, to be.

Like a jackal he waited until the monk was fighting with the strongest and largest soldier in his command. With the monk engaged face to face with the massive soldier, horse and rider moved in quietly from behind. For the task at hand, timing was everything.

The monk continued to fight with a strength that verged on legendary. The general paused while his archers took their positions, and then he shouted the order to fire. Horse and general charged forward and upward to take the head. He moved quickly now to silence the voice of inner demons as he charged toward glory.

To the eye all three things happened at the same time. Ten arrows hit their mark, the last sweep of the falling monk's blade cut through the huge soldier's weapon and found the heart, and the blade of the general was launched upon its deadly journey to an unprotected neck. But at the edge of life and death, time slows and events that seem simultaneous unfold in separate clarity.

Mah Lin did not see the severed tip of the giant's saber flying past his shoulder for the arrows landed and his body dropped. He did not sense the impending blow to his neck, nor hear the aspiring assassin behind him scream and fall backwards as that forged steel tip sliced through his face, cleaving bone from sinew. He did not feel the hulking weight of adversary crush out his last breath, whispering through arrow holes as it crashed down and buried him.

The lower jaw clung precariously by shredded flesh to its place upon the general's features. It tried to form the order to find and remove the library, but it could not. Through the pain and the fog of seething hatred, the general looked back to where the last monk had stood. The giant lay dead and fallen, and the monk as if by magic had vanished into the thin morning air.

The general surrendered to the darkness.

In the Eyes of
an Emperor

In the aftermath of battle the monk was nowhere to be found. This ruined monastery was now a place of fear and phantom. In great haste what remained of the battalion left the mountaintop. The dead, even their own, were left where they had fallen, and the living were gone before the sun had set. They tied their wounded general securely to his horse, and for the next three days and nights he slipped fitfully in and out of consciousness. The image of the fearless monk never left his mind. It haunted him in his delirium—the specter of his own inadequacy.

While this young general lay recovering from his open wound, the emperor's own men had reported that the scrolls had not been found. There may have once been a library, but a pile of bodies and barren shelves were all that remained. The empty structure was carefully combed from floor to ceiling for any clue, but the timeless collection of sacred knowledge had vanished as though it had never been. The black feather of a nameless bird went unnoticed by the men who searched unsuccessfully for scroll, silk, and parchment.

The vision of the Son of Heaven does not compare to the sight of an ordinary man. For the sake of a people, it must be clear from western desert to eastern ocean and from ice-bound northland to wild and humid southern jungles. The emperor stared through the wounded soldier that lay before him. He assessed the condition of the butchered general, and with his mind's acumen he surveyed the success and failure of the mission.

The monks were dead. The threat of their great metal was now removed. The method of its making destroyed beyond any skill of resurrection. The loss of this art was a regrettable casualty of war, but the security that it afforded balanced well against the deficit. The mind of the emperor did not stop there. It browsed within the missing library, and it hungered.

Throughout the ages its secrets had been guarded by the cloistered hands that held it, its reputation grown freely in rumor. This was not just the usual collection of monastic sutras and scripture. It was so much more. In reverent tones it was said to hold the wisdom of the ages, from both this land and places far away. Its fading pages were thought to have descended from the time of the First Emperor. It was whispered that among its yellowed parchments, the arts of war rested peacefully beside the way of enlightenment, and that even the enigma of immortality was recorded on its pages. Like the methods of their metal this treasure, too, was gone, but this loss could never find a balance.

The general moaned, fighting his way to consciousness only to feel the sting of his emperor's words. "You are an efficient killing machine, but much was trampled in the fray." The swollen eyes of the general blinked slowly as the emperor continued. "You are now the Supreme Commander, but do not dare think this a promotion for a job well done. It is not. Consider it merely a gift from the times. The people need heroes, and luckily your face destroyed in the service of your emperor has made you one."

It was officially recorded as a successful completion of mission, but it had taken one hundred and seventy three lives to do it. More accurate but unrecorded was the truth that under the direction of an ambitious and untested leader, the strength of the enemy had been grossly underestimated, and that the value of what had not been recovered far outweighed the measure of anything that had been gained.

The pain of the emperor's harsh rebuke and the emptiness of his movement up the ranks did not fade with the healing of his wounds. The commander, however, embraced the power of his title despite its dubious origin. When the wounded leader had healed enough to slur an order, a permanent sentry was posted at the site, but no order for search or salvage was ever issued.

The presence of a guard assured the new commander that the cinders of truth would never again be stirred, and he hoped that by taking no plunder he might seal up the ghosts of his past. For the next twelve years, the commander's man on the mountain had nothing of any consequence to report.

OLD WOUNDS REOPEN

The commander had changed much in the twelve years since the slaughter. His oily black hair sat in a topknot, and he had grown a beard to try and hide his ruined face. The armor that he now wore at all times was ornate and polished. His memory of that day had not faded or softened. The dead monks upon the mountaintop were silent and forgotten by most, but the figure of the last spectral monk still haunted the general. Hatred had taken root in the darkness of his soul and grown like a twisted leafless tree.

The sentry entered the hall of the commander and dropped in servitude like a stone. He moved forward on hand and knee, face to ground, grateful at least not to look at the grotesquely slashed features of the commander's face. He made his factual report of all that he had seen from his hiding place seven days before. He spoke of monk, woman, and wagon, the collecting of bones and the building of their resting place. He spoke of the prayers for the dead. Still prone, he finished his monotone and waited to be dismissed.

He did not hear the sound of the Supreme Commander's sword being drawn or the sound of his own severed head hitting the cold stone floor. He heard only the thud of a fated rock, dropped on the ashes of a distant and dying night fire many miles away.

The execution was justified by sighting cowardice, lack of initiative, and for not knowing the exact direction of travel. In truth, however, the commander was undone. To hear the monk still lived, and was indeed a mortal man, exhumed the buried demons of his past, and hatred had driven him. He felt the pain again as if his wounds were fresh. His right hand squeezed the razor sharp sword tip that hung like a jewel from a chain around his neck. He stared back into the darkness of events long past, oblivious to the blood dripping from hand to floor and joining the dark pool forming around the sentry's headless body.

For every two eyes there is one mouth, and three full seasons would pass before a tale found its way to the ears of the commander. He listened intently to the story of a monk of great stature and a fair young woman far to the west claiming and transporting the human refuse of war's far-flung campaign. This thieving monk from first meeting had come away the victor. He had stolen his place as aspiring novice, robbed him of his greatest victory, and now purloined the spoils of war. The commander sat, a hollow disfigured leader in a command that he had not earned by deed or merit.

He waited impatiently over the next season for more information, but none came. Here the trail would grow cold, not a whisper not a rumor, as if the earth itself had swallowed them up. The commander found this silence deafening. He knew by instinct that where this monk rested the scrolls of the lost library would be found, and that his redemption in the eyes of his emperor lay in their recovery.

FIRST BLOOD

Amid the rugged beauty of the highlands, forge and stable were sheltered under one thatched roof. While most of the men were raiding, the orphaned child stayed with the smith and worked as best he could for a meal and a sleeping place within the straw. Not family as most would know it, but these were all he had.

Some were kind most were not, his survival hinged on mistrust. At night the boy moved well among the men, filling cups when most were too drunk to walk or pour. He had his niche, slicing gracefully through the darkness serving wine and listening to the rambling stories of the warriors. At an early age he knew well to be useful, but not visible. He could tell by tone when to attend and when to escape, for mood in camp could change with a swallow. The boy learned well how to seize opportunity, for in the company of brigands and mercenaries mead loosened purse strings as well as tongues.

The men had fought that day, a bloody skirmish if the talk was to be believed. When coupled with a full moon, the boy knew well to be vigilant. By firelight he felt the eyes of a tattooed warrior upon him and responded cautiously to the signal for more drink. The small boy did not like the way this one looked at him or the way that he smiled when his cup had been filled. He dodged the arm reaching drunkenly through the darkness and moved with haste to serve in the comfort of others.

The night concluded without event. The boy had done his work well and was the last to find sleep, for the men now lay snoring around the fading fire. He found a private place away from the group. Standing before the small tree, he felt the soft touch of its wet leaves on his face and shivered as he released his water. Tired from his long day, he looked forward to the quiet warmth of his nest.

From the blackness the man pounced.

The cry that would have issued was silenced as all wind was crushed from his delicate body by the weight of his foe. He could smell the man. Alcohol and sweat mingled with the stench of bad intentions. A tattooed hand gripped the top of his trousers and roughly tried to pull them down. The boy knew what was upon him, what pushed his face into the night mud drowning him silently beneath the mire. He knew what rape was.

He moved past the panic of his voiceless scream searching for a solution to a situation that seemed beyond his control. No one could protect him, he was truly alone. Small hands grasped at anything that they could touch until the fingers of his right closed around a dried and broken forest branch. They were called lossoughs, and he had picked them on many mornings, for nothing was better to start the fire of an early forge than these. The familiar feel brought comfort, and comfort brought hope. There would be only one chance.

His attacker turned the struggling boy over and fumbled with the task of loosening his own belt. He pressed his filthy hand across the small mouth as he reached down inside his tunic. Here the boy struck. The thick, pointed stick found an eye. The cry of pain cut through the darkness. It was the sound that should have come from the lad but could not. With a kick of both legs, he was free and snatched the warrior's short sword away in both his tiny hands. He did not stop.

He hacked the kneeling giant savagely. He smelt the blood and felt its warm wetness paint his face and body, and still he slashed. The rage that was his life drove him onward, unaware of when the man no longer knelt or when the man had perished. The boy was still cutting with all his might when the others broke upon the scene. It was the smith that wrapped him gently in mighty arms and whispered soothing truths, "Vincent, stop now, it is enough."

All stood quietly in the forest, taken by the scene that they had come upon. The boy was blood soaked but unhurt, the warrior did not fare as well. His corpse was stretched upon the ground recognizable only by its heavy tattoos. The chest was open and hollow, and in the small clenched fist of his left hand, the boy held the dripping heart of his adversary.

As is common in the world of war and atrocity, nothing more was spoken of the night's event. The smith held the boy closely as he led him towards the stable. He saw the look in the lad's wild eyes and knew that this one now had the taste of blood. That would serve him well he thought, as would the short sword the warrior no longer needed. By midday he had finished sharpening it anew, and this small one had joined the ranks of men. The civil world of fire and straw was now behind him.

The smith was impressed with the sharpness of his own handiwork. This child is different he mused, and as he placed the freshly honed weapon into the boy's young hands he drew him near.

"Vincent, may the force that made you guide and protect your path, and may God have mercy on your enemies."

THE SHIELD

His first foray into the world of men was less than success-ful, and his first skirmish did not last long. With a child's fool-ishness he thought it would be the most memorable, but in fact, he was left with almost no memory of it at all. He picked his target, a large lowlander with a wooden shield, and attacked with all the spirit of a full grown Celtic warrior. That was his only surviving recollection.

By God's mercy a large mercenary had befriended the boy and kept a watchful eye. He was skilled enough to finish what the boy had started, fast enough to pull him from where he had fallen, and kind enough to bear the wounded boy home. Vincent had been unconscious for the two-day carry, the first and only casualty of this excursion. He was laid groaning upon the familiar straw and held down throughout the night as he thrashed violently against enemies that only he could see.

The one that had hauled him stayed with him, watching to see which way the lad would go. The soldier wondered to himself why he had worked so hard on the boy's behalf. The smith assured him that this one was worth saving, and that he was right to intervene.

Like the worst hangover, morning light brought agony and confusion. The dull ache in Vincent's neck contrasted with the sharp pains shooting down from his head. This sobriety was not a pleasant state, and his missing reality would have to be filled in by others gradually, one painful fragment at a time.

For now, however, he lay where he was dropped. Eventually he deployed tentative fingers to survey his damaged skull.

"A simple fracture, leave it alone," the smith told him, while the soldier added, "You forgot about the shield." In truth he had forgotten the entire encounter. The event, however, was not without lesson.

For a Celt the head is the seat of power, the house of the soul, and his would have to be rebuilt. He could not stand. His balance was undone, and there was no hearing on his left side. Fingers again explored, dipping into the clear brown fluid that leaked freely from his ear. It was the smell of it that disturbed him, for it seemed better suited to another orifice.

Over the changing of the next full moon, the boy lay restlessly for the time of his healing. On the nights when he was alone, the buried memories of the tattooed menace he had butchered surfaced. These were now with him forever, his first express direction from Death. He wondered why his brain would haunt him with these, but not release the events of his own wounding, for surely they would have been more valuable in his growth as warrior. Then again he knew that his mind, no matter how noble its thoughts, floated in a stinking pool of clear brown fluid. Its fluvial discharge still dripped occasionally from his damaged ear. So how much was it to be trusted?

In time he healed. Although his body was weak from inactivity, his hearing and balance had gradually returned. The boy came to know that death would be his life's work, and he accepted this without a struggle. It was clear to him that life was brutal and his would probably be brief. He held the short sword in his hand and ran a finger along its edge. His broken head and temporary frailty were a blessing, for with this wound came the strength of resolution. Vincent sought the one that had saved his life and begged for any lesson that he could give.

The man was rough but not stupid. There would not be another carry home. He introduced the boy to the way of the blade, and Vincent returned the favor by applying the lessons learned with ever increasing skill.

LIFE SPEAKS

I knew the dreams were upon me that first night, but after wakening to the sounds of warm conversation and the smell of the evening meal already beginning to cook, they quickly faded and disappeared. I heard a rooster crowing proudly over his domain, but continued to lie motionless pretending to be asleep and listening carefully for tones of treachery in a language I did not understand. For the next hour I lay with body still but ears active, expecting anything. Only when I was sure that there would be nothing did I stand up and walk into the main room.

Merlin and the Sea Lass greeted me warmly and bid me sit down upon the cushions that leaned against the thick stone walls. Together they examined and discussed my torn arm, obviously pleased by its steady healing. She held my wrist quietly with three fingers as if listening to much deeper rhythms, and then both looked upon my tongue as if it was a visual gateway to the inner workings of my battered body.

Finally and most strangely she steadied my head between her gentle hands and gazed directly into my eyes. I thought it might be her way of spell casting, but I had not the strength to resist and so stared back into the liquid brown beauty that were hers.

Her father interrupted tersely, indicating points on my body with a well-seasoned finger, and then smoothly she drew her pouch. My body was already jumping up and back even before my eyes told it the painless needles were coming. I would not bear this witchcraft again, and I braced myself for a fight.

The two were wide eyed at my agility, and their easy laughter rang in my ears. Sea Lass spoke for both as Merlin tried to collect himself. "Judging by your many scars, you have no fear of sword or spear, yet you are terrified by the small steel that will help to make you whole. Father, show him what he fears."

Merlin, still smiling, held out the tiny shard to me as if presenting a flower, and I looked at it with wonder. It was a perfect round bladed miniature sword. I took it and pushed against it with my finger. It bent like spring grass on a windy day. Remarkably it rebounded back to its original shape. I had never seen metal so small, so alive, and so skillfully created. "My father made them," the Sea Lass said, "He is a master."

I quickly caught the beauty of her eyes and spoke strongly, "Just because he owns me does not make him my master." She mimicked my tone and replied, "That is both honest and profound, but I was referring to his ability to create with metal." I realized as they began to laugh again that both her statements were indeed true, and that I had misunderstood. I pensively allowed the needle treatment to continue.

Afterwards I was served a delicious breakfast of rice-gruel, fruit, and honey, and felt more an honored guest than a slave. As I feasted, Sea Lass offered a well-packed lunch to her father as he turned to me and spoke, "I go now to tend the land. You are still very weak, stay with Selah and help her with the household chores. We will speak more this evening." With that he left, stuffing his lunch inside the chest of his simple work shirt, and I was alone with the one who had already begun to enchant me.

She moved with grace and lightness around the house, unconcerned by my presence and sometimes singing sweetly in her own language. I wondered why they trusted me, for even weak I am a dangerous man. As I stared at her back, I reasoned that she would not be hard to kill. She turned to me and smiled innocently, untouched by the darkness of my thoughts. Holding two buckets she invited me to follow her while she drew milk from the cows.

Outside she flung down oats for the clucking hens, stopped and stooped by the path, looking upon a bustling nest of large black ants. As we approached the fields, she walked to the hedgerow and seemed to speak to the briers. The cows came running to her like large happy pets, and soon both buckets were overflowing with their frothy white bounty.

As she looked up into the clear blue sky at the high flying birds, I found myself doing the exact same thing. "What is your forecast?" she asked softly. It seemed a strange question for such a beautiful day. "A fair and sunny spring day," was how I answered. Smiling now, she said, "If we move quickly, we will be back to the house before the rains unleash." No sooner were we inside placing the buckets of milk on the table, than the skies opened up and the heavy downpour began.

I was quiet for a while, grateful for the warmth and dryness of the house, unsure about questioning her arcane powers, but curiosity overruled and I asked her how she knew. "The hens, the ants, the hedgerow, and the high flying birds all told me the same story of the rainstorm coming," she said, smiling at the look on my face. "Don't worry; talking to the world around us is not witchcraft. It is the wisdom of the old ways, passed from mother to daughter since time was young."

I heard her words without really understanding, but knew clearly that those words, if uttered in my world, were more than enough to have her bound, burned, and scattered by the winds. As if reading my thoughts, she placed a comforting hand on my good shoulder and spoke in a tone that was both calm and reassuring.

"Vincent, when you see that the hens will not stray far from where they sleep, you know that a storm is coming." She continued evenly, "The dirt piled in beads around the opening of the ant's nest is spread wide and funnel shaped on a fine day. When they build the opening high and narrow, it is because they feel the changing weather. Not even the tiny creatures want their home flooded and their family drowned."

She handed me a cup of warm milk and tea.

"The leaves on the briers turn toward the coming storm and curl up like cups to catch the water. The birds that fly so high are riding and rising on huge pockets of air displaced upward by the next one moving in and under from the direction of the distant ocean. It is not witchcraft; it is just listening to the world of nature as it speaks to us."

I could hear Merlin returning from his day, and as his daughter rushed to meet him, I heard the raven's distant call carried upon the winds. The life that I had lived had evaporated like the desert dew. It had risen from me somewhere over the blistering sands. I weighed the memory of my former grim existence, and knew in heart that it was not worth fighting for. I had fallen helpless and frail into this strange world, like a child lost in an unknown wilderness. There was no escape. I closed my eyes to bring the darkness and drew deep breath to drink it in.

Exhaling long and slow, I took my first step on a road that I had never walked. Within my soul, the words gathered and then, "I surrender," tumbled out through my parched cracked lips.

DREAMS

Merlin's return was marked by a kiss from his daughter. If they had heard my submission they made no response. His sharp eyes smiled to me warmly. His hands were blackened and his clothes held the odor of a clean fire's smoke. As he prepared to wash, the Sea Lass threw in the finishing spices to the evening meal and bid me set the bowls on the large round table.

While we ate, the Sea Lass talked to her father happily about her day. She pantomimed as she spoke, so that I could guess her meaning. I was entertained by her gestures as she spoke about the state of the animals, the eggs collected, and the sudden downpour. The food that we ate was fresh and hearty, flavored artfully with spices the likes of which I had never before tasted. Sharing a family meal was also something I had never tasted, and I was grateful to be part of it.

Eventually the animated conversation came my way as Merlin knowingly caught my eye and asked, "Vincent, what did you dream last night?" I felt like one struck by lightning as the memory of my night visions flooded back into my consciousness.

I gathered the details in my mind and prepared to speak my dreams. "Merlin," I began, "I dreamt of a mountain of fire. The three of us were strangely walking toward it instead of running away. We could see the smoke rise up and darken the sun, and we could hear the mountain roar and cry out with the pains of birth, and in our legs we could feel the earth beneath us tremble and shudder. The wounds in its peak and sides oozed thick molten blood that ran down beyond its base like a slow moving river. We could feel its oven's heat on our faces, and white ash was landing on our clothes like a new winter's snowfall."

There was a deep silence at the table as Merlin and Sea Lass collected their thoughts. It was clear that my dream meant more to them than it had to me. The Sea Lass poured steaming tea into three small cups. Merlin sipped quietly before he spoke, and then he said only, "Your dreams are strong." With a wave of his arm they rose and proceeded down a large hallway. I followed them out and into a sparse lamp lit room.

The sword in its sheath lay alone upon a great oak table. The hollow shelves hewn in the stone walls were filled with parchment, leather, silk, and scroll documents of an age as great as the stones themselves. I had no words to speak and felt like a man cleaved in two. My hands and body reached to touch the star sculpted on the sword hilt, while my eyes and mind reached out to the shelves to touch the ancient words and symbols that I could not read or understand. It was the sound of Merlin's voice and the sight of his daughter's gentle face that brought me back to myself, whole once more. Nodding towards the weapon, "It knows you," he said.

I watched for permission in Merlin's eyes, as I lifted sword from table and drew it half way to study its blade. The steel was layered in a pattern of strength and beauty. Its flowing design spoke to me of chaos folded into unity. Its polished surface suggested the texture of boundless ocean waves and endless desert dunes. It was amazingly light of weight yet substantial, and as I held it, it became an extension of both my arm and mind. I could almost feel its birth and pulse, the clang of cold hammer on white hot metal that gave it life so long ago. I slid it back into its sheath reverently and set it down.

We all retired to the main room and sat by the earthen hearth, but the feeling of the monk's sword did not leave my hands. I watched the fire play and roll along the soot covered bottom of the large kettle, and listened to the steady clanging of its lid as the water within it boiled and bubbled. I scanned the hearth from bottom to top. I saw the hearth's earthen floor, its burning wood, the nimble flames, its silver kettle, and its bubbling water, and I wondered to myself what would happen if the lid could not rise up to release the pressure.

The Sea Lass broke my thoughts with, "Father made the kettle."

"I know," I said dryly, "your father is a master."

It had been a long time since I had heard the sound of my own laughter, and as Merlin and Sea Lass added theirs, I felt warmed and comforted by much more than just the glowing hearth.

THE MOTHER

I awoke once more to the bubbling sounds of their easy banter and the comforting smell of the delicious evening meal already beginning to simmer. I was sorry to have missed Merlin's departure, but grateful to share the simple chores of his daughter's day. The way of keeping a home was new to me, and I had always thought it woman's work, but now it held my interest. I realized that as my world had changed so too had I.

I watched her carefully from a distance, moving around the ancient homestead like a queen travels through her kingdom. Her domain was uncluttered and simple, elegant in both design and adornment. The space was functional in its layout. A small room filled with harvest bounty was attached to the simple kitchen, and it was here that Sea Lass spent the early part of her day. She sang as she worked and gestured for me to enter as she continued with her daily routine.

Sacks of the pale grain they called rice sat patiently on the floor, waiting to be cooked and presented for our sustenance and satisfaction. Her attention was focused on the many plants and herbs that hung root to tip from the substantial wooden beams that lined the ceiling. She had plucked a mixed handful and laid them sequentially on the table before us. Without surprise I recognized none, for botany held little importance in my past existence. Most were dry and brittle and seemed well ready to be thrown out.

Once again, she must have caught those thoughts, for, smiling, she rolled some desiccated foliage vigorously between her palms and held them up to my face. I inhaled deeply with closed eyes and drank in the infused power of the rugged landscape. The pungent aroma released by the heat of her hands spoke of the season of their past growth, the sun, the rain, the soil, and the gentle balance of their place within it.

Whether to season our food or to heal affliction, her purposeful actions freed the dormant vitality from the withered leaves of a plant that seemed long dead.

I held a stem gently between my calloused fingers, as I teased its clump of roots I saw the dirt land on the crude wooden countertop like the white soot from the chimneys of my homeland. She drew me from this idle action with a question, "Where do you come from?" was all she asked. From the roots and the soil I looked up into the wide brown eyes of a curious child, and realized I had all but forgotten my past.

I closed my eyes to banish time and distance, as memory began to conjure the dark phantoms of my own history. They opened slowly and fixed upon the delicate root and soil that lay before me, and speech gave my past both voice and life.

"Sea Lass," I began, "The place from where I come is a mother blessed with beauty and fertility. She wears robes of living green, and all its shades cover her hills and valleys in a complete and seamless embrace. In her western reaches she is adorned with rock and mountains. It is in place both harsh and generous, and she wears this landscape like precious jewelry. She has always given openly, so that man and beast may live and prosper from one generation to the next." My eyes closed once more to search with my thoughts the visions I had left behind, and she waited quietly and patiently for more.

"On all sides she is held by the sea, sometimes gently caressed, and sometimes savagely pounded by the fury of her wild lover. From ocean and sky she draws the weather, and it falls as rain. This rain is what keeps her and makes her whole, and it is the rain that speaks her very moods. Sometimes it falls light and gentle like a mist that delights the senses, but sometimes it drives heavy cold and hard and carries the taste of ocean salt, like tears. From these heavenly tears of sorrow and joy, all life does come." My memories now welled up within me and spilt out in truth unstoppable.

I spoke slowly so that she could more easily understand, "I knew no parents, my father died at the hands of the Norse raiders and my mother was taken never to return, but that was longer ago than I remember. When God takes with one hand he gives with the other, and for a child with nothing I had something beyond measure. I had the land of my ancestors written upon my heart. Its people, my people, were written upon my soul. With the passage of time, my body grew strong and I acquired the skills of war."

My voice bounced within the confines of the small room, "In this great land, my land, where farmers till and toil, a man with a sword has his place and purpose, for farmers are bound by land and family, and I was without either. The short sharp iron gave me a way to carve my niche and fill my belly, I did not prosper, but I did survive. Battles were my bread and their spoils my butter, for morality does not feed the body. The scarred furrow of war was the trough at which I drank, and at this trough I did drink deeply."

Silence settled in the room around us, my thoughts returned from my world to theirs. Her head was bowed, and her hands rested on the rough-hewn countertop. I had spoken for the first time of my parents and my homeland. I looked down upon the delicate plant that lay before me, and my thoughts journeyed home once more. Vividly my mind's eye beheld the savage Norsemen, and once again my mind's ear heard the screams from the darkness, but to these thoughts and memories, I could never give a voice.

As the lass looked down at the plant that I had been holding, a solitary tear fell upon its coiled roots, and the grey soil that still tenaciously clung to it turned mud black.

THE ROOTS ARE SEVERED

"Do not cry for me," I said softly, "For I have shed enough tears for both my homeland and my clan." I spoke no more, for although my words did purge my soul, they came with a price of awakened pain and sorrow. There would be no more speech, but memory tumbled and rose within my mind like a gollum made from the clay of what was once my birth land, and this effigy conjured from events long past emerged and walked with a life and power both terrifying and unstoppable.

At a young age I had my fill of blood and killing, and had in pocket enough coin to buy some land and make a family. The nature of thirst and hunger is a craving for what is missing, and family and land were the things of my childhood that I did not have, now I felt them for the first time within my grasp and attainable. I traveled back over hill and sea to the place from which I was born. The time of two moon cycles brought me home to the town called Kilkenny. From where I had come, I had at last returned.

I mixed openly for a fortnight with the local farmers and the people of this region. They knew me not, but my warrior past was marked upon my body and did at times bring glances of fear and suspicion. I enjoyed watching as they passed their days and lived their lives of commerce and trade. I knew I was no farmer, but I had some skill around a simple forge. I pictured myself settled as the local smith, creating shoes for the large plow horses and repairing iron tools. By night's quiet comfort,

I took meals within the local inn and drank the grains that grew in fields of wonderful peace.

I made conversation and soon made friends, as fear gave way to acceptance and suspicion fell to trust. I felt at the right place at the right time. I had for the first time a people and a clan. I felt sure that the short sword at my waist would soon find rest, and I would be free of this thing called war.

But that was not to be.

I was slow with drink and well relaxed within the tavern walls when the cry went up and the alarm was sounded. A boy much younger than I ran in and screamed that the raiders from the north had landed upon our soil once more, and would soon set upon us. It had been two decades since their last foray; a raid that had robbed me of both my parents, and a time still remembered with dread and terror.

Instantly the room cleared as all inside rushed to secure the safety of their wives and children, to collect, to assemble, and to fight. I was given the courtesy of the warning but was not asked for anything in return, for to them I was still a stranger, but to me they were my people. In the confines of this empty room, I continued to drink my ale and checked the sharpness of my hungry sword. By the time of four cups, I was stripped and naked, my sword and my mind my only armor. With the last of my woad flower dye, I painted my body for battle and emerged with the breaking dawn.

Men collected their families and brought them to the square. The wives, the children, and the elderly huddled in mass while men who were merely farmers gathered rusted weapons and farm implements. I walked among them naked with deep blue skin and sword in hand, the savage demon within me prepared now for its release. They questioned not why I chose to fight, for they had taken me in by full measure. I was ready for blood, and Death's dour purpose was written clearly and terribly upon my features for all to see.

I moved with the men, some of great bulk, for farming is not an easy living, and we flowed down to the river from where the enemy had emerged before. Their fleet had landed by sail, and moved swiftly up the Barrow River by arm and by oar. They took route by the left fork, a river called Nore which was named for their last incursion. My heart beat faster as my eyes saw the dragon headed prows moving high and swiftly toward our group. Six ships in number, it was a battle we would not survive.

At first blood it was clear that my people were brave but not skilled, and they fell quickly and painfully before the first onslaught. I killed two raiders in succession, but their fierceness in battle was greater than any sagas told. By sheer number we dispatched the first of their party, but the other long boats had now joined the fray.

The largest of our party held me in a tight grip and spoke with the intense clarity of one who has already seen his death, "They come for plunder and for slaves. Young prince, the treasure of our land now flees to the hills of Dunmore. There lies a cave that will hide and shelter, go back and get them to its safety. We will hold, we will delay, and we will die here among the banks." Without thought I saw the wisdom of his words and turned and obeyed his orders without a question.

With distance the cries of this battle did soften and grow silent, and in three hours I had caught up to the wandering mass. The children, the women, and the old ones moved painfully slow. Some carried babies, some carried parents, and all carried fear. Our pursuers gained ground, but at last I saw the great mouth and led them through its darkness. This great womb opened, and inside we numbered almost one thousand. Amid the crying I spoke for silence, and as I listened I heard the Norse men closing on our hidden place. Inside I urged them deeper and ran back to the opening hoping to lead the enemy away, hoping that the treasure of my land would be held safe by its mother.

In the bright light of day as my eyes adjusted from the darkness, they were upon us. I charged the invaders and knew that nothing would be safe. I moved fast and dodged the arrows that came my way, with a loud cry I set upon them cleaving limb from body. A strong right arm stained the ground on which it fell, and I continued my killing until a blow from behind cut through my arm and shoulder. I staggered and turned, and saw that the one-armed Norseman had pried his sword from his severed right arm and struck me with his left. More blows fell, and with darkness descending deeper than the cave, I thought that I heard Death call me by name.

In agony they held me roughly up and vision came to me again. Their Norse tongue was rough, but I knew its meaning. Alive I at least was of some value, although I had come at a dear price; for six were dead and three were wounded. I was lashed to a rough wooden shield to make my carry easy, and all but two descended into the darkness. With swords drawn and thirsty, they entered, and the slaughter of the innocents began.

From Dearc Fearna, "The Cave of the Alders," the screams and cries reached my ears but truly Dark Fear, as it sounds in the Saxon tongue, was now a more fitting name. For over one hour the painful cries rose from the mighty opening, as if mother earth herself screamed her pain. But no birth would come from this womb, finally still and silent, all inside were dead, left where they had fallen, a lesson perhaps for those that chose to resist or maybe a simple economic statement that nursing mothers, children, and the old, make poor slaves. Either way in the business of slaughter the Norse brood was methodical and efficient, for I lay now, its lone survivor.

Half mad and half dead they carried me on shield to the waiting ships. My journey through hell had begun. I was empty, a man without a tribe, a man without a country. I jumped back from the darkness of my recollections to the sound of the lass's voice, and I turned in her direction.

She stood now beside her father and without judgment or pity she replied to my desolate thoughts, "It is written that one day you will have both again, and these you shall have beyond your wildest measure."

By Sea and by Land

That night as I lay quietly in my bed I continued to rake through my pained memories.

I was cast into the dark hole of their long ship and did not need to be tied for, indeed, I could barely move. By oar to ocean the dragon boats raced, and once there the large mainsail was set, and we were driven only by wind and current. The movement of the ship made me sick beyond measure, and so I lay, in blood, in vomit, and in my own excrement. At first I knew not speed or direction, but by the gathering coldness and the shadows of the sun, I realized we moved northward and to the east. Rough bread was sometimes thrown my way, for even some of these men could still feel pity.

I watched and listened to them daily, to know if I was to be fed or beaten. I got to know their habits and routines, and at times they seemed almost like normal men. They worshiped their gods, ate their food, and drank as my people did. I remembered my mother and wondered if she had faced a similar fate so many years ago, and I hated them with all the power of my immortal soul.

Insects that thought to feed on me were quickly eaten by me, and occasionally a careless rat would find its way by my mouth to my stomach. I bound my wounds with rags found jammed between the planks of the hull, for I cared little if we sank or floated. I watched daily as my captors, men of great girth, little morals, and no fear, danced across the mighty ocean. I had been forsaken by God and prayed only for Death, but even his comfort would not be extended. Here in the cold blackness of my floating prison I knew that all had turned against me, and yet I still lived.

Time passed and ocean became river and direction changed to southward. They carried me to the deck where I saw banks of green and trees of great size and number. I knew we had traveled far, for here and southward the ones we called Viken and Norse were now called the Rus. The great river was named Volga, and it cut through the lands that these wild men called the land of the Slavs, and this vast region was where they hunted freely.

Sometimes we stopped traveling long enough for some of the Viken to run inland, only to return with women taken by force and held like me. At night I would hear the cries of the women as these fur-clad animals raped and violated them in unimagined ways. Some women chose death, but most were carefully bound because these, both fair and homely would fetch them silver coin, and I thought once more about the fate of my mother.

Scraps of food continued to come my way, and blood seeped darkly from my filthy wounds. All along the well-worn route my jailors traded. I saw furs for amber, and silver for the living. New supplies were taken on, and new women were captured. I wondered if they pillaged from whom they traded, selling them back what they had stolen. At places along the river the ship was pulled by rope and pushed by oar, until at last we reached a port called Astrakhan that opened to a huge sea. Here new supplies were taken on and stock replenished. For three days we remained, their mood was joyous for the river was now behind us, and sail would be set once more to cross the sea before us.

Green forest and stark mountain had yielded to sea and sand, and the icy cold had been replaced by scorching heat. On this Khazar Ocean we sailed without incident. The crossing was slow, for here blew only inland winds and not the gales of mighty oceans. I could taste the mist and knew that this inland sea was salted water, and not fresh like the lakes of my world. For two moon cycles we sailed southward until at last we reached another port, and leaving the ship we continued over sand by foot and beast. We traveled now with a desert brown people who on the surface seemed a cleaner race, much less barbaric than the Norse.

The long journey ended much to the south in a kingdom of great wonder. Ironically, it was this flourishing people who had a boundless appetite for slave girls of white skin and fair hair. These great people were the driving force behind this human trade. The trappings of civilization meant nothing, and may God swiftly judge them all.

Amid the sprawling city they called Baghdad, I was placed for sale. My poor condition coupled with the festering wound brought little interest from serious buyers, and I feared I would end as a one-armed eunuch amid a snow-white harem. Finally I was sold, only to be dragged eastward further through sand and heat to a place unknown.

I fetched only a few dinars, and was overcome with joy to know that for all their trouble I had profited the Norsemen little. Few felt I would survive the desert journey, and with so little paid there was little to be lost, and this was my victory. Pulled by chain across the dunes, I felt the constant presence of Death high above my shoulder, but I cared not for my life and so was bound by nothing. In fever I was free and swore that whatever would come I would peacefully embrace.

I pulled myself back from dark recollection and came back to my simple room. Since that time my agony has faded, and I am safe for now with Merlin and his daughter. I give profound thanks for my simple comforts and my fortune. Death had let me be. Instead of freedom from life, he had given me freedom in it.

With this thought I felt hope, and passed gently into sleep.

BALANCE

The beggar walked steadily bowl in hand for most of the day. The tattered black rags that he wore dangled precariously from his skinny shoulders. What remained of its hood covered most of his gaunt face, protecting him from burning sun or biting cold, depending on season and circumstance. In cities he sat cross-legged for brief periods of time at the center of life's busy world. Skinny fingers held the bowl in his lap, and his head nodded grateful acknowledgement for each small contribution it received.

His life was defined by the concept of enough. Enough to eat, enough to carry, enough to rest, and enough to move on; he was a migratory bird.

He heard the distant marching of soldiers in formation growing louder and getting closer. He watched the passing ranks of the infantry and smelled the sweat and dust of their rhythmic cadence. He pressed closer to the walls that lined the street, his delicate frame hugged a bricked-up archway so that the cavalry could now pass without trampling him. The common people looked down and away from the sound of the passing military procession to minimize the risk of confrontation.

This beggar, however, was far from common, and so looked up and directly into the spiritless dark eyes of its mounted commander.

The powerful steed whinnied and rose in fear, while its rider tugged the reins and fought to bring it under his control. The commander struggled to regain his balance and once again in charge, reached down to the blade at his waist. The steady coal eyes of the beggar did not shift or loosen their grip and seemed to look past the wrecked visage of face and eyes and into the depths of a soul in torment.

Rethinking the actions of reflex, the leader justified his inability to act decisively with the logic that the black-garbed vermin before him was indeed valueless and not worth the time or trouble of killing. He pulled the reins tightly and with a kick of the triangular stirrups, horse and rider moved quickly on.

The times were indeed strange, pockets of sanity in a world gone largely mad. Power was now stolen by sword edge, and human worth measured by the accumulation of material wealth. Both the world and the universe, however, exist in a constant state of shifting balance. The dry dust settled, and the sounds of daily life returned quickly and filled the silent hollow left by the military passage. Hawkers again cried out to pitch their wares, and the sounds of animals mixed once more with human speech. The timeless noise of children playing and laughing soon echoed freely along the city streets. Life moved all around him. The coins in the brass bowl drank up the sunlight and were enough. It was his time to move on.

To those that study simple things the act of walking is a straightforward one. It requires a decision, a direction, and little more. It is the steady and continuous process of releasing and regaining balance, a methodically controlled free fall.

Very few acknowledged his arrival, presence, or passage. His awkward gait caused people to look away uncomfortably, rather than look closely or empathetically. The blackness of his filthy garments set him apart, so different yet so perfectly invisible.

With concentrated effort the beggar swung his frame into an uneasy forward direction.

None saw this man, none saw this bird, and none saw the many pockmarked scars that littered his ancient parchment skin.

THE NEEDLE POINTS NORTH

An emperor does not retain power by being uninformed, and so in high imperial circles information has always been a commodity of extreme value. One high-ranking minister in particular had the emperor's ear. This man was a kind and gentle soul and was always in the company of his eldest son. This boy was being groomed for life within the imperial court; he would follow naturally in his father's footsteps. The generational passage of cyclic power would continue.

The minister was honest and above reproach, and he held nothing back as he shared his true opinion with his emperor. It was not malicious or self-serving. It was a warning of the most serious kind. Ambition is a plow with two edges, outwardly it is promoted and rewarded, and inwardly it is distrusted and feared because the fruit of ambition is power, and it grows and wanes throughout every dynasty. The wise emperor, like a skillful gardener, keeps it closely monitored, and finally must decide whether it should be nurtured or nipped in the bud.

The grounds of the military wing of the imperial capital were a safe and familiar place for the armor-clad commander. A young page took the reins of his lathered stallion and led the beast away to be brushed, fed, and rested. Moving quickly into the training yard, the commander scanned the men engaged in combat exercises. A few turned to acknowledge his presence, but none risked a long or lingering stare.

Groups of fifty were overseen by a master-at-arms. These overseers shouted commands, stopped action, gave advice, and demonstrated the physical meaning of their words. Inactivity and lack of concentration were not tolerated and usually had direct and severe repercussions. Often a man would leave to nurse a broken rib or injured limb, the pain a better lesson than any words an instructor could provide. It was easy to tell the seasoned from the novice. The difference lay not in the sophistication of the techniques practiced, but in the soldiers' confidence in their ability to apply them properly.

Still unsettled by the bold stare of the old beggar, the commander sought an outlet. Passing by the arena of wooden blade, he walked directly into the intermediate field of live blade training where steel rang out against steel in the sounds and motions of parry, thrust, and cut. Immediately he saw what he had been looking for in the form of a young soldier whose demeanor spoke loudly of preferring to be anywhere else. He would be a fitting target for the day's lesson.

In a matter of minutes he was standing in front of the reluctant enlisted man, and in much less time than that, the youth had fully registered the peril he was in.

Fear is the mind killer, in battle or in training. The commander's eyes ordered the young man to attack. It was clumsy and halfhearted; the clang of metal on metal rang out and the commander's foot found the boy's unprotected abdomen. In pain the young man stood up and tried to gather himself, urged on by the barking and jostling of his peers, wild dogs tracking the scent of blood.

His next attack was at best a confused step forward. The monk blade wielded by the commander bit deeply into the soldier's upper leg. The finishing strike was already in motion and would have found its home had the disabled youth not been brought to his knees by the kindness of gravity. Composure regained, the commander shook and sheathed his dripping blade and left the wounded man to be dragged away by the instructors.

With eyes averted and with as few words as possible, the young page approached the commander and spoke. "Sir," he began, "the Emperor wishes to speak to you." The summons received, the commander marched past the archery fields and into the lavish inner quarters of the imperial palace.

Three times from both knees his head knocked on the stone floor, and on one knee he waited to hear the words of The Son of Heaven, still wishing he had taken the young man's life.

"In the far north there are still those that do not bend to my compassion," the emperor intoned. "You have always been the faithful hammer that shapes the steel around the anvil of my purpose." This situation required ruthless abandon, and his sources of information indicated clearly that this commander was the right tool for the job.

"My Lord," the commander began," with four battalions at my disposal I will travel north, for the protection of the empire and enforcement of your divine will." Even on bended knee the cold heart of the commander was grateful, knowing that he would once again be free to kill, and that he would enjoy the work.

The emperor was, in turn, pleased to have found a use for the commander's unspent rage and dangerously idle fury. Even a small rebellion if not crushed promptly can spread like fire. He understood clearly that while his power waned, the influence of his disfigured commander was on the rise. With the insight of his trusted advisor, he gave his orders thinking he would at least for now, be rid of him.

The Supreme Commander left the city with four thousand soldiers. They marched out through the main gates with all the pomp and ceremony that protocol allowed. He and his men were headed one thousand *li* north in the service of the emperor. The orders were clear, and the intentions of the Supreme Commander were as crystal. There would be death and blood, and much of it.

In the wake of the massacre at the temple mount, he had reevaluated the merits of direct confrontation, and had, in fact, begun to study the virtues and methods of siege warfare. This campaign could well be a lengthy one, and although his body traveled northward, his mind wandered from arid desert frontiers to rugged southern landscapes.

Despite the direction of mind or body, conflict raged within the darkest corners of his being. The very life of this monk still mocked him with its every passing breath and heartbeat.

THE BEAR

The army trekked with mechanical precision and morale was high. The veterans were once more happy for a chance to prove their worth, and the young were anxious to apply the lessons learned in training. Supplies were fresh and plentiful, and night encampments had an atmosphere of celebration rather than serious military campaign. Through night's haze the commander could hear the drunken revelry of his men, the piercing laugher of the camp whores, and the music of flute and drum that occasionally sounded from around the dark night fires.

Four thousand men, fully half on horseback, traversed their way through peaceful valley and along simple winding roads as faithfully and steadily as the north pointing needle of their navigational compass. The trail they left behind was littered with refuse. It was picked clean by the scavengers that followed them, some animal, some bird, and some quite human.

Mimicking many good leaders the commander remained aloof and spoke very little. There was no need. The men knew the task at hand and where they were going. During the nights as the men relaxed, he would fixate on finding the last monk and the company he now kept, but that was a mission for another day. For now he would just drink himself into a state of bitter oblivion and wait.

Both terrain and mood changed rapidly over the next few weeks. The novelty of the new mission was beginning to wear off, replaced now by the monotony of mindless military routine.

The quick pace that was originally set was slowed by the difficult terrain of the highlands, as wide road was replaced by narrow mountain paths. The day-to-day drudgery was punctuated by the occasional rockslide or the loss of man or beast over a steep edge. They were entering the lands of the long winter, and supplies, while not yet dangerously low, would soon be rationed.

Hamlets were raided as required, and any weak pack animals were consumed. The drunken night parties were more subdued. By full moon's light the howling of unseen wolf packs cried that this was their domain, and that all others were intruders.

The imperial troops met no direct resistance along the way, for that would have been a blessing. Men in numbers if not productively occupied can turn on themselves. On one particularly slow day, the commander summoned his page and snarled his orders, "Bring me sword, bow, and quiver." He watched the boy painfully avoid eye contact and continued, "and summon my generals."

The generals quickly assembled, curious yet leery of their commander's unexpected summons. Terse orders were given. "Hold here while I scout ahead, I will return in two days." The generals acknowledged the order and tried to hide their confusion. The commander was not a man who did his own scouting, nor one known to venture out without guards. In truth, however, his purpose was twofold. He sought a selfish escape from the monotony of the mission and thought to show all that he still firmly held the reins of power.

Less than a day hence, alone and for now content, he found tracks in the new fallen snow that drew his interest. He followed the large, fresh paw prints of a moon bear. He was careful not to be taken by surprise, and paid close attention to the nervousness of his battle-tested horse. The tracks led eventually to the mouth of a cave.

Tethering his steed to a leafless stunted tree not far from the cave opening, he climbed quietly to a rocky outcrop twenty-five feet high and directly above it. The plan was a simple one, and one that he had seen executed many times as a boy. He sat in patient silence and watched his exhaled breath fog in steady bursts, as it mixed with the cold, crisp air.

The image of the blackened beggar and his bowl filled his mind. He sat like him, but instead of a bowl he cradled a forty-pound rock in his frost covered lap, and to his left he laid carefully his war bow and quiver. The wait would not be a long one.

Already his horse whimpered and tugged skittishly at reins that secured him like a lamb tethered for slaughter. The commander could feel the heat rise from the opening as the large grey head appeared below him and sniffed the air cautiously. Hunger has a powerful pull, and his wild-eyed horse as if on cue began to panic. As the huge grey shag shoulders cleared the entrance, the commander dropped the boulder and let gravity do his dirty work.

It landed square where the bear's neck meets the shoulders and crushed the spine. While the bear roared in shock and agony, the commander reached gingerly for his bow and full quiver, firing arrow after arrow until the bear was finally silent and lifeless. A crimson blanket stained the powdered snow. Satisfied that the animal was now dead, the assassin's heartbeat and breathing slowed closer to their normal rhythm. He climbed down, sword in hand, as he approached the steaming carcass.

This bear was surely a Great Bear, a throwback to the times when ice covered half the world. The commander jumped at the animal's last death rattle, and listened coldly to the cries of the cubs that remained deep in the dark cavern. He first removed the arrows some as deep as the feathered flights. From around his neck he removed his talisman of pain. Methodically he wrapped its icy metal links several times around his wrist until the shard of broken blade rested firmly between thumb and index finger. Looking down, he saw the edge that took his life, and the chain that held him bound. In the cruel bite of new winter's day he began the process of skinning, picturing once more the monk upon the mountain.

The first cut cleaved the white lunar crescent on the animal's powerful chest neatly in half and tore right down to the pelvis. The bloody work continued until separated from the body the hide stretched upon the open ground, like a dark and greasy carpet. Six hours later the last remaining bits of flesh and tissue had been scraped off, while mountain winds cried their soulful mourning. Ironically, for at least this night, his trophy would protect him from the elements. In the falling darkness the wolves howled as if grieving the dead, and in the morning horse and rider started back to where the troops were waiting.

By the afternoon he rode proudly into the encampment. The result of the two-day sojourn made a deep and lasting impression on all. The commander, usually garbed in meticulously polished armor, was now dressed in blood.

His helmet was covered by the skull of the bear, and his mangled face stared out from a visor of jaw and fangs. The right claws of a once mighty paw were flung over his left shoulder like a barbaric cape, held firm by the chained sword tip encircling the leader's neck. The large hide flowed down and over the horse's hind quarters. The rear claws as long as a man's fingers draped down and dangled on both sides of his horse's flanks, and the stallion's well-muscled legs twitched at their each and every touch.

The soldiers stared wide eyed and open mouthed. Hushed whispers flew around the compound, each man's imagination filled in the fantastic details of what might have transpired. What was true was far less powerful than what was imagined, and this was fitting, for both truth and reality were beginning to flee the commander's grasp. The young page led away the terrified steed as the commander retired to his tent. He was, at least in his own eyes, more than a man, more than just Supreme Commander, perhaps even more than the Son of Heaven himself.

Alone again and safe, the commander drank himself once more into the blind and guilt-free numbness of the living dead.

Entrenched

The final leg of the army's campaign was by far the most difficult. The snows had come early and their northern climb had steepened. The weather and terrain had formed a united front, as if nature herself had turned against them. They had cut deeply into rebel territory, but neither the commander, nor his generals, nor his men, ever saw the face of their enemy. Instead their presence was felt like a mist. It enveloped all but could not be touched; it could be seen but not seen through.

It changed from ethereal to solid when least expected. On treacherous mountain conduits, stones materialized from the mist and dropped down from above. Random showers of arrows and bolts came in the night with the wind, piercing the dark and finding their mark in beast and man. By journey's end the imperial forces had lost thirty-seven men and sixteen horses, but what they had lost in confidence and courage could never be tallied.

When the walled rebel city was at last in sight, the men were as nervous as their horses. In bitter cold the commander's cloak of bear skin hung stiffly from his broad shoulders and still carried the lingering odor of death and putrefaction. On horseback and out-of-arrow's range, he rode a circle around the fortress and took survey of its defenses. While from the high wall the staid rebel leader silently took survey of him.

The city was ancient even by the standards of the capitol. It was the former jewel of a much older dynasty's crown. Double walls of brick and quarried stone stood higher and thicker than the strongest man could hurl a spear. Slotted ramparts lined the top, and a pagoda tower stood protectively at each of her four corners.

One imposing arched entrance marked the middle of the south facing wall. It was built just low enough to restrict the full gallop of horse and rider, and fortified from above by the large archery tower. This solitary entrance was blocked by doors of oak sandwiched between palm-thick and ornately decorated cast iron. This was a city that had been built to stand a thousand years and launch a million lifetimes.

The leader watched the commander with intense conviction. There was no secret about the slow, steady approach of the imperial force and no mystery about what the rebels were up against. The stronghold's reinforcement had been as methodical and relentless as the army's northern journey. North and south had matched each other step for step.

For four months the rebels had been arriving at the enclave and had swelled its population to thirty thousand strong. The surrounding farmlands were now abandoned and fallow, and although fear was not unreasonable, it was held in check by the will of these brave people. Life went on within for the civilian population, but its direction had shifted from production to survival.

The business of stockpiling food, water, livestock, and weapons had not been ignored. Throughout the fortress vacant buildings now stored grain, unused vessels now held water, and idle courtyards now housed animals. For four full moons, the normally dark and quiet nights had been lit up by the fires of forge, and filled with the steady beating of hammer upon steel, until every household could draw a blade. A triple ring of sharpened wooden stakes now encircled the square fortress, the final parting gift from the summer's short-lived abundance.

Everything that could be done had been done; everything that had an edge to be sharpened had been honed. The leader had organized and supervised the work through every stage. He knew by name the elderly, the women, and the children that called this place their home. He knew they were not fighting for glory, power, or wealth, this was simply a battle for life. The leader's actions had been meticulous with regard to the protection of his people, and now he would wait.

In heart he knew that no quarter would be given by the southern troops, and in sorrow he knew that no matter how much had been done, it would not be enough.

THE ORACLE SPEAKS

When the commander had taken stock of the city, he had ordered the machines of war to be assembled. The first and tallest of these was a mobile observation tower, followed by seven large trebuchets for hurling the largest of boulders into and against the fortress, and sixteen low crossbow catapults. The work progressed well, and their encampment spanned all four sides of their target. It was a circle of cloth tents around a square of stone walls. It was the hardness of stone surrounded by the softness of silk.

The imperial commander tried to see clearly. Organized siege would make this rebel city a prison, and time would make this prison a tomb, but an overwhelming assault might end things quickly and bring greater glory. To his young page the commander ordered, "Bring me the hag." The young page left quickly on his mission, surprised that his Supreme Commander had even noticed her.

It had come to be that an old woman had been following their passage to scavenge from the camp refuse. From her mind's state it was clear she had but one leg in the world of reality, and among his men it was well known that she had a gift for divination. The page found her picking and foraging near the camp latrine. Her innocent smile and what seemed a look of recognition caught the page off guard. He was prepared for mental imbalance, but saw none. She bowed before the page and said in a tone of reassurance, "One day your virtue shall be your shield and purity your armor." The young man wondered if this was the start of a long rant, but she continued evenly, and said only, "Take me to the coward."

She entered his tent and smiled toothlessly, eyes bright beyond her years but never focused on the obviously present. Across her shoulder her bag held the tools of the oracle.

"Sit," said the commander as if talking to his dog. "Tell me what I want to know," he whispered. At this she began to cackle and taunted, "what you want to know, or what you want to hear?" His patience thin, he barked, "cast it now," and to these words she settled by the fire and into a state of cool and systematic resonance.

He heard the age-old songs of her craft emanate from the core of her being as she rocked back and forth, the opened bag upon her lap. With crooked fingers she scrawled upon a tortoise shell the questions for the ancients, and placed it on the fire's embers while rocking and singing the sounds of the dead. It grated on the commander like a growing toothache, and ended suddenly, with a splitting snap.

For a long silence she sat and stared at the cooling shell reading its cracks and shadows. Her eyes saw past the commander and into the beginning and end of her own long life. "I will tell you as I have been told," she offered and then began in the voice of one much younger, and of one much farther away.

"Your victory will stand like the tall and hollow lion, and the oak that knows its parents. Its father is destruction from on high, and its mother the worms that move below the ground. It stands and throws its shadow between them both. It binds them together by root and by leaf. The colorful seeds of victory shall hang in high places and bring you praise, but their germination shall bring the end to many."

She paused and drew a labored breath, "The bear's steel is the two-edged sword. One edge priest and the other edge warrior, both sharpened by the same stone, she the healer of great suffering. This is the blade that will separate a slave from a king."

The commander took this phrase of bear and steel to refer directly to him, and was flattered by the description of warrior, priest, and healer combined. He pressed on, looking for more acclaim as her word 'King' echoed through the hollows of his mind. The crone was tired now and silent. Finally the commander ordered, "Explain."

"I see and I say, my lord, but I do not explain," she replied evenly.

"Will I have victory here old woman?" he pushed.

"You will," she intoned, still far away in time and place.

He tossed the pouch of meager coins disdainfully in her direction. She held them up to her useless eyes and smiled her toothless grin. Collecting herself and her belongings, she packed up, and as she took leave of the sullen commander and his tent, she began to rave, voicing only the meandering thoughts of a madwoman. She spoke of finding the bird that shared her dreams and of the solace of the raven. Cloaked in the shadows of night she left the cold comforts of the camp, and in the morning light she began leaving with absolute haste this vast region of the north.

Alone in his tent, the commander smiled an ugly grimace and snatched up the coin pouch that had been left behind.

THE SIEGE

The rebel leader was young as rebels often are, handsome and strong by standards, a leader not because of age or standing but because of will and courage. This young insurgent put no faith in the trappings of formal rank or title. Among his tribe he sometimes stood apart, but never above. To all that followed, he was known only as the rebel, respected and loved simply because of who, not what, he was.

His people had always been farmers and merchants. What they would never be, however, were sheep led peacefully to the slaughter. If the inability to pay taxes was rebellion, then they were guilty, and if pitchforks must become spears, then it would be so.

He watched the cloaked one circle the city on horseback tantalizingly close, but just outside the range of arrows bite. He knew the bear whose skin now draped across horse and rider, and thought about the wolves of the highlands and how they circle behind the young, the sick, and the starving. There was no chance to win, survival meant compromise, and reluctantly he sent the city's four best negotiators out to plead for peace.

The answer came swiftly and loudly. He watched the four taken by sword and led to their fate. Within the hour the trebuchets were fired from each of the four directions. Their ammunition wailed in terror. Their screams increased in pitch and volume as far became near, and then only the sickening thud and cracking of bone and skull, as the four emissaries crashed and rolled from on high into the market square. Unrecognizable now except by clothing, silence was their bitter eulogy.

The blessed act of dig fill and cover renews in season the soul of every farmer. This time, however, it was not seeds of life that they planted, but the seeds of death; and this strange reversal would soon come to define their norm. The season of the grim harvest had begun.

The rebel watched the commander's troops dig in on every side. The eyes in the high tower had already drawn out the fort's inner layout. His mind now turned to the civilian population and how best to serve their needs, whatever could be done would be done under the cover of night. This game of chess afforded little movement and no mistakes, but the first strike would come from the enemy troops. The one advantage that the rebels held was that this was their territory, and if civilians could reach the forest unnoticed, they could escape.

His footsteps rang from the bare stone walls as the rebel walked steadily and effortlessly to the room at the far end. This was the last vestige of a life before war, it was bleak and unadorned, a room not fit for habitation, a room now used only for idle storage. The young man stood before the large machine, which to the untrained eye seemed a complicated contraption. It was built and used by his great-grandfather, and it had passed from one generation to the next along with the skill to make it sing.

The young hands that had first used it were now bone within the earth, and yet they reached down to him from ages. What he saw, touched, and heard was what his forefathers had seen, touched, and heard, and it bound them both and gave him strength. With rough cloth he wiped away the dust layer that bore witness to abandonment and disuse. A spider scurried from its woolen threads. Another time he would have carelessly wiped it away with the dust, but now he watched it and was sorry to have destroyed its home and sent it scrambling.

'Regrettable, another casualty of war,' he thought and then he sat before his instrument. His feet and hands moved with the speed of practiced lightning. Working the loom had always set his mind at peace, but he was not concentrating on the weaving, he was going through the motions of movement and strategy. Time had no substance here, and the afternoon passed as though it had never been.

He continued effortlessly, a man both totally present, and yet, very much far away. On this day he cared naught for composition or color or sequence, he cared only that this work would bring him mental clarity. He stopped his work at the loom only when his mind had stopped its working. All the possibilities had been considered, all the permutations had been exhausted, and he stood, now confident that his next course of action would be the best one.

Darkness had fallen, as he stretched his tired and weakened frame he thanked his ancestors for the life he had been given. It was time to get back to the serious business at hand, and time he realized, was now everything. Before returning to the company of his men and those he protected, he looked upon what he had woven. Strangely, it was a color he had never used or ever noticed. Before him stretched a sky of blue, dyed from the leaves and flowers of woad that grew with abundance in the hills of his old home region.

He touched his work with a curious fingertip and thought, 'Too small for a carpet, too plain for a prayer rug, mindless effort with no real purpose.'

SACRIFICE

The small children that were by nature so active, now slept with mothers and elders; they were heavily sedated. The ones old enough to walk were left alert, but their faces were wrapped to muffle any cries of pain or fear. All faces were blackened with soot from the lamps, and the clothing worn was also dark. Meager rations had been evenly distributed. The major components of the plan had been explained. There was nothing more to do but wait, and waiting of all the tasks was by far the most difficult.

Now they sat in groups of one hundred with each group being assigned one soldier from the rebel forces. Talking was not permitted, and so only their eyes held their conversations. Some spoke of defiance, some of fear, and all spoke of love and farewells. Hers spoke clearly of loss and sorrow, but much more loudly of strength and resolution.

The rebel's wife kept her oldest by her side and nursed the baby one last time. Her milk was drying, but her breast would soothe her infant while the sedative took effect. Her husband entered like the wind of a winter's day. No longer hers alone, he moved with purpose through the throng. His eyes took in all. He stopped to tighten a darkened blanket across the shoulders of an ancient, he moved to wipe a child's tear and lend his courage to one too young to speak.

In whispered tones he spoke to his soldiers, assuring that each one knew his solemn purpose. As she watched him from her distance, her heart ached within her chest, and she held him within her mind's embrace. She knew this final one, must last for her remaining lifetime. The moonless power of the night was upon them, and to this power he prayed to keep them safe.

He moved finally to his wife and children and held them tightly one by one. Smoothly he slipped her the sharpened dagger, the loud unspoken truth, that their death was better than their capture. She quickly tucked it under her sleeve. Too soon it was their time, and en masse they moved to the southern wall. The soldiers descended rapidly, the lust of battle was already coursing through their veins. Into the darkness they dropped, and in the blackened silence that followed, the civilians waited with anticipation.

When the sounds of the nighttime battle reached their ears from the far end of the surrounding field, they knew it was their signal. They were lowered by scaffold roughly to the snow-covered ground. Their sentry watched over them with sword drawn until all in their group were down. They wove their way through the protective stakes of sharpened timber, and although they rushed, their pace was a limp with the old and the young. The weaving amble through the angled stakes reminded her of peaceful times spent watching her husband work the loom, and with fierce resolution she shook those memories from her mind.

The smell of death cut through the darkness as they passed near the forgotten carcass of man or beast. She was glad the darkness hid the view, and that the rags that silenced the sound of children also kept them safe from the stench of war's true horrors. Their party moved as one, spread out upon the killing field like the great mythical serpent. They undulated away from the clanging of steel and the cries of the embattled, until to the ear it sounded merely like the distant drone of children playing.

The leading sentry pawed the snow covered ground frantically. For a time brief by normal standard but an eternity by theirs, he searched. He reminded her of the hungry wolves that dig for a dead elk buried beneath winter's white blanket. He held his panic in check until at last he was rewarded. He pulled away the canvas cover to reveal the opening of the well-placed tunnel, and into its cold blackness they descended.

They moved as the blind move, an outstretched hand on frozen wall, silent and with only one direction—forward. Under the enemy camps they pressed on, moving quietly but for the occasional stumble. Finally they reached the hidden exit near the forest's promised safety and emerged from their underground corridor under the watchful eye of their armored guardian. She drank the cold fresh air like a baby fresh from the womb, and even in the thick darkness she saw their protector was not much more than a child himself. The noise of the distant fray was carried softly to them upon the night winds.

She held her children close, one by hand and one at breast, and looked with gratitude to their young protector. No cry escaped his lips as she saw the sword emerge from his chest. She saw his pain upon his face, and knew his silence was his last heroic act. As he fell where he was struck, she released her hold on the small hand and made distance. With a brief struggle the imperial soldier had freed his saber and now rushed to cleave her lone-standing son. From behind, her blade was drawn across the enemy's throat, and if he could have screamed he would have, but he fell in silence as the white snow pooled black within the darkness.

She helped the others move to the safety of the forest, and only after many miles did they rest and recoup their strength. No man should come between a bear and her cubs. By dawn's light she looked down at her hands stained red with blood, and in the growing light she remembered they wore this gown after both her children were birthed. She thought with love about the one who led them, her husband and the father of her sons. His sacrifice would not be in vain, he would be remembered by his children and his people. It would be woven into song and story for all to know and for generations to recall.

But for now she pulled her rough wool scarf up around her face, to keep her from the cold and to hide her freezing tears. She gathered up their people and with her as their protector, they moved on.

FIRST STRIKE

The first major strike came the following evening. The catapults were positioned and the targets picked. Fire bolts the lengths of two men were launched systematically, accurately, and in seemingly endless array. The urine and grey water miserly collected for four months could not extinguish all the fires, and so it was that the main granary went upward as flame. While the imperial forces watched and cheered this, their first spectacle of war, fully half of the children and women had been lowered over the great walls, and spirited through darkness of tunnel under enemy lines and to the safety and freedom of the protective woodlands.

In morning's light the full extent of the damage could be seen, and its seriousness was written in the smoke and embers that hovered in the icy air. Over half of their stockpiled food had been destroyed and the charred bodies of human and live-stock alike lay strewn upon the alleys, squares, and streets.

The young leader organized the burial detail amid the wailing and weeping of the wounded and the grieving. For the next four nights, by the sliver of the new moon, his men would by rope descend the walls. In the darkened pitch with arrow, spear, and sword, they launched a noble plan of harass and divert, while giving the innocents the precious time needed to flee.

At week's end food was strictly rationed. The civilian population had escaped and continued to move onward seeking the safety of distance. A mere three thousand men were left to stand their ground within the walls. They faced two enemies. The first was the tangible weapons of wood and metal. The second hung in air like a ghost, the specter of starvation. It haunted the city fortress from the rising smoke that danced with the gathering of the crows.

In the imperial camp the commander's elation had begun its bitter fermentation as he realized that the sounds of civilian life no longer came from inside the rebel city. He understood now that the dark night skirmishes had been a ruse, and in fact a most successful one. When all the tunnels were destroyed, he would turn his hatred and animosity fully on those still living within the fortress walls.

When the night forays came no more, the commander sent a full brigade against the southern wall with siege ladders and grappling hooks. They were slowed by the concealed pits dug months prior, and the ladders offered no protection from the maelstrom of arrows launched upon the impeded forces. In all, on that one day, one hundred and sixty three men died and forty-four were seriously wounded, all imperial troops.

Drunk with anger, the commander, twice more, on different walls and different times, tried again and obtained almost exactly the same results. A night raid launched by his cavalry was also disastrous. The field was well mined, and in light of early morning, seven lame and abandoned horses were coaxed through the soundly protected gate. The rebels ate well that night.

Finally he accepted that although siege by attrition was far less glorious than direct confrontation, it was in fact the correct strategy. He would stand down and allow nature to take its course, very much like he had allowed gravity to carry the boulder to its target at the shadowed cavern entrance.

Famine would be their just retribution, and their death would come at his command. He did not realize that he had underestimated both the tenacity of the rebels, and the sovereignty of Death, and that his forces would remain entrenched here for the next eleven months.

At night, sated and besotted with drink and wrapped within the fetid bear hide, he would feel his mangled face and long for his return to the capital and his next chance to hunt down and kill a monk and all who are close to him.

THE OAK

With the coming of each new day, I felt much better. I ate breakfast with Merlin and the Sea Lass and watched him dress warmly for his work upon the land. I continued to stay with his daughter and help her within the house. With Merlin gone, her home routine was patiently attended until at last we were free to tend to the outside duties. With the closing of the large wooden door, the sun and breeze welcomed us into the open.

She smiled proudly when she saw me crouched and watching the nest of ants along our path. "What is the forecast?" she inquired, and nodded her approval when I answered, "Sunny and bright here, distant storm moving closer." Together we filled two wicker baskets with mulberry leaves and carried them to a shed some distance from the main house.

I was not prepared for the sight that greeted me as she lit the shed lamps and emptied the leaves into round woven lids. I saw the pulsing of the worms, they looked like the maggots that feed upon the dead, and I recoiled in horror. Her laughter calmed me, and she quickly said, "Don't worry, Vincent, these worms work for us."

The sound of a heavy summer downpour somehow filled the room. I forced myself to look once more to the lids and she continued, "Listen to them eat, when they are full and ripe, they will spin themselves a sleeping place with threads of splendor, comfort, and protection. I will boil them, unwind them, and color them, and from these I will make you the clothing of kings." I knew that for the Sea Lass even this wondrous intention held no trace of witchcraft or magic, but was quite ordinary within this world. But for me, it was still bound by the threads of mystery.

My repulsion faded as we closed the door behind us and walked on across the vast and open beauty of the land. We followed the river, where she stopped to peer quietly into the clear calm pools along its edge. Her hands darted in scooping out a speckled fish that now thrashed upon the dry land. A few more steps brought another, and then a third, cleaned and deftly tied with reeds through gills and handed to me for carrying.

Eventually we approached a large tree that stood majestic and alone in an open field, and we made our way in its direction. It towered against the clear blue sky and pulled at me steadily. I turned to the Sea Lass and heard my own voice rich with excitement, "I know this tree," I exclaimed, and sprinted toward it.

With eyes closed I pressed my body against its dry rough bark and embraced it like a long lost friend. I deeply inhaled its spring musk and, in turn, it took me back in memory to the land of my people. I backed away with head cranked up looking at its great height, still leafless, adorned only by the green brown buds getting ready to burst forth. A raven flew down from the highest boughs, and Sea Lass lovingly fed it scraps from yesterday's evening meal.

"To my people this tree is both guardian and gateway," I told her, as the large black bird raised its beak and dropped another morsel down its gullet. I should not have been surprised that its leather cupped seeds had reached as far as this distant land. "In my language it is called oak." My refreshed memories had loosened my tongue, and I told her of the Norse Landers whose people also held the great oaks sacred.

Sea Lass listened to my words like a child in school, "Their warrior god was named Thor. During a great storm Thor sought shelter beneath a huge oak tree, and it was here that he was made immortal. He was given the power of lightning and thunder, a power he took into battle as he wielded his massive steel war hammer." Spellbound she stopped feeding the greedy bird that bounced happily beside her.

Sea Lass pointed to the tree, concentrated, and said, "ark." "Oak," I responded, "ark," she repeated. Over and over, although in fact her pronunciation improved very little, I smiled and nodded to reassure her. Making a hammering motion she questioned, "Thar?" "Thor," I corrected. This word's lesson went on much the same way, but for considerably more time and with much the same result. "Thar," she mimicked.

As a teacher I accepted my limitations and was content that I had tried my best. I did not care that her pronunciation was stilted, and I rested in the pleasure that she had tried so hard to wrap her tongue around the words of my world.

Suddenly a sound that seemed from another world pierced the quietness. Clearly and loudly, through the heavy black beak of the contented raven came the eerie and unearthly squawk, "Arkthar."

I was shocked by a bird that speaks, and Sea Lass laughed loudly at her pet's contribution to her language lesson. We both turned quickly as Merlin's voice rang out from behind us, "He thinks to name you Arkthar." The monk saw the bright colors of the fish, and chuckled to himself at the appropriate meal choice.

In the midday shadow of the great oak tree, we cooked and ate fish and rice cakes, so delicious that I licked the last flavors from my greasy fingers. After lunch Merlin stood directly from his cross-legged position. "So the god of your enemies is the lightning bearer," he said. "Like you, he has transformed with time and distance. From north to south and from east to west, the wielder of lightning has known many incarnations.

We owe much to a foreign monk that brought us his ways of combat and religion. When the time is right, I will show you form and symbol, and you will study the meditation and movement of the fist he called vajra."

Much of what the monk had spoken had no meaning for me. Graciously Mah Lin did not press it but let me digest peacefully until at last he spoke again. "Vincent, your wounds are many, some to your flesh and some to your spirit." We three walked farther along the river until we came to a high waterfall, where following Merlin's bidding and example I stripped to loincloth.

Together we stood in the flowing curtain of cold spring water, while the Sea Lass sat on the short new grass and watched. Merlin shouted to me above the river's roar, "Let the blood of your past be washed from your soul." He drew breath, "Let your new body grow strong." In a short time I could take no more. Merlin, in contrast, looked comfortable as I stumbled from the rushing torrent. Sea Lass dried and warmed me by rubbing my rough clothing against my blue-white skin.

I looked back to the monk, who had vanished as though he had never been.

Sea Lass and I walked together back to our dwelling place. I did not talk about a monk that could evaporate like a mist. Instead I asked, "Do all the animals of this strange land have the power to speak?" To that she smiled and replied, "They do, but in their own language." The sunshine of the afternoon had begun to be replaced by dark grey cloud cover. As we passed the great tree, a solitary lightning bolt flashed across the distant sky. The raven saw the far-off brightness from its high vantage. Looking up, it spread wing, and took flight.

Between heaven and earth it spoke for the sacred oak, to all the creatures of its great kingdom that could hear, as once again it looked down and screamed the name, "Arkthar."

WATER AND FISH

As Sea Lass and I approached our home, I felt like one carried upon winds of magic. This was surely a place of wonder and beauty. It had once been an ancient temple, and kept from that time the mantle and energy of grounds long consecrated. It held the harmonious power of great tranquility. From communal worship, its robe of peace had descended to envelop even us few who now lived under its protective roof. Its power had even given voice to the croak of the black feathered bird, and I wondered what other wonders it would share with me.

We made ready to enter by the pond near the massive wooden door, and as if responding to my inner thoughts, the fish rose up to churn the surface and seemed to speak. They wagged impatiently as the Sea Lass scooped some dried silkworm nymphs from a small stone grotto and cast them to the hungry mob. Heads and eyes stared from under the circular green pads and pushed into the open surfaces of the pool. The image of cloud and sky disappeared from its mirrored surface, broken now by the happy undulations of both fin and body.

I hunkered close to catch a glimpse and remembered her words, 'In their own language.' I closed my eyes in concentration and strained to hear their words. I wanted desperately to understand them, for their world of water was so different from my own. At first I heard nothing, but then it came, it was not a language of words at all, but the language of gentle laughter. I was astonished, but this broke as quickly as the image of cloud and sky had broken, and my eyes now opened saw that all the gentle laughter came not from the fish, but from the lass.

She was by my side once more and only by great effort regained her composure. She knew at once what I had been trying to do, and looked at me with kindness, impressed I hoped with the sincerity of my efforts. Into my hands she placed more nymphs and worms and bid me to cast as she herself had done. Although they still did not speak, they did seem to greatly appreciate this and as the last morsel disappeared so too did they. I looked to her with eyes that still questioned, and her response was simply, "Food is a language that all creatures understand."

We lingered there a while, the clouds of the woad blue sky visible again on the flat quiet surface. The direction of our gaze was down, but our vision did not penetrate the tranquil depths. It was thrown upwards by the dark calm water, past where the black bird flew, and up higher into the heavens that cover and protect all. But my mind still lingered on the fish, and if they could speak, wondered what lessons they would teach.

The Sea Lass broke this reverie and seemed to speak to me for them. "In my language they are called Liyu," she said. "I think in my world they are carp," I replied, "although I had never seen them so beautifully colored and so well behaved." We laughed as she said the word "carp," her lips mimicking the mouths of the ravenous fish.

We entered our home, and the Sea Lass explained to me why these fish were fed instead of eaten. "For us the liyu are a symbol of many things," she explained. "They are bound closely to the god of literature; they speak of endurance, perseverance, and courage." She measured me with her look while her body moved comfortably in the final preparation of the evening meal, and she continued. "To monks like my father they symbolize the mind's freedom from—" She stopped here unsure of the words, but gently touched the angry scars on both my wrists where the chains of iron had held them for so long. "They swim in all the directions of the compass, like the enlightened mind that has moved beyond any restraint and obstruction and is now truly and fully free."

The Sea Lass lifted the lid from the cooking pot and discerningly inhaled its aroma. Glancing toward me she smiled and said, "They swim in pairs and so have also come to mean the union of great opposites and all its harmony and bliss." I knew instantly by her smile, the nature of what she spoke, for sexual union is a constant in any world. My mind was pulled abruptly from these thoughts as Merlin's voice sounded from behind me. As always, he moved so effortlessly that I heard nothing as he entered.

She smiled at my discomfort as she added more salt, and her father spoke to me. "These carp can jump over the rapids in the Yellow River leaving all others behind. Some believe the legend that if one manages to climb the falls of this great river they will be transformed into...." Here he stopped and searched for the word he needed. Looking to his daughter for help, they made motions of an enormous flying description, and both said the word "loong."

I did not understand, and in truth I did not see how fish could grow huge and take wing, then I remembered a bird that could speak, and so said nothing.

THE TREE OF KNOWLEDGE

I awoke to the now familiar sound of the rooster's call and the clinking of breakfast bowls being set upon the table. Merlin and the Sea Lass were deeply engaged in conversation as I entered the room. Merlin was the first to speak as the Sea Lass graciously handed me my breakfast. "We will begin with the names," he said, "Mah."

"Mah," I repeated. He continued, "It means horse." "Horse," I mindlessly repeated, and was met by the raucous laughter of father and daughter. Serious once more, "Lin," he said, "Its meaning is forest." "Lin," I chimed back, not fully aware that I had a mouthful of rice porridge and fruit, which drew even more laughter from the pair. This was quickly silenced and replaced with looks of wide-eyed pride when I swallowed quickly and the sound "Mah Lin" came forth from inside me in the perfect tonal pronunciation of their dialect.

The Sea Lass was the next to speak. "My mother chose for me a name from the distant land and ancient language of the Hebrew people. She hoped it would make me comfortable with my family differences, as from birth I was one already set apart. It was her desire that I grow into the timeless strength, serenity, and endurance of my title; for the meaning of *Selah* is stone."

Without thought the name "Selah" came from my lips as easily as my delicious morning breakfast had gone past them.

The monk and his daughter left the room and bid me to join them. I promptly followed the two into the library where the sword still lay upon the table of thick oak. Beside it now were sheets of mulberry paper made from the bark of the trees that feed the worms. Ink stick, stone, and brush sat nearby, and beside that, a long robe of shimmering blue. Selah offered me the robe, clearly on the behalf of both herself and Mah Lin. I was deeply moved as I put it on. It was perfectly tailored, and it cleared the ground just above my feet.

Mah Lin stood by as Selah checked her handiwork against my frame, and after a few small adjustments, she humbly said, "I have made you the robe of scholar, so now let us begin your journey." I was almost without words, but spoke sincerely from my heart, "I have never worn so wondrous a garment." I saw her eyes look toward her father and saw the blush come to her face.

I looked again at my new attire and wondered how she had decided to make it 'warrior blue.' Whispers of understanding pushed through the voice of my own superstitions. This cloth was made by the worms; a marvelous transformation guided not by witchcraft but by wisdom.

I knew the fears of my past were yielding to faith, as Selah, composed and serious, prepared the ink, grinding a black stick on a stone dish until she achieved the depth of color she desired. Watching her movements I felt myself being calmed into readiness. She dipped the brush into the black ink, and I watched like one under a spell as she painted the sound of 'Mah.' I could see the mane, the body, and the four legs come together with deft strokes. Then she showed me 'Lin.' I saw clearly the trunk, the ground, and the reaching of its three roots. Then she painted another, and the two trees stood side by side to capture the sound of forest. "Lin," I breathed.

She handed the brush to me, and Mah Lin searched at my discomfort. I explained, "I have never written, nor can I read or write. The only instrument of communication I have ever held is a sword." "Good," said Mah Lin, "That is the perfect place at which to start, in truth, sword and brush are closely connected." He gestured toward the brush in encouragement.

I held it straight between my fingers and dipped into the ink as she had done, and I looked nervously at the fresh white mulberry sheet. I calmed myself further and steadied the breath within my belly. I had seen the horses rutting wild in the meadows of my homeland. I let the blackened tip bring their sound to life as the character 'Mah' galloped freely from its bristled tip and onto page.

Mah Lin and Selah studied my first written word in silence. Mah Lin moved it aside and gestured towards the fresh new sheet. Like before I became quiet from the inside, went in mind to the woodlands, and then began to write the sound of 'Lin.' When this character was finished, Selah came to my side quickly and began to examine my work.

While she and her father spoke about my efforts in their tongue, a language that I was only beginning to know, I reached for the sword that seemed to speak my name. I peered closely at the pentagram on its hilt and saw the half word of my ink. "Yes," Mah Lin said, "two together means forest, one apart means wood."

Selah moved my fingertips around the star beginning with the symbol that I recognized. "Wood, fire, earth, metal, water," she chanted softly, "these are the five elements." The feel of her touch lingered long after her words had ceased, and I looked where she directed me. I saw in each the shape of sound, the concept captured by symbol. I studied each carefully and deeply, the upward dance of fire, the mountain and mines of ore, the fertile sprouting earth, and the turbulent movement of water, the root and trunk of wood, and they spoke to me in a way that I cannot explain, from a place I did not know.

I was aware once again of Selah and Mah Lin who were looking at me closely as I held the weapon. My mind followed my eyes to the library shelves. I could sense the wonder, knowledge, and mystery locked within these ancient documents, and I could almost hear them speak. I touched the hem of my sea blue robe and felt its shimmering texture between my fingertips while I heard the wisdom of ages call to my soul from the rock-hewn shelves.

I was drawn back from my reverie by the sound of Mah Lin and Selah as they tried earnestly to pronounce my name.

"Vin-cent?" they chanted in unison, and they spoke it like a question. I saw the sincerity of great effort in their eyes. In my life that had past I had never known family, companionship, or peace. Now I knew absolutely that I had found all three treasures, and my answer came from the core of my being.

"Arkthar," sprang loudly from my soul and flew up beyond the library wall and sailed on dragon ships far past the dark bird that flew on high. "Arkthar," I said again, "Its meaning in the language of the Celts... is Bear."

STANDING AT PEACE

Mah Lin and Selah seemed pleased with my desire to learn. I had always loved the spoken word, but life had not included the skills of reading or writing. Since a mere boy it had been a stark and sterile tale of survival; my reality was one of kill or is killed, and it left no room for the arts to flourish. Save perhaps the art of sword and the art of staying alive.

In truth, however, I had hungered for it as much as the planted seed craves the sunlight. A new child learns an entire language in the time of two years. I was new again, though not a child, and would do much better. I sat often at the oaken table with Selah at my side, and my mind cracked and parched for so long could not seem to drink enough. My fingers trembled as I cast eye and heart over the open and endless manuscripts in front of me.

I was rough but not completely ignorant, and I knew the significance of what lay on the table before me. These were the treasures of the ages, the collective wisdom of humanities' greatest. Poets, sages, warriors, kings, priests, astronomers, and healers alike all collected, protected, and preserved, invited me to reach back in time and share in their wealth.

I saw the cursive and mysterious script of Arab, the harsh stark lettering of the Roman Caesars, and the scrolls of this empire's picture language, and I grasped the depths of Mah Lin's understanding. For me, however, the pull and hold of this land's picture words were more than enough to demand all my efforts. The mornings passed with the speed of flight.

Selah nudged me from my focus and brought me back to afternoon's chores, I was sorry that I had not noticed that Mah Lin had taken his leave. The work itself now had a new purpose. Even the simple tasks, I was directed to do in a way that built the strength of body or mind. Full milk buckets were carried arms straight out from shoulder, and the catching of fish was done with just two fingers. She was a hard taskmaster and a brilliant teacher.

Together we walked the land, and Selah showed me more of its secrets. Many of its features were new to me; in places it rolled gently like the green hills of my homeland, and in places it was stark and bare. Parts of it were folded in alternating layers and colors of rock, some hard some brittle. The river sang through it constantly. It was loud and savage at falls and rapids, peacefully subdued at other parts. I thought the river carved the land, but Selah assured me that it was the land that had formed the river.

Medicinal plants were always collected while we walked, and she patiently explained their nature. By this I mean the plant's effective area, whether root, stem, leaves, flower, or bark, and its method of harvesting. Some were used fresh, others dried and ground. She spoke often of the five elements and the union of opposites. She tried to explain that these concepts were related to the application of healing and the connection of man to nature, but I was not clear how or why. True understanding I knew would come only with great effort and much time, but in her company time spent was effortless and seemed always to pass too quickly.

We arrived at last to the great falls, where her father already stood in meditation. The water beat against his body as if he were a great stone eternally part of the river. Selah bade me join him, which I did. Just as before, the numbness quickly reached my bones and soon I could take no more. I looked to the face of Mah Lin, and while mine was cast in grimace, his wore a mask of peace and contentment. Indeed, the monk had a body of iron.

As Selah revived me on the grass beside the river, Mah Lin smiling came to stand beside us. He knew that I enjoyed the rough feel of the fragrant herbs rubbed into my skin, and knew as well that his daughter was pleased that my personal hygiene had inadvertently improved.

"Don't worry," he said, "like your tree you will grow strong ring by ring." We ate lunch listening to the river's voice, and I was well content and to my surprise invigorated. After lunch, Mah Lin stood up and stretched his body like a cat. His body was as flexible as it was muscled. He sprang like an animal and his leg flashed like a whirlwind. I had seen much military training for hand-to-hand combat, but I had never seen anything like this.

The practiced movement of his art flowed like the river itself, soft yet powerful, punctuated by the savage snap of leg and limb. The hardness of his strikes was surrounded by his fluid movement, like rocks that jut from raging rapids. As I watched his saffron tunic flash and whirl in measured pace and perfect balance, I lost all sense of time. With one last mighty flurry all movement ceased, leaving only the silence of the sunny afternoon.

Back from his physical journey, he smiled in our direction. Mah Lin bent from the waist with his right fist cradled in left hand. I took this as a salute, and I mirrored it back to him. We laughed like carefree children, and he pointed to a thick oak bough that had washed ashore by the river. "Arkthar, bring the staff," he said. Selah was clearly enjoying the show which I was soon to learn had not yet ended, and I went to fetch the long, water-heavy club of tree limb.

Mah Lin stood unmoving and of calm expression. To Selah and me he said, "An indestructible body is built upon a tranquil mind." The monk stood with eyes closed, his outward features a true reflection of his inner serenity. Suddenly and without warning Selah took the club and swung it mightily. It cracked like a lightning strike across his chest and was broken jaggedly in two.

Reality for me was once more undone. It seemed that I saw a loving and gentle daughter try in earnest to kill her unsuspecting father. I had never seen such a powerful strike, and I had seen the battle feats of many a powerful man. As impossible as it seemed, the monk Mah Lin still stood. His features wrapped in peace and stillness. They both looked at the fear and horror written upon my face, and they laughed once more at my expense.

Mah Lin sprang once again like a large wild cat. This time he flew directly into the roaring falls. It was a leap at least the height of two tall men, and then nothing. I saw him with the vision of my own eyes instantly disappear. In this strange world I was once again lost between the real and the impossible.

To Selah this seemed nothing unusual, but I was without words. I ruminated over all that I had seen, as we walked home. Selah seemed to feel the heaviness of my thoughts and confusion, but did not want to disturb me further, and so, she too, was quiet.

By the time we reached the dwelling, she was singing sweetly and it soothed me much. I heard the raven that shared this land call me by name once more. If Mah Lin was a sorcerer, he must be a most powerful one. Selah turned to me as if she had read my thoughts, she placed her palm gently upon my healing shoulder and looked deeply into my eyes and mind.

"You must trust your heart rather than your senses sometimes," she said. "Now be of good spirit while I finish preparing the evening meal, my father will reveal all to you in time, and know this, Arkthar—you have much to learn."

HEAT

Mah Lin returned to the house that evening, his clothes once again holding the pleasant smell of smoke. It mixed happily with the tantalizing smell of the well-cooked evening meal. I had aided Selah in its preparation, and she had guided me in the use of fragrant spices.

It was as a feast. A roasting pheasant that had been snared earlier near the oak tree was now lazily dripping fat onto a bed of green garden vegetables. I myself had fertilized the garden with the buckets of dried bat manure that she had been pleased to have me mix and cast. That such delicious vegetation came from the application of such a concoction spoke eloquently of nature's power to transform.

Mah Lin savored both the meal and the conversation as Selah told him the details of her day. They spoke in their language, and I could now hear familiar words and was, in fact, beginning to understand the root of their conversation. He was intent while listening and questioned her about details. Sometimes he would stifle a smile or try unsuccessfully to suppress his laughter.

At these points I knew they were usually discussing me, and often I found myself laughing as well. At meal's end we were all well satisfied, and Selah had placed sweet treats to steam upon the cooking stove. Mah Lin pointed to the handle on the square wooden box attached to the stove and indicated that I should work it back and forth.

This I did happily, for I craved something warm and delicious. I had watched her make these treats and imitated her motion at the box. As I pumped the handle, the heated embers glowed from below, redder and hotter at each pull and push. Even the simplest things, when never before seen are fascinating, and this machine was a puzzle to me. Mah Lin watched me carefully as I played the wooden handle in and out, and he stopped Selah from interrupting my activity even though the dessert was surely done by now.

As a boy in the forge of a weapon maker, I had worked the bellows. It was day-long toil for a morsel at daylight's end. This device, however, was not the same. The bellows of my past world work like the lungs of a strong soldier blowing through a reed at the base of fire's heat. It is a panting climb to glow the iron, a huffing and puffing. This simple kitchen device, however, was radically different and far superior.

This bellows did not pump out air by panting. The air stream was continuous; it was forced out on the push stroke and exhaled steadily on the handle's pull stroke as well. Constant air must mean more heat. Intrinsically, I knew that in the working of metal, if heat increased so too did possibility. I began to open up the lid of the wooden box to see its inner workings, and then remembering where I was, looked for permission from Selah and Mah Lin. They nodded for me to continue. I explored with the wonder of childhood and saw that its functional beauty lay in its simplicity.

Pushing and pulling I studied its wooden mechanism. I saw the inner flaps open as the air was pulled in, and close as the air was pushed out. I saw the piston lined with a layer of feathers that sealed it and helped it slide. It was a wooden box of genius, so basic and yet so profound.

Selah rose quickly and dragged me away from my fascination in an effort to save the sweet treats, which were by now quite overcooked. Despite their dark appearance, Mah Lin ate them with zest and abandon. Only when we had finished the last treat and washed it down with tea, did he speak.

"Thank you, Selah, for the meal," and to me he spoke with the sound of satisfaction in his voice. "You perceive well, Arkthar. Without that simple machine there would be no Five Element Sword." He paused now to collect his next expression, always careful to speak with accuracy and truth. "Before you learn the art of steel, you must understand the powerful softness of the moving air.

Only by the steady and constant air from the double pump bellows can a forge reach the temperature needed for iron to give birth to steel." Mah Lin sipped and continued, "Bellows of this type have humbly served in our kitchens and in our forges for more than a thousand years." After his last sip of now cool tea he added, "Since the time of the First Emperor." He was lit from within by his reflections of mankind's long history of invention and ingenuity.

"How interesting it is that the greatest achievements of human beings are built directly upon the modest and humble accomplishments of those that have gone before them."

CHI

I spent each morning happily huddled over the library documents, with Selah by my side instructing me and answering my many questions. The mysteries of reading and writing were slowly beginning to unfold, as the pages of my past life were quickly beginning to dry, fade, and crumble. Gradually and steadily the words of the ancients began to replace my life-long ignorance.

We worked and we walked upon the land. It was a land that I was beginning to know. After our chores, Selah the healer directed me in the slow breathing movements of dao yin, a series of exercises whose name she said meant 'guiding and stretching.' As I practiced each movement I felt myself sinking deeper from the surface of my raging past.

At the end of my lesson, I felt rejuvenated and at peace. My teacher smiled openly at my calm demeanor, and said cryptically, "If practiced faithfully, the road of dao yin may one day lead to purity of heart." "Purity of heart?" I remembered my first kill, and how I had held his, briefly beating within my hands. "Selah, you don't know my life."

In the serene afterglow of physical expression, I wondered how so small a woman could strike so hard, and I wondered about the monk that could vanish into the afternoon air. Long I pondered the idea that the foundation of an indestructible body is built upon the bedrock of a tranquil mind, and I enjoyed life and all its simple blessings.

The world of nature had now become both my friend and my sanctuary. I often looked for the raven who shared our food and our existence. The radiant blue silk robe that was the combined effort of worm and woman gave me great comfort. It was cool in heat, and warm in breeze.

We neared the massive oak and beneath it we could see Mah Lin sitting peacefully, as was his way. Selah smiled and explained, "Today my father will show you a new exercise." She stopped and looked at a small spring flower, then broke the stem and put it in her hair. She was radiant, and with great effort I did not stare, but listened as she said, "The beginning of true power starts with the discipline of mind and breath."

As we arrived at the oak, Mah Lin walked toward us. He was inclined sometimes to use few words, and now laid hands on me to adjust my position. He faced me toward the tree and bent my legs with a nudge of his knee. A palm on my lower belly and the motion of the bellows indicated that I was to breathe from there. He raised my arms in front of my body and rounded them as if I were holding the great trunk of the oak. Again he reminded me, with gesture of the bellows, that I should use my abdomen to draw breath.

Standing back he looked at my position as if I were a statue he was sculpting. He seemed satisfied after a few more small adjustments, and indicated to me the oak and its connection to my mind. A finger up and he said, "the heavens," a finger down—"the earth," a slap to my belly and, "Arkthar." His last adjustment was to my lips, as he turned them up to smile, and his last word before he and Selah ate lunch and watched me stand, was "Chi."

At the end of twenty minutes my legs trembled. My arms held in front were heavy beyond description. The earth's pull was the constant hammering force that would build my body to the strength of steel. "Enough for today," he said. "Every day, ring by ring, you will grow stronger." As I dropped my tired arms and moved my shaking legs, he said, "Let the oak tree be your teacher."

We three walked on now, and I ate the remains of the lunch that in kindness they had saved for me. Mah Lin and I sat by the thunderous falls and with a sweeping gesture of his hand he said again the word "Chi." Selah reached for a small stick and scratched its character into the dirt. It was composed of two parts she explained.

The middle was the character for a grain of rice. This was surrounded above and to the right by a shape that she said meant steam or vapor. It danced on the earth, and I took the stick and wrote it anew. "Draw from here," Mah Lin said and indicated his belly. In truth I did not yet make the connection between steamed rice and this mysterious energy, and finally Mah Lin looked to his daughter and said, "I will show him."

She brought me to my feet and put me to stand. "Tighten," she said gently. With a wide slow gathering motion he seemed to collect the energy from all around us, and then in an instant he released it. From a distance no longer than a finger, his palm clapped against my mid-section in a flash. I heard the air empty from my lungs as I felt both my feet take leave from the ground. There was at first only darkness and then the flooding of pain and light.

I lay on my back a good distance from where I had been standing. Mah Lin and Selah hovered over me, concern written on their faces. Mah Lin was contrite, but I knew, that in truth he had not issued anywhere near all his power. In time and by degree I came back to myself. I came first to my knees, then sitting, and finally back to my feet. I could say only one word, and that was "Chi."

"Yes," they said in unison and then came the relieved laughter of two who now knew that I would be all right.

All afternoon we three lingered by the falls. The mood was spirited and joyful. I reflected upon my present situation, and the beauty that cradled me, and wondered perhaps if I had died somewhere along my desert journey and had not realized my demise. Perhaps this was paradise, though truly I could not think of anything I may have done to earn it.

In heart I was completely grateful, and in body and mind completely alive. I remember the sword cutting my bonds of iron, and Mah Lin's first words to me, "From today I am your owner. Your life sentence has just begun."

I had never before been taken in war, I had never before been owned by another, I had never before been a slave, and, in truth, I had never before now been so free.

THE GUARDIAN

There were many things in my past life as a soldier that I had never experienced, and there were many experiences in that life that I wished I had never known. I had previously kept only the company of assassins, mercenaries, and murderers. Some were good soldiers, all were rough men, and I was harder than most. I had never regretted killing, but now in this home and ancient temple, my understanding of life's true value was changing.

A warrior's armor is designed by purpose to keep things out. As I looked down at the light and comfortable robe of scholar that I now so proudly wore, I realized that it helped me greatly to take things in. Ironically, the blue color of its fibers is boiled from the very plant that paints my skin for battle. Within cocoons the worms transform, and now like them, metamorphosis was upon me.

I moved daily in the slow martial movements of the exercise Selah had taught me. The strength that flowed all around me had begun to move through me. Selah watched, adjusted, and encouraged me, and together there was release and renewal.

My mind was opening like the wild flowers of the summer's landscape. I had only known the cold imposed order of a soldier's routine, but now upon waking I looked forward to breakfast with the monk and the doctor. The library was stark and cold by standards, but as I sat at its oak table with Selah beside me and the images and words of past masters before me, I felt only great comfort and warmth.

Selah on this particular day seemed even more jubilant than usual, like a child with a secret, bursting to tell me but holding it in trust until the time was right. After our exercise we tended to the household chores and walked with pleasure to the great sacred oak where the monk Mah Lin was quietly sitting with eyes closed and legs crossed. The raven flew down from above at our arrival and begged excitedly for scraps and morsels.

Father and daughter ate their picnic lunch while I stood contemplating the great oak and all that it nourished and protected. Even in its regal immensity it shared in kindness its bounty, giving home to squirrel, bird, and insect alike. With half-closed eyes I could hear the distant breathing of the great falls and the peaceful speech of priest and doctor. Here between heaven and earth, I held my stance.

Through the slow motions of the dance of dao yin I was learning 'stillness in movement,' and here in the company of the oak I was learning to feel the 'movement in stillness.' I could feel the rhythms and cycles of heartbeat, breathing, and digestion, and was at the same time quieting and taming the uncontrolled direction of my mind's unbridled thoughts.

Almost an hour had gone by before I realized that the priest and his child had long finished eating and were patiently waiting for me to finish standing. "Every day, ring by ring, Arkthar," Mah Lin said once more, and then added mysteriously, "Today we will show you something more of this place." This was the secret that Selah had been holding.

We walked onward past the roaring of the cold falls. Selah stooped to dig the odd root, or pluck a savory herb and tuck it carefully under her tunic. This she did sometimes for medicine and sometimes for food. She had often told me the two were intrinsic branches from the same tree. Mah Lin seemed also well animated and spoke much more than usual.

"In ancient times, the monks of this temple were renowned for their skill with metal," he said. "Some of their work still stands in the palace of the emperor." He paused briefly to take our bearings and then continued in both travel and conversation. "Those were the days that saw the birth of peerless weapons; those were times when art and spirit drove the powers of war." He pointed now as we reached a clearing, and said, "Arkthar, behold."

I was stunned to silence as I approached and touched the massive form that stood before me roaring from the stillness of a bygone age.

Rising above the afternoon mist of the sheltered but enormous clearing towered a fierce and regal lion. Vines of the spring had already climbed and spiraled up to the knees of the statue. It was metallic cold to the touch, and a slap of my hand told me it was substantially thick but hollow. Of how the metal had been worked on such a grand scale I could not say, for I had only seen the working of hand-held hammer bend and shape.

In my past world no wonders like this existed, it seemed crafted exquisitely by the hand of giants. I stood enraptured until Mah Lin broke my trance. "This iron is melted to liquid and then cast," he said. "It was made here by imperial order, and bequeathed back to the monks of this monastery to mark their artistry and loyalty." I could hear wonder and respect in the usually even voice of Mah Lin.

Selah reached high and rubbed the inscription carved across the creature's powerful chest. When the accumulated dirt of eons past had fallen to her hand, she read and translated; "From the First Emperor, the date unreadable, forever will this guardian protect these hallowed grounds, against this temple no evil will prevail."

She paused briefly before turning towards me and adding, "The First Emperor and his army has been sleeping under his mountain for the last one thousand years." Although this sounded unbelievable, in this world I had learned the wisdom of not rushing to conclusion.

I wanted to stay here for a long time. Mah Lin and Selah were also in no hurry, and so they left me to my thoughts. The idea of metal so hot that it flows brought back my dream of the rivers of fire. I remembered clearly the red molten streams flooding down the mountain as we walked towards it. I winced, seared with the heat of its memory, and the feeling that it held the delicate balance of primal creation and utter destruction.

Reluctantly we gathered to leave, and as I looked back over my shoulder it seemed the great beast could easily come to life at the command of a powerful monk. I weighed Mah Lin against the clerics of my old land and realized that falsehood is often wrapped in the trappings of fear and power, while truth stands tall, clad only in the mantle of its purity. Selah gently coaxed me from my contemplation, "Arkthar, where are your thoughts?"

I stopped walking and faced her. "Selah, the ones that know Latin preach that the ancient prophets of my old world have a similar portent. In the Book of Revelation, one wrote of a Conquering Lion that shall come to trample and destroy the wicked at the time of the end," I replied gravely.

I turned away and added to myself, "the time of the Apocalypse," and we walked on.

THE FIRST EMPEROR

Time is the great transformer of all things. The rhythm of its steady passage is the beating heart of change. Under its watchful stare newborns turn to ancients, generations pass from old to new, and empires rise and crumble. In the world of men, it is time's passage that converts the deeds of history into tales of legend. It is the ice that grinds the mountain, the water that transports the scree, and finally it is the mist that shrouds the remaining foothill.

The old woman walked slowly upon the high green knoll. She placed her steps carefully, climbing steadily higher between the heavens and the earth. Adjusting the bag slung across her brittle shoulders, the old one sat and rested, hoping here to gather strength.

Built to last forever, it had already outlived the collective memory of those that saw her new. To the scattered villagers that lived in its shadow, it was just a hillock, an obstacle in the way of their travel and progress. To the ancient oracle, however, it was much more. She knew that her wandering had carried her not upon a hill whittled from mountain by nature's blade, but a mound cast upward by the labor of a united people.

In the cloaked recesses of her tortured mind, she toiled with the hands of a near million, and she drank up the lifetimes that passed in its creation. This forgotten monument now lay serenely sleeping. Its origins hidden like the hills, by the earthbound fog of time.

Breathing easier she closed her eyes, perched high on the sacred tomb of the First Emperor. In one steady exhalation she voiced a name that only the birds could hear. "Qin Shi Huang Di." Beneath her rests the Son of Heaven, sealed within a bronze model of his world. He lies under gold painted stars, surrounded by seas and rivers of flowing mercury, and treasures beyond imagination.

History records that this ruler's tribe bore the totem of the bear. He set standards of measure, language, philosophy, medicine, and commerce that have entwined a diverse culture ever since. Through superior tactics and military might he was able to unify the empire, and he held it with an iron fist. It was the stones of his wall that kept his enemies out, but it was the blood of his people that cemented them together.

Legend holds that his birth was announced by a thunderclap from a clear sky, and that he was a god made into the form of a man. After living for more than one hundred years, he arranged his affairs and prepared for his journey into the afterlife. Some say that a dragon descended from the heavens and took him away, while another account holds that the First Emperor himself turned into a dragon and departed.

Entombed with an army of ten thousand, all sleep, he in death and those that serve rendered mortal by the clay and kilns of the surrounding hills. Poised to protect him on his journey, or be woken from Death's slumber to rise and conquer once again.

There are some things that only time must know.

The Entrance

We continued to walk back, the voice of the falls growing steadily louder as we drew near. Once there Mah Lin and I stripped to loincloth and stood in the turbulent icy downpour. The rocks were round and slippery and footing was precarious, but seeking a balance in the midst of adversity was cleansing. I held my stance beneath the river's power, pleased that my resistance to the icy cold had steadily increased.

Mah Lin stood calmly beside me. After some time he shouted over the rushing water, "There is more." I took this to mean that I should continue to hold my stance, and I turned toward him to seek some sign of confirmation. He had disappeared, and before I could once again wonder how, his muscled arm had wrapped my torso from behind and pulled me through the frigid fluid wall.

The water's sound was instantly muted; its tone deeper as it bounced off the walls of the cave. His laughter echoed all around me as he set me down and allowed my vision the time it needed to adjust. An opaque blue light poured in from direction of the falls, and the size of the cave grew and expanded as he lit the torches that flamed along its walls. I could now see the movement of the wooden machinery as it turned and churned, wheel to wheel, and cog to cog, driven by the interplay of water with gravity.

Within its dark walls the shadowed memories of my past reared up within me, unrestrained and unbidden. 'The Cave of the Alders,' was my only thought. My body shook without control, and I felt once more worthless and ineffectual, unable to protect those who were entrusted to me. I felt the failure of my past rise up again to tear me asunder.

Returning now that all the lamps were lit, if Mah Lin noticed my plight he ignored it and said, "Welcome, Arkthar, to the temple forge. It is ancient, and was in great need of repair when Selah and I arrived, but with hard work we have brought it back to life. Its heart beats once again," clearly referring to the water wheel driving the in and out pumping of the large two-stroke bellows. He looked to the vast cave like a proud parent and said, "This is where your Five Element child was born over six hundred years ago, and this is the cave from where the guardian lion emerged.

From the far end of the cave Selah approached us. She was dry, and it made sense that there would be other ways in beside the grand hidden doorway of the falls. Indeed, light did shine in from higher elevations to make a natural chimney for the forge's smoke, and I could smell the familiar aroma of bat manure that I had often spread upon the garden. "Show Arkthar the cave," Mah Lin suggested, "while I tune the mechanism of the bellow pump."

I pushed the terror that had initially gripped me back into the crevice from where it came. There was much to see as we each took a torch and I began to explore. She told me that this place was once a mountain of fire as in my dream. "Time," she said, "has altered its appearance much."

There was the regular forge, fueled by charcoal from willow wood, and its familiar tools of hammers and anvil. There was charcoal enough to fill a mighty enclave, the byproduct of industry that had continued for so many generations. Further back was a huge smelter. I had never before seen such a furnace; it was a large enclosure covered by a thick layer of reddened clay to trap the heat. It drained from the bottom onto a sandy surface. Around it were a variety of thick-walled molds, some to shape kettles and pans, some urns, bells, and the like. Raw ingots lay beside finished tools and farm implements.

Deeper inside the cave the bat guano was layered thick and dark, the accumulation of eons. Water dripped from above it and leached out small white crystals piled thick now like heavy snow. Yellow brimstone clung in various cracks like the bats that hung from the roof by the thousands. Upside down they waited for the freedom of the dusk. Theirs was a life of moonlight raid and insect pillage; they were as a mighty army, these soldiers of the night.

There was a flat expanse lined with crafted thick wood trunks, some padded, most not. Selah made a gesture of kick and strike, and I remembered the legs of Mah Lin and understood completely. I walked closer to a lone wooden table, low and substantial, Selah close by my side. On it rested a pillow filled with iron pellets. Mah Lin stood with bended knees and began to drop his hands flat down upon it. The sound was murderous within the cave. "Iron Palm," the monk said, and I jumped back in reflex as he feigned a mid-strike.

Much later I would come to understand that the hard striking arts, they called external, and these they trained inside. The soft and sometimes still movements were called internal arts, and these were practiced outside. It seemed they favored this linking together of opposites to make one harmonious whole.

We ate well when we finally arrived back home, both in quality and amount. Selah and Mah Lin talked much and the conversation seemed centered around my progress and my perspective. I knew now the names of food, and I was able to ask for more, or graciously decline. Over time I tried to follow their manners for the table and even bathed my hands before we sat.

I had mastered the use of their utensils, merely two wooden sticks, which if held properly could subdue a hunger quite efficiently. It was fine to shovel the food into an open mouth from a closely held bowl and spit the bones upon the table, but wrong to impale a morsel or rake the common dish for a tastier bite.

Often I learned more by mistake than example. We finished the last of the tea, and as I stood I stuck my sticks into a bowl of rice that had escaped consumption. I tried to hand Selah the leftovers thinking that she would place it safely for tomorrow's meal, but she was frozen. I saw the color leave her face as she looked first at my offering and then to her father, and I knew that I had erred. Mah Lin moved smoothly to pull out the eating sticks and quickly remove the bowl of grain.

Breaking the cold awkward silence that followed, Mah Lin kindly offered a correction. "Arkthar, the sticks in the rice call to mind the incense offered at a funeral, they call to Death."

SLEEP

My day had been full. My body was tired when I lay down that night, my mind however, reared up like a wild horse. I was its rider, but not its master. It jumped and raced past memory and half thought, from place to place with no control or guidance. It carried me to the iron monument in the open clearing, where once again I stood humbled before the mighty effigy.

From the towering lion to the jagged flight of bats and the steady syncopation of the forge machinery, my psyche charged onward. It brought me from the darkness of the cave through the churning falls and into the sunlight, where I emerged and drew fresh breath. My imagination slowed from its untamed gallop, and I stopped to survey the vast landscape that stretched before me. The last thoughts of my day had become the first dreams of my night, and I was not alone.

We three stood looking at the mountain of fire. Our location was as before, but now the fire and molten rivers were long gone, and instead of the blackening smoke, its rocky peak stood wrapped in blue white ice. The high altitude winds carried snowy powder up and off, painting feathers on its frozen cap.

The once blistering terrain was now a fresh spring meadow. From the lush green lowland a forest climbed the mountain's base like an advancing army, front lines halted far below the snow and ice. Thick mist cloaked the cliffs and craggy outcrops; it hung and lingered in the trees caressing the forest in its damp embrace.

A mighty river snaked and coiled its way from high to low, undulating like the mythical serpent of old seafarers' tales. It remained ever humble in its almighty power, seeking only the course of least resistance. It cut deep and moved fast on high, but slowed, widened, and finally wandered like an old man as it arrived at the gentler slope at mountain's foot, its energy spent by the length of its journey.

Water is the ice, the river, and the mist—one element, three forms. I felt his presence behind my back, but I would not turn around.

"You have done well, Arkthar, since we last met above the desert sands," Death said. If within the dream Selah and Mah Lin heard him, they gave no indication and continued to look silently in the direction of the mountain. "I have done my best," I replied, and this too, they seemed unable to hear. "Well at least so far you have kept your feet on the ground," Death quipped, and we both shared a chuckle. Still I dared not turn around.

"In the world of men I am much maligned. They see only that I take and never see that I give in great measure. I alone release them from their suffering. In times of great dying, men point to me and curse, but it is they that have overturned the balance." I felt Death move much closer, and my body shuttered.

"I am Death, and I am the natural law. I have walked this world since life began. From primordial seas I helped life thrive, it was I that pushed it up upon the solid ground, and it was I that gave it wings and launched it to the heavens. I am the keeper and the one that weeds your earthly garden." I listened carefully to the words he spoke, and when he paused, I heard the earth begin its lamentation.

"Arkthar, we are moving into strange times. Mankind is new upon this platform, and from their beginnings they have fought against the natural order, it is your kind who work me to the bone." He spoke again with purging energy, "It was I who gave you back your life when you died at the hands of men. You intrigue me, and I am not done with you. Study well the wisdom of the monk and heed the lessons from the past, for as we speak a storm is gathering to come against you. The dark tempest is driven by hatred and revenge. It seeks your end and the ruin of all that you hold dear." I listened silently and stared off at the mountain, and Death continued.

"Remember me kindly, Arkthar, and remember this as well—to unleash the Dragon you must first imprison it. Heed me, once the Dragon is released there can be no returning." Death spoke again but it was not with words. Instead, the cries of the earth rose and trembled with the voices of the past. It was the growing cry of age-old pain, and it shocked me to the core. Spurred by terror I tried to run, but the sound followed and engulfed me.

It trailed off, then started up and filled my room again, until it became the familiar sound of the rooster's morning crowing.

THE FIVE CUTS

Selah handed me my breakfast bowl immediately. Mah Lin sat amid a pile of shavings whittled from the handle of a garden hoe. The Five Element sword was sheathed upon his back. As he rose, his hands traced the patterned smoothness of his work and he was satisfied. The farmer's tool he handed me had been transformed. It had been sculpted quickly but with great skill. I held the hard wooden hilt and felt its heft. It was not steel, but it was a weapon. No longer meant to work the garden, clearly it was now a tool that the priest had crafted to train me. Mah Lin's tone was jovial, "No more a handle," he said; "now it is an oar."

The room had been cleared, and as I shoveled in the last of my gruel he began to speak with both his voice and his body. "Five Elements, five cuts," he said dryly. With his right arm he traced a large X in front of his body as he faced me. Then, holding an imaginary sword with two hands, he began.

From top right to bottom left a diagonal slash, "One." He turned his hands rotating the unseen edge and then back on the same line, from bottom left to upper right, "Two." He drew the imaginary blade back slowly past his ear and down in a graceful half circle until it rested at his lower right. He brought it up and to the left, "Three." At its apex his hands moved again rotating the invisible edge like a swallow's flight, and then down smoothly from top left to bottom right, "Four." The momentum of the phantom blade spiraled steadily forward as his two hands came up to torso height and then became a center thrust. "Five." The sword tip's target was the intersection of the X, the middle of the body line.

His body faced me squarely, and he began the count once more. Both hands flew up to the handle at his back. The sword came up, out, and down to the left. "One." From lower left it retraced its path up and to the right. "Two." It drew back gracefully, circling down to the bottom right and up. "Three." The blade turned over and from high left cut down, and to the right. "Four." Moving upward it gathered momentum as its point flashed precisely through the center. "Five."

"Eventually the five cuts will become only one cut." He moved again, and in less time than a nod the sequence of five blurred together and became one. It was faster by far than the eye could follow. He laughed at my open mouth, and said, "Ring by ring, Arkthar. Now five cuts, but not five elements, for before there was steel, there was wood."

We moved outside into the clean morning air, the wood felt heavy in my hands. Once I had gotten comfortable with the five cuts from a square unmoving stance, we began again. The first cut with the right leg leading, the second with the left stepping forward, third in harmony with the right step, the forth with the left, and the fifth thrust with the planting of the right. "Five cuts, five paces." Mah Lin said and asked, "How fast can you run?" I didn't have any real answer and so I replied, "As fast as I have to." His frown told me he was not joking, and he sprinted to the count of five, covering about four body lengths along the ground.

Mah Lin raised the sword and ran at full speed toward a bamboo grove. This tall plant stood in clusters everywhere upon this land. It was most utilitarian, used to craft everything from furniture to cutlery. It would grow the length of fist to elbow in a single day, and it would reach the thickness of a man's arm. What made it unique was not its girth, but that inside it was completely empty. So it seemed that it should have no strength at all, but like many things of this world the opposite was, in fact, the truth.

By the time he reached it, he was at full stride and the sound of steel on wood rang out. Every step a cut, he had traversed four body lengths in the time of one breath. Only as he impaled the last trunk with the metal tip did the diagonally severed victim of first blow reach the ground. With a tilt of his head three more in sequence followed suit.

Sweat glistened on his muscled chest when he rejoined us, sword in hand. "Arkthar," he said as he touched the wooden sword within my hand, "Keep it with you and let it grow to become your fifth limb." I was touched by his gift and bowed with deep respect. He had called it an oar, I knew that it was now a necessary part of my journey, an implement that if used well would propel me forward. So it was that a new element had been added to the structure of my day.

Before first meal and with Selah near me, I voraciously studied writing, reading, and wisdom past. To the accompaniment of morning birdsong, I practiced the slow movements of the dao yin. At midday from flower to acorn, and from bud to leaf, the oak and the raven would watch over me as I held my quiet stance beneath them.

The daily pounding of the falls with my friend and teacher, signaled and conditioned my body for the fast and hard training of limb and movement that we practiced inside the cavern. I returned home every evening and with arms held at shoulder height, carrying two pails of bat dung to feed our thriving plot.

During the day my heavy wooden blade never left my back, but the time of its training was sunset. Bathed in the warm blood red light of day's end, I held the oar within my hands, and traced the pattern of five cuts until every muscle of my body held their memory. I remembered also the sword art of the fierce Norse raiders, and learned from it. With every new skill that my right arm learned, I trained my left to be its equal.

As well as arts of war, I mastered what I once considered women's work. I tended the livestock. I learned to flavor well most of what we ate, for I enjoyed the new experience of spice. At evening meal I learned to follow by ear their conversation, and now could add my simple point in the language of this land. Sometimes speech switched from my language to theirs, and like spice, perhaps a flavor of Latin, Norse, or Celt would surface in the mix.

In my new world, the monk Mah Lin taught me the ways of the warrior priest, while with Selah I learned the arts of the scholar and the methods of traditional medicine. I had often heard father and daughter speak of the natural world reflecting the movement and balance of opposite forces.

Through conflict to peace, from soldier to healer, now with the passage of time I was beginning not just to understand this concept, but to embody it.

THE LIGHT WITHIN
THE DARKNESS

Within the darkened shadows of the cavern's forge, my training with Mah Lin continued. He spoke of the new form that I would learn, "It is older by far than many," he said, "first brought by a brown southern giant to the temple we call Shaolin." I recalled the name from our conversation of long ago in the presence of the sacred oak. The priest nodded with pleasure when I remembered its name, "vajra fist," and nodded once more when I remembered that its meaning is "thunderbolt."

He began his instruction without fanfare; the form opened slowly, and was initially not unlike the "dao yin sequence" that Selah had taught me. After its slow opening all similarities vanished. I watched in awe as his movements transformed from the slow power of twist undulate and coil, to the blinding speed of limb and leg. This speed was not yet within my reach, for full mobility had not yet returned to my battered body. The priest assured me, however, that it would, but for now I was to be content to imitate his motions as accurately as possible.

By month's end I had learned all the movements, but the real skill would come only with practice. Day by day we trained the motions of the vajra fist, and day by day I did become more fluid in its powerful execution. Steadily I grew stronger and more confident, I was indeed happy to push myself once more beyond the limits of flesh and mind.

Satisfied at last that the form was in my body and that my mind no longer needed to focus on recalling the next sequence, Mah Lin bid me pause and reflect. "Now that the first stage of your training has ended, the hidden truths of this ancient exercise can be explored." He reached high into a crevice and drew forth a work of wonder. It was beautifully crafted and old beyond measure. "This relic, too, came to us with the journey of the southern monk. It is a steel they call *wootz,* and its making is the secret of our sacred forge.

He held it with reverence in his strong hands and showed it to me to examine only with my eyes. "It is the earthly symbol of what you now study through the flesh," he said, and as I looked upon it he continued to explain. "This is the vajra. In a time long past it was held by the hand of the Bodhidharma, and aided his meditation." I looked at what he spoke of and could think only that for such a powerful object it was indeed quite small. It rested comfortably upon his outstretched palm. It shared the texture of Mah Lin's sword, perfectly symmetric in shape like two oaken acorns joined by a straight silver bridge.

Mah Lin was not one to use words carelessly. With explanation he was more than sparse, assuming, I think, that my understanding would catch up over time. He stated simply that, "this object is a symbol. The twofold meaning of vajra is thunderbolt and diamond—the blinding light of enlightenment that crashes unexpectedly to permanently illuminate the darkened mind and leaves in its wake a new consciousness as clear and resilient as the hardest jewel in nature's crown."

As I listened mindfully to his words, he added one more thought, "The hammer of Thor has traveled far."

He led me now to a small grotto at the cavern's far end, where he bid me sit in the uncomfortable cross-legged style of his custom. He had me close my eyes lightly and direct my breath to my center. My fingers he placed in a specific way, he called "a mudra." The fingers of my right hand surrounded the extended index finger of the fist of my left.

He answered my bewildered look with another short explanation that was not much of an answer at all. "The vajra mudra transforms ignorance into wisdom and symbolizes the five elements: earth, water, wood, fire, and metal." I accepted his request that each day following the physical movements of the Vajra Fist, I continue in darkness the quiet seated practice of the mudra.

The words of my teacher were still well beyond my mind's understanding, but in the monk and his daughter my faith was now unwavering, and I would do my best in anything that they asked of me.

The Vajra and the Mind

The seated meditation of the vajra mudra was harder for me then the movement of the vajra fist form. But eventually and with work I became comfortable with both. As always Mah Lin knew the moment of this transition, without ceremony he passed the vajra to me, and I touched it for the first time.

I held the solid but beautifully delicate object in my hand and in my mind. It was short and heavy, double-ended, perfectly symmetric, and balanced. Its size was the length of my palm, a figure eight, like the symbol of infinity. It felt familiar, the echo of a distant memory. I knew it was a sacred object of symbol and ritual, but I was already in motion. I had a fighter's knowledge and a pugilist's mind. Many times for sport and money I had held a weapon like this, I knew well the feel of a caestus strapped into my hand. But this was not strapped, it was free, and I could pass it hand to hand. It moved my body like lightning and made my fist as hard as diamond, and I thought then that they had named it well.

Mah Lin said nothing but allowed me to move as I felt. When I was finally spent, Mah Lin said, "You move well, but a striking tool was considered by the monk who carried it only the basest of its properties. In the hands of healer it is a tool of massage," and he bid me to push against my muscles and source out any pain. Mah Lin made a motion like striking and suggested a beating rhythm. "Light now, every day a little stronger, for health," he said. "An instrument of healing is a much more worthy purpose than a weapon of destruction."

He held out his hand and I gave it back. He drew fresh breath and released his mind from the strict channel of rational thought. It swirled and tumbled over time and place like a mythic river. It flowed freely southward from the cold homeland of Thor to the kingdom of the ancient Aryans, where the northern god was embraced, altered, and released into the world. The mind of the monk surged eastward, tracing the thunder god's course, as he streamed out over vast distance and desert sand, only to spill and gather in the lush and fertile valleys of the vast southern continent. The monk saw the northern lightning bearer take root there and transform once more. He saw him rising with hands that reached to heaven, remade as mighty Indra, 'the wielder of the thunderbolt.' As the speed of turbulent thought slowed to pools of quiet reflection, he saw this wielder carried northward across the roof of the earth by the Bodhidharma himself, and settle here, reborn now, as the guardian Vajrapani.

The glint of the metal vajra caught my eye as the monk smiled and bid me, "Take it." As I reached again it was not there. I could feel only its lightest touch against my wrist, and then with only the slightest of his movement, the pain came. It made my body shift, and Mah Lin followed and interpreted these shifts like the reading of manuscript. From wrist to elbow, shoulder to neck, and then down again to wrist. He controlled my movements both offensive and defensive over the entire expanse of the forge. The harder I tried to retrieve it the more intense the painful lesson got.

Mah Lin pressed or pulled me at will with never anything more than the strength required to comfortably shake hands. He, finally tired of this sport, released me. "The real martial power of the bolt lies in the skill of softness coupled with the knowledge of healer. The full power of the timeless vajra, however, lies only within the mind of the enlightened." In the darkness of the cavern, Mah Lin left me to nurse my aching limbs and injured pride. He bid me only "breathe deeply and grow quiet," and left me to myself.

The monk strode through the raging water of the falls without slowing and burst into the bright open sunlight. Suddenly his vision was pulled skyward by the distant cry of a bird of prey. On high, two mighty eagles crashed together. With talons locked they began the dangerous free-falling spiral of their courtship ritual. The priest watched the speed of their earthbound plummet increase and their wing tips trace the graceful outline of the double helix, the timeless pattern of life. Mere seconds from earthly impact they broke apart to climb and begin their mating ritual anew.

Mah Lin contemplated the mystical divine energy of the universe itself. He knew that Arkthar and the symbolic metal thunderbolt were also joined, locked, and entwined. He understood that both had somehow plummeted through vast distance and far place, falling and for now intact, through the ascending layers of history, legend, religion, and myth.

To See Beyond

She had wandered for months through the blind madness
that took her mind whenever it desired. Her gnarled fingers
clutched at her bag of bones and tortoise shells as if its touch
might keep her sane, but it did not. She no longer controlled
her walks between the world of spirit and the world of flesh.
Visions emerged unbidden, reflected in full moon's light by the
shattered mirror of what was once a healthy mind. She could
not remember clearly what she had seen and from what she had
escaped.

The old one ate when she remembered and that was incon-
sistently. When her mind was lucid she picked the roots and
berries of the wilderness. Safely stowed within her bag, she
would find them later, and devour them hungrily. She was
grateful that at least her bag had somehow retained its power.
The steady supply of refuse from the marching soldiers was no
more, and so her body withered. What was consistent was the
need to put distance between her and them, and this burning need to be far away from the commander and the cold
north region. From north to south blew the winds that filled
her ragged sails.

The oracle moved like a strange animal, from hamlet to
house with little rhyme and no reason. She would on occasion be asked to divine, but since her night in the commander's
tent she could not see clearly in any direction, and so no coins
would come her way. She had assumed the habit of looking to

the sky, and searching every bird that flew there. The one she sought was oily black, but it did not fly above her.

He was a creature living and moving on the instincts of his kind. The beggar did not rave, nor was he mad or possessed. He was workmanlike as he went about his business. He traveled mostly at night, for the stars gave him comfort and direction. Patiently and methodically he moved from south to north, and moving as a bird flies, he followed a long dead trail that he saw from his great height.

He avoided the society of men as much as he could, not because he hated them, but because their world and their way was simply not his. His way was the way of forest paths and meadow streams, or the way of clouds that cross the sky. He knew where he was going, but paused occasionally searching for her among the shadows. He at least was not among the lost.

Long before he saw the twinkling firelight, he smelled the smoke and heard her howls rise up into the heavens. She was astonished when he came upon her, relieved that her cries had finally drawn him from the skies. They sat with few words, and on her fire he cooked a meal for her that warmed and nourished her fragmented mind. She had settled now that she had eaten, and looked at him anew, and wondered how he came.

She saw the feathered rags that adorned him, and thought that his plumage was the darkest of his kind. She wanted to reach out and touch, but she dared not take the chance that he would fly away. He offered her a warm twig tea which she held between her palms and sipped. "You have seen much old one," he said gently, and was warmed by her toothless smile and eyes that sparkled almost human. "It is time to let it go," he soothed, "You have given freely of your gift." "It is gone now," she answered, not sure if this was good or bad. "I saw too much."

With a slow deep breath the beggar answered, "If men could see their fate, they would not rise from their beds." The beggar looked deeply into eyes almost blind with cataracts and said lovingly, "You have seen enough."

In stillness and at peace she rested and sat quietly by the dying fire. At half-moon's highest point, the beggar stood. He arranged and smoothed his ragged plumage, as the oracle watched and wondered if she could make him stay. But she could not, for he was a wild bird, and he was free among the stars. With bowl in hand, he reached out to touch her wrinkled face, and then in an instant he was gone. He disappeared into the dark night, yet she had not seen him fly away.

Alone once more, she thought of looking up into the blue-black sky to see if she could catch another glimpse. She rose with a mind as clear as crystal, and to no one but herself she whispered, "That would be foolish, for he is walking as a man."

THE MANNER OF
KILLING CROWS

The rebel lay flat and still in the main square beside the ten dead that had passed over during the night. He stared upward along the barrel through cold skies at the fattened crows that circled and squawked overhead. His breathing and heartbeat slowed, and his finger squeezed the trigger of his rugged crossbow. The bolt flew upwards with a thump, and carried through and well beyond the ugly bird.

The rebel listened with closed eyes for the position of two sounds. The first was the hollow crashing of the bird; the second was the metallic thud of his returning ammunition. He rose, retrieved, and repeated the process again and again. The dead had fed the birds, and now the birds would feed the living.

Of twenty thousand men only four hundred remained, and these four hundred were more wraith than human. The everyday sounds of urban life had ceased long ago. All livestock had been consumed months prior, right down to the last emaciated horse. Conversations were rare, as speech now took the tones of whisper, and walking had regressed to an act of limp or shuffle. If black was the color of the birds of the sky, then grey was the pallor of these few men, the last of the living.

The young leader often thought of his wife and children. He pictured them in his mind's eye far away and warm. When he tried consciously to remember their faces he could not, but

then a sound or smell or movement would bring their faces
flooding back whole, detailed, and plump. He did not miss
them and would never miss them, for that would mean wishing
that they were here, and he had learned enough in his short life
to appreciate even the strangest of favors.

He called to his second in command as he stood in the
corner high tower and looked out at the enemy encampment.
They scanned the outer plains, and as he took stock he spoke.
His voice was low and gravely now, the effect of no food and
little water. "This has never been a fight that we could win." He
was weak and paused for breath, "Our position is simple, we
can die like animals or we can die like men. We did not choose
this fight, but this at least, we can choose."

He could hear the distant sounds of the enemy and see the
disciplined structure of the foreign camps. Their dialect and
manner was not so different from those of his tribe. He wondered how long people had been killing people, and wondered
to himself if it would always be so. He wondered how in the
equal balance of the great opposites, is war is so permanent and
undying and peace so transitory and short-lived. The leader
knew answers did not matter, for these were just the foolish
thoughts of the dying and the soon dead.

The machines of war stood idle. The cast iron layered on the
oak gateway would never yield, and against the massive walls even
the trebuchets were of no use. The rebel forces had stung well and
stung hard at the early attempts to breech. The enemy did not
know that ammunition was scarce and that their arrow count was
now merely fifty-five. It seemed to the rebel that the great commander was not really much of a military tactician at all.

Perhaps strategy was not his strength. Maybe he was the
type of leader that inspires by example and charisma. The rebel

studied him often from the distance. The man who had killed the bear was aloof and alone, more feared then loved. This type of officer is more likely to die at the hands of his own than those of the enemy, for the battlefield is a place of chaos and a place where any manner of dying is possible.

For the entire afternoon the rebel and his officer explored the inside of their destroyed capital. The walk was unhurried. When they found a body or part that had been missed, it was recorded for burial. This was a mission of evaluation, and it was clear that there was nothing. Everything had been consumed, if not by men then by fire. The act of walking was exhausting, and the business of appraisal was depressing. Finally like a child the rebel's chief officer sat, put head to hand, and cried.

"It is alright," the rebel soothed, but in fact he looked around hoping that no others would see this sight. "Stop the tears you are no woman," he said curtly, and quickly added, "I wish now that you were, to serve me in my bed and not in my battles." They both laughed loudly at this, and, at least for now, despair flew off like a greasy crow.

"You are a good man," the rebel said, "you have seen much, but now is the time to use fresh eyes." He had his comrade's attention. "You have seen the stables long empty where once our mighty cavalry fed and rested. We have walked together through the empty larder where there has been nothing to fry for months, and still you have seen only what is gone, not what is left behind." His man waited for more of an explanation.

"We have clean dry straw, and that we have in great abundance. We have the cooking oil that has been idle for far too long. We have fifty-five arrows, arrows that if aimed well can do damage. They may return to the capitol with their victory and our heads, but they will leave without the catapults, the trebuchets, and their tower. It is time again for one more night excursion—our last."

Hope is a powerful force in the movements of men and war, for without hope there is no life. The young leader spoke again and said, "Do you remember how often I have killed the circling crows?"

"Yes, my lord, everyday," was the answer that came.

"Do you remember when I am by far the happiest at this grim task?"

The reply came without pause, "When you impale two birds with one arrow."

The young leader smiled and nodded.

"Gather me eight of the finest and stealthiest. I will need skillful bowmen and men who are prepared to kill in silence and up close."

THE LAST MISSION

Eight of the best remaining men were assembled within the tower, along with the rebel, their company numbered nine. By any standard the strongest here would be the weakest anywhere else, but now strength was a measure of the mind. The leader knew all eight; six were seasoned veterans and two had barely reached manhood.

The rebel was comfortable with six but questioned his second-in-command's choice of the young ones. His second spoke from the heart, "They are boys no doubt, but war makes men at an early age, my lord. These two are brothers. At our arrival they were civilians and worked diligently on the mining of the field. They toiled together, while one dug the other sharpened and planted spikes."

There was no argument that the knowing of the field hazards was useful but the leader was still hesitant. "These boys are farmers not soldiers," the rebel said. His second passed a youth his dagger; scanning the room for an instant, the youth hurled it full force into an apple-sized knot in a door at the room's far end. "Point taken," was all the leader said.

The raiding party entered the once empty livery. It was now a hive of activity, as more than a hundred men toiled at their task. The straw with cord and twine was being shaped into the form of men, and these straw men were being clothed in the lightest of armor. The youths and the veterans alike looked to this task with confusion, but asked no questions.

The second in charge fielded the unspoken question. "Pay these efforts no heed, your purpose will occupy you fully. Killing a man when you are close does not have the filter of distance." This he directed to the young boys who fidgeted in discomfort and stared to the floor. The response from the seasoned was only a smile.

The rest of the afternoon was spent training for their mission. They had assembled a reasonable copy of the armor worn by the imperial sentries. They discussed in broad terms its strengths, but focused in detail on its weaknesses. The lifting of the body scales by dagger point just before thrust was mentioned and discarded; death must come quicker and quieter.

In the end the oldest and most experienced would have the final say. The grizzled one taunted the youngest and said, "Scream for your life when first you feel me, and for now just march with awareness back and forth here before me." The youth looked around the room reluctant to be the victim. The old soldier chuckled at this and urged, "Come on son, don't disappoint an old man."

So there it was; the complete reversal of the timeless natural order. It was now the oldest that had challenged the youngest. The grizzled soldier sat, tightly securing a filthy blindfold around his already feeble eyes. Emboldened by the blindfold, the youth complied and marched back and forth in front of the sightless soldier who for now just listened. In his mind the youth was already preparing to scream.

On his third pass the old one flew, catching the youth on the half step. The offbeat is the no man's land of movement's rhythm, the place after a step is launched, and before it has landed. The soldier with a gift of this rhythm does well in combat; and this man's age was no accident. The young scream did not escape; instead it was trapped and silenced by the old right hand that did three things simultaneously and in an instant.

His jaw was held firmly shut by hand heel from below; the pushing up of jaw turned the youth's face to the ceiling, and the palm sealed the mouth, as the thumb and fingers had already closed the air from the nostrils. As the ceiling passed before his eyes, so did his entire life. The flash of the left hand and the cold feeling of steel passing roughly across his throat was the last thing he remembered before the blackness.

As they revived the young man who may have wet himself slightly, the old one removed the grimy cloth from around his eyes. He helped the shaken young man to his feet. Graciously, this time he had used only the dull side of his blade. The old soldier now held the floor and the attention of his eight comrades. He spoke well and demonstrated better. His two arms showed the motion which was as simple as tying a knot. "Two arms, one motion, and death is served in silence," he said.

Making contact now with the eyes of his peers he continued, "The skill of its application lies in the secret of the off-beat rhythm, and this is best learned from the ears and not the eyes, for in the dark only those that must see are truly blind." This lesson they practiced well into the night within the barn and beside the army of straw that was now taking shape. The last preparation was the study of the field and enemy encampment. The rebel had scratched its detailed image upon the brown dirt floor.

The fort was a thick-walled square, which sat upon a huge open square plain. Where the plain ended the dense forest began on all four sides. Positioned as close to the forest and as far from the fortress as possible sat the huge ring of enemy encampment, four tents thick. Beyond this in the four corners where the ring of tents pulls away from the square of forest, were positioned the war machines. With the combined help of the two youngest, they marked out every hidden trap upon the open field. Their starvation was all but forgotten as a hunger of a different kind now took over.

All remembered the trebuchets and the screams that answered the diplomatic entreaty, one more wrong that would on this night, finally be avenged.

OVER THE WALL

It was the walls of their city fortress that set it apart from all others and kept it safe. Their method of building had been lost to time, and many say that this method has never been surpassed. A northern outpost of the First Emperor, it had already stood its ground for more than a thousand years. The rebel stronghold is protected by both an inner and outer wall. It is the outer wall that is the most imposing. Along its top, soldiers once rode chariots, and the men that had died in its construction were buried within it.

Legend says that this is the reason it could never be destroyed in war, but the very thickness and slope of its base is probably the more accurate explanation. The defending army could move anywhere along the top providing they pass through the corner towers. From these same towers any attacking army could expect withering arrow fire launched from its upper murder holes.

As the men stood on these timeless walls and looked out in each of the four directions from this great height, their mission became focused in their minds. From each of the four high walls they would depart, and with good fortune they would return to their starting point. The rebel pondered this circle; even as he surveyed the distant ring of the enemy's surrounding tents.

They were divided into three groups of two and one group of three, and each group took their place in the middle of each great wall. The leader was with the two young brothers for their safety and to his peril. To each was given a large bundle of oil-soaked straw, a bow, and six fire arrows that were also charged with oil and straw, and finally to each a dagger of the finest forging. Each man, blackened, hunched beneath a cloak of shimmering white. In snow or in darkness, they were prepared to blend.

Quickly and smoothly they descended over the walls, lowered from above by ropes. His second in command embraced the rebel just before the descent. With wet eyes and a voice wracked with emotion, he said quietly, "Stay safe, my lord, and bring these boys home unscathed." The rebel looked at him steadily before replying with a smile, "You are indeed a woman." With a curt nod, "Point taken," was all that his friend said.

All four parties reached the ground simultaneously and moved silently off in each of the four directions. The moon favored their task and stayed hidden behind the clouds. They crawled like lizards across the wide, snowy field and lay still under the white cloak when the need arose. They crossed the open plain and then between and through the four rows of enemy tents undetected.

Upon reaching the cover of the forest, they removed the white cloaks and used them to bundle the oiled straw. Black shadows shifted through the moonless night, silently they moved through the woods to the resting siege weapons. The silent killing began at each war machine, and indeed it was easier than expected, most of the sentries were asleep or drunk or both.

Proudly the youths took the sentries that were upright and moving on the half step. They planted the straw well and then moved on to the next target repeating the process throughout the night. The work went well and no alarm was sounded. All the parties returned and hunkered near the fort once more.

Their position on each of the four fields was chosen to gain the best advantage from the hidden traps and the cleanest line of fire to their straw-mined targets. They carried all of the remaining ammunition, fifty-five arrows in total, six to each of the nine, and one fitted to the string of the rebel in command. He sat now resting from the night's ordeal as his two young allies lit a tiny smokeless fire upon the field. This act was done on each of the four fronts.

The benevolent moon emerged from behind its white cloak to light the targets. The distant machines of war and destruction glowed in its cold pale light. He dipped the straw-packed arrow to the flame, lay back, and fired straight up.

Thus the signal was given in much the same way as the manner of killing crows.

THE WHORE AND
THE CRONE

The commander had fallen into the steady routine of idle nights and wasted days. He enjoyed both the visibility and invisibility that the robe of bear hide afforded. To his men he was a grotesque annoyance. He barked useless orders at stupid times; their only purpose was to show clearly that he was still very much in charge.

His appearance was a wound that gnawed at his soul like a parasitic worm, boring its way slowly and steadily out towards open light. It would never heal; it would constantly and increasingly fester. The only expression that escaped his tattered face was hatred.

The siege had turned into a slow death by strangulation. This would not be an epic or heroic battle, but there was no cause for concern, the outcome already written. They were almost four thousand strong. His biggest adversaries were boredom, dissension, and desertion. Any slackness was dealt with quickly and harshly, cruel attention paid only to the military discipline of others.

The end of the campaign was now almost within sight, the night excursions that had secured the freedom of so many in the early days of the siege had long since ended. From all sides they could see the circling of the crows; and all knew that these were the harbingers of the final outcome. The oracle had spoken true.

The rate of the dying within the fortress was always hard to estimate. If intelligence was right it was now between twelve and fifteen each day. That number would increase over time, and the four hundred left could hold out perhaps three more weeks. The complexities of siege warfare in these final stages had been distilled down to basic mathematics.

The commander should have been elated, but he was not. As the number of rebels within the fort dwindled, the pain of soul and face increased. This battle had done little to quench his thirst for blood. With nothing else to distract him, he would attempt once again to obliterate the memory of the monk, with strong drink and a stronger whore.

On this night it seemed he could not drink enough to forget, and got even less satisfaction from the company of the whore. Eventually, however, he managed poorly to do both, and fell asleep across the rancid skin that had come to be his blanket as well as his cape. Even in sleep he knew that the slut had not performed well or earned her money. He had seen revulsion spoken by her eyes.

He knew as he had finished and fallen into a sleep-like stupor that she had found both his appearance and the act in particular to be disgusting. Even the poorest of actors could have better cloaked their abhorrence, and even the stupidest of whores should have known well to do so. At this thought the commander decided to teach her a lesson, and in a drunken fog with leg and with arm he spun the sleeping woman to him once again, breathing his stale alcohol stench closely into her face.

With effort he focused his eyes for close sight and began to blindly thrust his loins, it was not the whore, however, that he stared at, but the old and wizened oracle. She was toothless and smiling as she wrapped him in her withered legs, and then laughing as his screams reached a crescendo and mingled with those of his men outside the damp, cold tent. With a groan of great relief he crashed through the tent flaps and stumbled out into the cold, smoke-filled air.

The eerie flicker of flames reached skyward like grasping fingers, and he was knocked to the ground by men running each a different way. They scattered like blind bats emerging from the cavern's mouth at nature's dimming twilight. But this was no natural flight, for these creatures were men and they flew on the wings of panic and confusion.

This blind and directionless human flight was the uncontrolled flight of mindless terror.

FIRE AND STRAW

The commander fought with the alcohol and the sightless scattering of his men to regain his footing in the mud and snow. He saw the flames licking skyward from the siege engines. He saw the dark smoke rising and the grey smoke migrating over the encampment. He could hear the screams and the panic of his soldiers.

Looking upward toward the sailing embers that danced now like burning stars on velvet sky, he saw the flight of the flaming arrows hit their mark. They were coming from the open plain near the fortress. "Arms," he shouted above the din, "To arms." Going back inside his tent he hurriedly strapped on his armor. He looked nervously to the whore and was relieved now to see that she was just a whore, and sent her flying as he ripped away the hide and threw it over his shoulders.

His page had his horse at the ready. He swung his leg up and over the saddle, and steadied the charger for control. Almost trampling the page, he kicked roughly into the animal's sides and galloped out to gain control of the madness unfolding all around him. The stumbling, waking men followed suit, and soon the commander had wrestled order from the chaos. The damage was confined to the large war machines, and within twenty-five minutes, the soldiers were assembled on all four fronts.

The small fires on the plain were clearly his destination, and the guerillas were dark against the moonlit snow still shooting the last flames in the direction of the engines.

The Supreme Commander, with monk steel held high he screamed the order, "Charge." From all sides the troops and cavalry flooded forward towards the men who stood alone in the open. Some horses dropped and toppled riders, some infantry fell and were trampled in the fray. The traps had done their job, but the tide of this attack would not be stemmed.

Like fools the men on the plains waited, unconcerned by the forces coming against them, and then finally almost within arrows range, they bolted. Like rabbits they ran towards the walls from which they had earlier descended. As the commander and the full charge of men and horse closed in on the prey, ropes were flung down the massive walls. The fools clung as they were drawn up, but no protective arrow cover was forthcoming. The commander was elated as he saw many men being lowered simultaneously on each of four walls, dangling now between heaven and earth.

It was at best a dim-witted rescue attempt or a poorly executed second attack. It mattered not; this was the slaughter he had been waiting for; his taste for blood mingled with temple mount memories. He saw the archers set their arrows and take aim.

Now closing at full speed he shouted the order for all archers to fire, an order that was repeated on all four sides of the fortress. As the men of the night incursion approached the top of the wall and safety, a hailstorm of arrows and crossbow bolts sailed up and rained down, filling the brightening night sky. Just before the many shafts began to land all around them, they were up, over, and down onto the other side of the wall.

They lay exhausted but safe as the monstrous barrage hit with a deafening ovation. The second in command was there to meet them, and he kept them low and safe from the hellish storm. "All back and accounted for, my lord," he roared above the missiles' thunderous applause. All were covered in the blood of their mission, and the loyal second took survey to make sure none of it was theirs.

After what seemed an eternity the noise subsided. The Supreme Commander could not understand what manner of men were these that would not fall. He shook himself from the fog of drink, but his eyes still saw what his mind could not explain.

The nine were now together on the wall beside the steady second in command who happily informed them, "My lord, the last-minute rescue attempt was a complete and utter failure, a slaughter of great proportion." Along the thick wall top he shouted the order, "Pull." And in unison the grunting of weakened men pulling for their lives began on all four sides.

To the amazement of the two young brothers, the straw men were pulled up and over the wall. It seemed to them like the motion of fishermen hauling in nets. They lay where they fell, one atop the other and more than three hundred in total. All seemed now more porcupine than human in shape. Every quill was an arrow, and each straw warrior had more than forty quills. They had collected well over one thousand arrows and three hundred bolts.

They laughed at the sight, and the success of the plan. This was the jubilation of men who had faced great danger and returned untouched and victorious. It was the joy of soldiers who have earned survival.

The second in command looked to educate the young lads and said dryly, "This is the manner of killing two crows with one arrow. Learn it well." To which the youngest of the boys said, "I too have killed two crows with one arrow." He opened his shirt to reveal three bottles of strong drink stolen from the sleeping sentries he had killed that night. "Have I learned it well?" he proudly asked.

The second in command smiled, "I think so, youth." he said, and then, with more composure added, "But we must drink those crows to be certain."

CHANGES

The aftermath of the night raid could be seen clearly from the great height of the walls. The grey-blue smoke filled the entire clearing and glowed purple in the red morning rays. The once ominous machines of siege had been reduced to smoldering, blackened stumps. The scavenging crows that had held dominion above the rebel city for so long had now expanded their empire to the plain as they picked at the flesh of horse and man.

His men had done damage, but the final outcome would not be changed. Sixteen more were being lowered into the earth within the walls, once brave men, reduced now, to fodder for the worms. The young leader was thankful that he had given the few that still remained this small taste of victory, a true delicacy in the midst of their great famine. He allowed the enemy to retrieve their dead even though they were well within range. He had never had a real appetite for war or for blood.

In the time before strife he was a carpet weaver, and after his wife and family this was his one true passion. This northern region of his homeland was once famous for the intricacy of its patterns, the boldness of its dyes, the density of its knot work, and the quality of its wool. This art he learned from his father who had learned it from his. Since childhood he had expected and accepted that he would be nothing else, but Death held other ideas.

Life had made him a weaver of a different sort. He always carried within him the songs of the weaving sequence and the wooden rhythms of the looms. He saw full patterns when others saw only the chaos of an unfinished work, he saw color when they saw only grey, and he saw works of beauty where others saw only a place to walk and trample.

Now he wove the hearts, minds, and actions of his men, for what was an army if not a tapestry of men bound strategically for a common goal? What was a tribe, if not the timeless fabric of a people woven together in harmony, durable and complete, to cover, claim, and keep warm a tiny patch upon the earth?

From the height of his fortress he watched the commander galloping back and forth on his powerful steed, and even from this great distance the rage was almost tangible. The young leader smiled to himself because, as hopeless and bleak as their position was within these four walls, within the enemy encampment the atmosphere would, at least on this day, be much worse.

The fires of the nighttime raid consumed the commander. Once again he had been taken by surprise. The loss of life was a part of the equation of warfare and could be easily explained. The loss of the emperor's war machinery was a different matter entirely. The imperial courts ran on taxes and money, and machines of this caliber did not come cheap.

In the workings of military discipline this was somebody's fault, and punishment should come down from on high as the natural order. The problem was that there was no one left to punish. If the guards were still alive they would be publicly beheaded, unfortunately they were not. Apart from their initial panic, his troops had performed adequately in the execution of their duties. There still remained the matter of his whore, but she was wisely nowhere to be found.

An anger that seethes is an anger of the most dangerous kind. There is no release, and so it builds. If he could lay hands on the men within the rebel city, it would quell at least some of his fury, but he could not. His young page promptly received an undeserved and unprovoked beating. His anger still an ember in his gut, the commander was left alone to comfort and soothe his wounds with the knowledge that all of them would soon perish, no matter how many arrows they had gathered.

From his position among the tents, he turned towards the fortress and reached out with all the poison in his heart in the direction of its young leader. The leader from his high perch was still looking out over the plains at the charred skeletons of tower, catapult, and trebuchet, and smiling peacefully.

The Book of Changes is a manuscript of great antiquity. The rebel had often seen it consulted to glean insight into the way the universe will unfold. He had seen the casting of coins and the reading of the hexagrams. He did not need this book to tell him his fate; he read the changes with his heart and interpreted their meaning by his actions. This young lion was a man well versed in fate's moving landscape, and a man that could see patterns rising and emerging from the tangled colors of so many life threads.

Looking out over the plain, he absent-mindedly rubbed the coin in his pocket. He liked its cold feel. It brought him back to a time of normality; a time of family, commodity, and commerce. It was a time that now existed only in his dreams. He drew the brass coin from his pocket and stared at it anew.

It was a round coin with a square hole cut in its center that sat on his square palm. The small inner square symbolized earth and the round perimeter, heaven. This he had always known, but now he saw that his square palm mirrored the distant square of the surrounding forest. The outer ring of the coin's edge mapped out the enemy encampment, and the bordered square hole within modeled exactly his walled fortress. As he gazed down at the brass piece resting on his calloused palm, his mind and spirit took flight.

He saw what the crows see as they look down from the heavens, and he knew now what Death would see on its winged approach.

A Bargain Refused

The young page came running to the commander as fast as his legs would carry him. He still kept his eyes averted but was no longer afraid to speak loudly. "Commander, Commander." Bent over fighting to regain his breath he pointed towards the fort and chose his words minimally "Man," he gasped for air and continued, "on the field." Once more he drew breath and stood taller, "flag of truce." The commander was already charging towards the lone figure even before the youth had finished his report.

The commander resisted the urge to fly full gallop, he had seen what the field pitfalls could do to both horse and rider. He approached with caution, and checked from saddle height for any signs of deception. Emboldened he moved within speaking distance, and resisted the urge to slay the emaciated rebel immediately. "Speak," he said, "but select your words carefully, for they may well be your last."

"My proposition is a simple one," the rebel responded, "My head for the safe passage of my men."

"There is nothing in that for me, you are already all dead men," and indeed the commander was perplexed.

"All you need know is that I am offering a bargain for both of us," was the dead calm reply from the gaunt young rebel.

The commander sneered through his broken face, "Your death and my victory are not negotiable. If I wanted bargains I would be dealing with a carpet seller," he hissed.

"You are," the rebel said proudly. "Remember always that you rejected this fair and honest deal," the rebel continued in a voice now charged with conviction, "and remember this promise," the rebel locked eyes with the Supreme Commander, "Only after your total victory, will our great battle really begin."

He spoke to the commander like one in the throes of a fever. To the ears and eyes of the commander, something in the rebel's voice and manner echoed the ways of the old oracle. He spoke with the unearthly power of a mighty prophet, "As specters and phantoms we will strike at the heart of your empire, and there will be no mercy. We will inflict more damage in death than we could ever have done in life." These words were not spit out like a curse, but delivered faithfully—as absolute truth.

It was clear to the commander that this rebel's mind had broken under the strain of siege. The thought of killing him here and ending his raving passed through the commander's mind, but the placement of the rebel's firm grip on his battered sword handle caused him to hesitate.

As the commander turned his horse with a harsh pull and made distance between the two, the young leader walked towards the fortress and looked towards the heavens, as if summoning the dark and approaching clouds.

ON TWO WINGS

His second was there to greet him as he passed through the massive front gate and almost tumbled from his horse. At a glance his second knew that the talk on the field had not gone well, "My lord, I am sorry to tell you that inside these walls the news is also bleak," he said. The rebel did not need to be told that Death had arrived, or that it came from on high, and flew on two wings.

One wing of the shadow of death was malnutrition. It had decimated his men steadily for the last three months. Those who had not fallen had been weakened, and these men were now touched by death's second wing, the wing of pestilence. It was the last cry of a deteriorated system, and its lament was heard throughout the stronghold. Death rose after landing like heat rises, and of the remaining two hundred, a full two-thirds now burned with the fever.

The rebel, his second in command, and the last six men of the night raid who could still stand moved directly to the treasure vault of their ancient city. It had been cleaned out long ago and now echoed hollow and empty, a cavernous barren cathedral. Of all the valuables that it had safeguarded over its entire life, a life that stretched back to the time of the First Emperor, only one remained. Against the back wall in a place where the light from wall torches did not reach, reverently untouched, rested the last and perhaps the greatest treasure of all.

The men picked it up in unison and with much effort hoisted it upon their shoulders. It seemed like a great tree trunk the length of four men and the weight of three. It was bound with ropes of silk, and its spiraled ends did give it the appearance of a thick oaken branch. Only its flexibility in the carry did speak that it was something else.

The rebel would share with his dying men a taste of luxury that they could never have touched in life. They would be treated as emperors.

Like a prisoner released, its bonds of silk were cut in the open main square, and it rested finally free where it was solemnly unrolled. Whether skilled weaver or crass soldier, it lifted the soul to a place beyond words. The carpet cast two dragons, one of north and one of south that danced among its fibers. They faced each other amidst clouds above a distant mountain range, while a plume of smoke rose into the sky from the peak of the middle mountain.

They seemed so alive that indeed they might rise up at any moment and fly up into the celestial heavens. Its texture, color, and pattern were the combined effort of all that was civilization. It was a symphony of living and breathing immortality.

For the next two weeks the infected soldiers of the rebel defense force were gently placed upon the unfurled carpet, where they passed over to the world beyond. The changing light of day cast life into the fibers of wool and silk, but Death ultimately had the final word in the fabric of men. The blisters of the growing pox hardened on the bodies of the afflicted, and these men fell in great number with great speed and in great suffering. The northern carpet from the time of the First Emperor was the definitive and silent witness to the suffering of the rebel troops.

The living worked feverishly to bury the dead. Within days only a few remained standing. The carpet had become a sacred gateway, one that marked the point of departure from world of flesh, and point of entry to world of spirit. It was the elegant platform for the rite of passage, the place of liftoff for the final inevitable flight.

The two young brothers shared it equally; each embraced by one dragon, until they finally stirred and raved no more. The blisters and fever eventually and inevitably brought them cold and lifeless peace. These two were the last to be laid to rest in this manner.

After the boys were buried, the rebel, his second, and the thirty that still remained, fitted their armor, secured their weapons and ammunition, collected the last of their strength, and marched out of the fortress to embrace their destiny.

Bow and Shield

In the surrounding camp of the imperial forces, word spread quickly that events were unfolding. The fort's large front gate opened, and a ragged group of thirty-two rebel soldiers marched onto the fortress plain. Behind them the enormous gates remained open and the fortress silent. These men had no need for words. They shared a single strategy; a short march into the open and then patience.

The Supreme Commander immediately had their position surrounded at a distance.

The last thirty-two men of the rebel outpost were paired shield and archer. One man protects and one man fires. The sixteen shields formed a ring around the sixteen bowmen in the center. The arrows were placed point first in the snow, ready to be nocked and fired. The rebel held his bow in a left-handed grip. His second on one knee held the shield; his life would end defending his friend and leader, and this was as it should be.

The northern siege had lasted almost a year, and it was time to end it. Once more the rebel looked toward the sky. He did not see Death but thought it strange that the crows had gone. He did not see the raven perched behind him, high atop the fortress wall. The young lion and his second in command were vigilant and at a place beyond fear.

From horseback and cloaked in bearskin, the commander watched the measured amble of shield and bow make its way steadily to midfield. It brought to his mind the slow movements of a tortoise, and he thought about the old one reading the cracks on the sacred shell. He thought also of the victory that she had promised, and knew that today it would be his.

His sword was held high, and with its drop the arrows flew. They were launched from all directions like apocalyptic rain. They were answered in kind but not quantity from the tortoise shell. The falling of men on both sides had begun. The commander regretted now the loss of his catapults, but no matter the finality of conquest was at hand. He watched from a safe distance, both horse and man breathing heavily in the bitter highland air.

It was over in less than one hour. Thirty-two men were now only a tangled pile of human wreckage in an open, snow-covered field. He gave the signal to cease fire and approached the twisted knot of shields, weapons, and bodies. The imperial arrows embedded in the ground around the rebel's last stand looked like the tall wheat of a summer's meadow.

In death the young leader smiled, still protected by the arrow pocked shield of his second in command. The commander finally had the victory he had come for, and with a flash of his monk steel weapon he had the rebel's head. He held it high and turned it to the four directions for all his cheering troops to see. He sheathed his weapon and carried the head by its hair as he walked into the beckoning fortress.

With an arrogant stride he entered the empty city fort, now just four walls and rubble. In the main square, so awed by the treasure before him, he dropped the head and stared in silent wonder. Hatred had so consumed his soul that little touched his heart anymore. The carpet's powerful beauty awoke the remnants of his humanity and a tear rolled down his ruined face.

VINCENT PRATCHETT

Between the dragons was the character for two. Not the number but the concept, two as one, or two under the same roof. It was the embodiment of his mission, for this godforsaken northern region and the temperate and civilized southern state were now as one. He knew little about carpets, but it was clear that this one was both ancient and a masterpiece. This was truly a treasure worthy of an emperor, and compared to this, the loss of a few war machines was minor. He was pulled back from his revelry by the arrival of his generals.

He reached down quickly to snatch up the head, and so cover his moment of weakness. Looking into the open eyes of the rebel he mocked loudly, "What fool leaves a carpet like this exposed to the elements." Both he and his generals laughed raucously. When they had stopped he ordered, "Pack this carpet carefully for transport," and added harshly, "Should anything happen to the emperor's carpet between now and our arrival at the palace, you will all be executed."

Once more atop his horse he tied the rebel's head by its hair to his belt. Leaving the generals to their task, the commander rode back towards the tent that had been his residence for the last eleven months. Horse and rider passed by the rebel heap and saw the snow, covered now by a pond of dark red gore. The slaughter of the moon bear flashed through his mind and sent a chill flying up his spine. He saw her blood spreading in the whiteness, and thought he heard once more the sound of orphaned cubs.

He looked up toward the distant cry of a black-feathered bird, pulled the bear hide tighter to ward off the bitter cold, and rode on.

THE BEGGAR'S BOWL

The walled city was empty when the imperial troops finally entered the gate. There were no survivors, but more importantly there was no plunder. Loot is life for the foot soldier, and here there was nothing. The imperial soldiers now tasted vinegar when they had expected wine, and even the hastiest return would not be fast enough for most.

The troops of the southern region flew from the walled city like a plague of locusts that have finished decimating a once fertile field. They had grown to hate this cold land, its rebellious people, and now their impoverished mission. It was whispered among them that the mind of their scar-faced commander had finally lost its delicate balance.

Three days after the rebels' final stand there remained only desolation. The land had already begun to reclaim the area marked by the occupation, now just a waning ring upon the earth like the scar of some great pox. No crows flew, and no animals roamed, the entire area mirrored the condition of the fort, empty and barren. Only the wind and its ghosts blew across the desolate plain, and the thirty-two dead were left to rot where they had fallen. At forest's edge something stirred.

The shredded black rags moved slowly across the great snow white field. They seemed like living calligraphy, perhaps not a character or word at all, merely an accidental spill of coal black ink, dripping down a fresh new page. Slow and determined they made way past the heap of dead upon dead and into the abandoned ruins. As they moved they measured the substance of space and time and spoke the language of persistence, onward toward the dead stone fortress.

Just as outside, inside there was nothing. Nothing at all to speak that here brave men had walked and here brave men had lived, or indeed that here brave men had died. Only a large rectangle outline in the square where once an ancient carpet had lain, spoke that at least here no enemy had dared to trample.

In the middle of this fading print, the black rags hunkered down and skinny arms drew forth the metal begging bowl and began to scrape. It was a task of epic proportion, like the draining of a lake using only a tea cup, but slowly the frozen earth did yield to an old one's unbridled determination. For six days and six moonless nights the futile task continued, until finally, from futility the beggar's bowl had gouged success.

The pit was as deep as its hunched digger, and the dirt was piled around its perimeter like the walls of the ruined fortress. He stood and shuffled from end to end of this dank tomb, and said aloud three simple words, "It is enough."

He wiped the sweat that ran down his pock-scared face with the filthy hood. His black eyes darted over his monumental effort, and he was satisfied. He climbed up from the even-sided crater and rolled down from the mound piled high around it. He saw beneath his broken fingernails the caked remains of blood and dirt, but he would not allow himself to feel pain or fatigue until after the completion of his task. Only then would he allow himself to feel everything.

Thirty-two trips the beggar made from plain to fortress square. One by one he dragged the frozen bodies to the large rectangular hole and laid them down, with weapons and shields. The last one placed was the headless young leader, and this one he lay beside the second in command.

Once again he muttered his comforting phrase, "It is enough."

The loose dirt was shoveled back methodically bowl by bowl, until the living earth had finally claimed its dead. Now he was free once again to feel. The ancient beggar staggered in the direction of the southern lands. He wanted to escape the coldness of this place. The beggar quickened the shifting balance of his awkward gait, aware now of the quickened shift of the changing universe.

As he continued his southern walk, he offered silent prayers for the dead of this place, and the many more that were soon to die.

Reaching for the Rain

Through the nakedness of three spring seasons, I had seen birds build nests in its branches, and squirrels homes within the hollow rooms of its trunk. I often saw the raven from its great height study me as I stood in silent stance. Ring by ring and day by day, I had grown stronger.

I watched the oak tree as it watched me. I borrowed its strength as I took my stance before it. I had seen its leaves emerge from buds and gracefully unfurl over days like a butterfly emerging from its chrysalis. The long catkins grew and dangled from delicate branches as the small yellow flowers formed. My oak was by nature's hand both male and female, and so spoke loudly of the harmonious union of two great opposites. From these flowers I watched the acorns grow and fall, some to be eaten and some to be carried far off and take root.

One late summer's day I was standing in stillness beside my great oak. Men are as trees, with feet that root in the earth, a mind that mingles with the heavens, and a trunk that unites and binds the two together. Selah and her black bird seemed never to tire of watching me, even though in tranquility I could now stand for hours.

On this day Selah asked, "Arkthar, did you consult the ants?"

I knew by the smell in the air and the darkening skies that their opinion was unnecessary, for it was certain a major storm was gathering. Just as I had finished my training the rains began, and from under the protective canopy of the oak we stood together and watched the warm afternoon downpour, and listened to the music of the worms. With wind and with fanfare the skies instantly released all the water that they had greedily been hoarding.

I thought of Thor who in his Norse land had done exactly the same as us, and I thought of his lightning, but luckily it did not come. The rain poured down as if from buckets. So heavy was it that from our vantage we could not see out past the length of three horses, but we were warm and dry, and we both enjoyed the power and presence of this storm.

In my thinking of trees, I had always felt them passive. I thought that they grow where they are placed and receive only what they are brought.

It began quietly at first, a soft trickling song. From somewhere behind us we heard the gentle sound of water like the spilling of a single cup. At first not much more than a dripping, but soon it began to increase. It was like listening to a single voice being joined steadily one by one by a choir of great number.

The great oak canopy trapped the sound, and it emanated from all around us. The noise grew quickly from a steady trickle to the sound of a brook, and it continued to grow. I shouted to Selah that I had found its source. We both turned and looked towards the base of the mighty trunk.

From the roots to the heavens the great trunk rose, from this trunk sprang and spiraled boughs like mighty arms. These rose up to forearms and these to hands of branch. Every finger grasped the leaves that reached to touch the rain.

From the heavens to the root the raindrops collected. They flowed from spring to brook, brook to stream. All water was directed by the cracks of the bark as it flew along the underside faster than it could fall to the ground, and was guided precisely to the roots where it was needed. Four rivers were pulled from the sky and from each direction poured onto the roots with the sound of a steady waterfall.

I knew then that my oak, that I once thought so sedentary and passive, reaches actively to the universe to take what the heavens provide. On this late summer's day I understood the power and strength of the oak, and the softness and beauty of water. This tree was truly one of my great teachers, and with this lesson Selah and I turned to each other.

We pressed our lips together for the first time, and felt our souls together for all time.

In bliss we lay beneath the protective canopy of the sacred oak. The rains had settled to the steady beat of passion released, and now sang only its gentle song. I held her tightly against my chest to keep her close and safe. We had no words, our actions had spoken for us both, and upon the ground we listened only to our steady breathing.

It was clear that I was her first man, and although I had been with many women, it was also clear that she was simply now, my only.

CIRCLES OF WOOD
AND STEEL

The monk enjoyed watching his charge practice with the oar in evening's soft light. He was a good student, dedicated to the physical effort needed for success. What impressed Mah Lin the most was that Arkthar was never satisfied. Any lesson given was always taken further. Not content with just the two-handed grip, he had with great effort learned to cut equally well with both the right arm and the left. Over the course of the passing years he had come far.

Selah and her father marveled how Arkthar had harmonized his foreign ways with theirs. Inspired by the striking posts for training limbs within the cavern, he had built from wood a Celtic cross as big as a man and set it firmly in the ground near the river. This he punished with all five cuts but added also short strikes with the butt of the handle. Every evening the sound of wood striking wood could be heard thundering across their peaceful homestead.

Now it seemed that the five cut method was transforming into a different art. Arkthar had listened well to Selah's explanation of the Five Element Theory. For his warrior mind the idea of subjugation and generation fit neatly into what he knew. He created movement and mindset modeled on the properties of each element. Before long he had captured in body the essence of all five and pushed further to make them one. Mah Lin watched the warrior dance through fire, water, earth, metal, and wood, and was deeply moved.

In the fading light of day, both monk and daughter watched him cut with fury against the cross. When he had finished his work, Arkthar turned to greet them and was surprised to see his teacher holding the Five Element sword unsheathed and in two hands. Although it was unusual, he did not question the monk's purpose. Mah Lin approached without ceremony and exchanged steel for wood. Each now held a different weapon, and each tested the weight and power held within their palms.

The steel that Arkthar held was light compared to the wooden oar. It spoke to him like a young horse urging its rider to loosen the reign and bridle, and fly to furious gallop. Meanwhile the monk assessed the balance of the warrior's wooden weapon, and the range of its cutting arc. He raised the oar slowly above his head, locked eyes with his young student, and attacked ferociously.

For Arkthar all thought and reason disappeared, fled perhaps to the safety of the thick-walled library. Here and now remained only the sound and reflex of flesh and steel defending against real danger. It was the quiet place of an unfettered mind, the place where Death would quickly answer any thought. The forward fury of the monk abated but his eyes remained vigilant. Arkthar realized that with great luck, he had not been touched. This revelation amused the monk, for he knew that the line that separates luck from skill is at best a thin one. Quietly he stood and awaited Arkthar's full reply.

Selah stood frozen, shocked now by the warrior's answer. She had heard of bloodlust but had never seen it. And now she stood mute, a witness to its terrible power as Arkthar released full force upon her father. If Mah Lin was concerned it did not show upon his face, for his features remained focused and serene. When the sound of the attack had finished, her father stood uninjured, but the oar he held was shortened, cleaved neatly in two. Arkthar fought for the reigns of his savagery, trying desperately to halt the finishing blow of his advantage. Through this hesitation the monk flashed forward once again.

He closed the distance in a blur and passed through the warrior as if a ghost. Silence filled the space between them. Looking down, Arkthar saw that his palm held the shortened oar and looking up realized that the blade of Five Elements was now back in the hands of its owner. Both men smiled. Arkthar now understood that the line that separates skill from magic is at best a thin one.

Over the evening meal Mah Lin inquired about the martial school of Arkthar's past and was surprised by his student's answer. "There was none. I learned as I went." Intrigued now, the priest delved further, "That being so, do you not have some deep conviction?" Arkthar replied, "When I was a child, I once became suddenly aware that a warrior is a man who does not hold his life in regret. Since I have held that in my heart for many years, it has become a deep conviction, and today I never think about my death. Other than that I have nothing." Mah Lin was deeply moved and said in reply, "The perceptions of my predecessors were not the least bit awry."

The monk gestured to the severed wooden oar that Arkthar had discarded near the hearth. The warrior thought to feed the useless remnant to the fire when the flames died down. Arktar held it once more and reevaluated its dimensions. Its weight and length was exactly the same as the short sword of his old world, long since buried in his Viken enemy.

He tucked it humbly into his belt and bowed his head to his two teachers.

DRAGONS

The morning light within the library grew steadily. I heard the rooster rouse his harem and mark the arrival of the new day. As I poured over the original temple manuscripts, my interest was captured. I had seen this word before but was unsure of its meaning. Selah entered quietly, and before she shed the heaviness of sleep I asked her, "What is the sound and meaning of this character?" I looked at its shape undulating on the ancient yellowed page and added, "It seems familiar."

"I know why you would be intrigued," Selah always thought carefully before she explained anything, but now she seemed to be thinking longer than usual. She began searching, for she knew that a painting would greatly aid my understanding. "Look, Arkthar," she said, as she carefully laid a yellowed illustration beside the written character that had caught me in its grip. While I stared at the detailed artwork in disbelief, she added, "Its sound is *loong*."

I looked at the written word. The fish that climbs the river falls becomes this mythical beast, and I remembered the carved oak prows of the Viken longboats as they churned through ocean waters. I shook this memory from my mind and stared again at the ancient seal script character.

My eyes saw a concept made of two pictures. On the left it seemed a man in armor. Like the tales of legend he stood adorned for battle, and by his side perhaps a sword. On the right a different image, I saw its four thick legs and long neck. It seemed almost grazing upon the landscape of its meaning. Side by side I saw both man and beast. From this written word I looked to the fine details of the ancient painting, and touched the scales, teeth, and claws of the long coiled body. To me it was both beautiful and frightening.

"Selah in the world of my old life we also have this creature, as a child I have heard many stories about this beast we call dragon, and it was a dragon that took me by sail from my home." My mind was alive now with the creature, and in the way of a novice scholar, I set aside my fears and carefully voiced my rational thoughts, "It is fascinating that such an imaginary creature is a concept in the hearts and minds of people of all places." The space of her silence, which I mistook for respectful listening, I filled with, "The dragon is a universal myth of great size and significance."

It sounded like a very wise and well-grounded statement to my ears, but Selah's confused expression quickly transformed into her bright familiar laugh. Laughter of the type that usually meant I had probably said something monumentally foolish. I turned now as Mah Lin entered the small library. He had heard my words and scanned the image on the table, and he too understood, and joined the merriment.

Now it was my turn to be confused, and Mah Lin's turn as a compassionate teacher to alleviate it promptly.

"Arkthar," he began, "myth often grows from reality, just as it does from the recording of history to the telling of legend." He paused now to catch my eye and my attention, "Dragons are as real as you and I, and so rightly exist in the hearts and minds of all mankind."

I felt alone. Dangling once more in the place where solid reality meets with the magical and the fantastic, a place now well familiar in my new land. "You have been training hard with the passing of the seasons," he said. "Tomorrow we will saddle the horses, and we will ride to touch a dragon. Selah, you can replenish your supply of medicine bones."

With that he went out about his usual business, and I finished my studies and went on with the day's routine. In the late afternoon, I trained hard my kicking and striking with Mah Lin inside the cavern, but half expected to see two fierce eyes watching me from its corner shadows. In truth I could think of little else.

That evening during our family meal, I ate much and spoke little. My mind was already on horseback, long before the morning came. At sunrise as Selah and Mah Lin fitted out the horses, I thought it prudent to add an early cutting practice with my shortened wooden sword. Although I worked purposefully, the monk and his daughter still managed to laugh at my last minute preparations. I didn't care; I would be ready for any danger that might come my way.

With the shortened oar at my waist, we three began riding out. I felt like a timeless adventurer moving steadily into the unknown. Past oak and raven, past the falls and cavern entrance, and past the great metal lion, we moved progressively forward past the boundaries of the comfortable world that had become my new home. Soon we would reach and enter the world of myth and legend.

For five full days we traveled up river, resting when we were tired and moving when we were refreshed. The landscape changed with our journey from lush and green to brown and sparse. We entered into a land where the very crust of the earth folded upon itself in layers. It reminded me of the metal worked within the forge, folded, hammered, and folded again. Like the metal, this land had long since cooled and hardened.

The horses were tethered, and on foot we traveled along the mighty river's edge where it cut through the landscape like a powerful sword. Walking now high up along the shifting banks, we arrived at our destination. With Selah by my side the monk turned and pointed.

"Arkthar, there sleeps your dragon."

I moved warily to his right and surveyed the ground before me. At first I saw nothing, but as I stepped forward I began to see the bones, some whole and some shattered by the hand of time. Like the many pieces of an enormous puzzle, my eyes began to piece together the whole. I saw the ribs and vertebrae of a monster of immense size and proportion.

Selah began collecting tiny bone fragments as my eyes collected the overall scale of the creature that lay before me. I saw leg bones that were longer by half than me, and I saw claws the size of a farmer's scythe blade. I was beyond speech and so said nothing. My hands were drawn to touch what was once a living pelvis. I had seen much of Death's handiwork and so was easily able to bring this creature back to flesh within my mind. Slowly I searched until eventually I found the object of my quest.

It rested aloof and alone imbedded by profile to the bedrock that cradled and protected it. I sat now beside the skull almost as big as the horse that had carried me. I saw empty sockets that had once housed seeing eyes, stare sightless but immortal. I saw nostrils that had once breathed the air of life, perched above the jawless mouth. I saw the serrated and still sharp teeth aligned in rows, teeth as big as daggers that I knew had once pierced living flesh.

Here, in the presence of this ancient creature, I was humbled.

"When did he die?" I asked Mah Lin.

"Before the time of men, when the earth was still young and our cave was still just a mountain of fire, this dragon brought the rains," was the monk's inexplicable reply.

A Father's Gift

The ride back to our home was a time for quiet reflection. My mind was fully occupied by the dragon that I had actually touched. We had walked the same ground and breathed the same air, but Mah Lin said that dragons were from a time before men. Everything the monk had said was simple, but it would take me much more time to understand these words. For now at least I knew that it is the dragon that brings the rain.

In the evening the three of us sat near the fire and roasted a snared rabbit. Mah Lin enjoyed the catch, and when I was almost finished he taught me to break the bones and suck the marrow, sharing the importance of the lesson, he said, "Without the marrow the hare's meat will only bring starvation." Looking back from where we had come, we could see the distant lightning flicker through the dark night sky.

In this strange land I had received life and intended now to serve my full sentence. I was a seed dropped into fertile ground and I was, with much help from Mah Lin and Selah, growing. Now sitting by the fire, I spoke more freely in their tongue. Tears of laughter in the middle of serious conversation spoke plainly that I had not yet mastered all its rising and falling tones.

Ironically, amid the strict framework of routine and discipline, I found that never were any two days remotely alike. Everyday I pushed myself harder and further than the day before. It was the skills of a seasoned warrior: patience, focus, persistence, and discipline that aided me in acquiring the skills of peace. Everything was changing, and yet there was comfort and security in the underlying consistency of transformation. Every day was new, and everyday I was new.

"Arkthar, in the great movement of life, the only thing of real permanence is change, and once you realize that all things are changing, there is nothing that you will try to hold onto."

Sitting with them now in the comfort of the firelight brought me back to that night long ago when they had bought me from Death, and welcomed me fully into their lives. My feelings for Selah held both warmth and promise, and I wanted to tell Mah Lin, but it was clear that he knew, and that he was comfortable.

By the light of the dying fire relaxed and well full, Mah Lin began to talk about the sword and the art of its making. But, when he spoke of the Five Element Sword he was speaking also of the patterns of life.

"All blades harness the power of elemental transformation, but only one in a thousand is truly a Five Element Sword. Arkthar, draw the sword and look upon the blade in the firelight."

The pattern of the folded steel seemed to dance in the shimmering glow. The ancient blade looked as if it had just come from the monastery forge. From the razor edge to the sturdy spine, I saw what the priest was showing me and heard what the sword was telling me.

The metal's edge held the pattern of flame. From hilt to tip was a flickering panorama of battles past and battles not yet fought. Hovering above the flames was the unmistakable pattern of living wood; the grain and the knots, and above this the metal captured the waves of the ocean. From the water the steel lines framed the shore and became the dry and open earth that stretched along the blade like the horizon. Finally above this nothing but the clear sky of polished metal.

Mah Lin gave me time to reflect upon the soul of this sword before he continued.

"You have seen the power of Selah's striking. You practice the slow guided movements of dao yin to cultivate this force. We call it the power of steel wrapped in cotton. The secret art of our sword making is also based on this concept—the hard must be wrapped in the soft.

The metal used to cast the lion is called raw iron, the iron of the plow is called ripe iron, the metal conjured to create the blade is known as the great iron. The sword maker's art lies in his ability to combine the raw and the ripe to form the great. Arkthar, this is the art you will learn beside me in the forge."

Mah Lin adjusted his position and adjusted his eye to include both me and his daughter before he continued.

"Children, listen carefully. A great sword can also speak clearly about other matters. Its metal from edge to spine is very hard and takes a fine edge, but it so hard and brittle that it may break. It is like you, Arkthar."

He continued, "In a blade of legend like the sword you hold, this edge must be wrapped with the soft raw metal. This softness gives it flexibility and strength. This softness is like you, Selah."

Now she blushed and glanced almost undetectably in my direction, but she smiled also, reading into her father's description her growing love for me.

"The hard wrapped by the soft is accomplished by folding, cutting, and hammering, but it is the heat of the fire and the coldness of the quench that marries the two metals to become one."

The monk was thoughtful as he drained his tea.

"As the testing of your metal approaches, feel confident with the hard wrapped by the soft, for this method has stood the test of time, it will be your strength and insure your survival."

Mah Lin's gaze tilted toward the northern night sky where lightning flashed, and a deep rumbling sounded in the great distance, and I read concern beneath his calm features.

THE SHAPING OF STEEL

The day after our return I was back to my daily routine of study and exercise. That morning I had begun to decipher documents of metal and its working. Among the works of this monastery were several extensive volumes on the making of swords. With words and pictures they catalogued types of forge and the method of its working. They spoke mysteriously of a rare and valuable southern ore, and I found myself somewhere between the worlds of magic and religion.

Within these documents were many concepts beyond my grasp. When I sought clarification from Selah she explained, "Method was often hidden by language as a code to safeguard technique. The true art of working steel must be passed directly from master to novice. The understanding of metal comes from the hammer and the fire, not the paper and the ink. You will find understanding only in the forge, Arkthar, not the library."

I worked hard that day with Selah and the raven guiding the soft movement of my body and the serenity of my mind. The falls refreshed and hardened my body like the quenching of forge metal, and my lesson from the monk within the hollowed cavern came like the blows of the hammer's beating. Mah Lin seemed pleased with my efforts, and after we had finished the exercises that condition my body, he brought me over to the forge to show me at what he had been working.

He reached with the tongs and drew forth a long black rod from its sandy mold. This he plunged deftly into the quenching trough with a great hissing amid the clouds of rising steam. He removed the cold dark form, ugly even by the beautiful blue light of the watery entrance. He smiled as he tested the weight and passed it to me for the simple task of grinding away the charred debris. As the hours passed the beauty of his labor was gradually revealed.

When I had finished I was soaked with sweat, a combination of the forge heat and my polishing efforts. I had discarded my blue silken scholar's robes for the blackened loincloth of common slave, preferring comfort over status. In my hand I now held a metal object of ultimate wonder and workmanship. It was a rod longer by a head than Mah Lin was tall, and cast in the perfect likeness of the bamboo plants that had fallen to his five cuts.

So life-like was it that it captured even their nodes and hollow form. It was the strength of steel welded into the lightness of the living wood, perfect in length and balance. Mah Lin, who had been resting beside the pumping bellows, approached me now to see what my efforts with the fine grinding sands had revealed. He smiled again as he handled it, at first as a simple walking staff, and then with the blinding circular speed of a lethal weapon.

"It is beautiful, Arkthur," he said, as if I was its maker rather than just the laborer that had merely released it from its blackened cast. "Tomorrow you and I will begin to make the blade to fit its end."

Our household was one of many dimensions but no secrets. The smell of smoke from my robe spoke pungently of my day's activities at the forge, and the oily blackness of sweat and charcoal on my skin screamed loudly of my new vocation. Selah smiled as she handed us the soap and water before she allowed us to enter the house. The food tasted especially good to my palate that evening, I was tired in body but energized in spirit.

We sat contentedly after dinner in front of the hearth, and spoke of many things. I drained my tea and thought carefully before I chose my words. There was so much about my feelings for them and for this place that I wanted expressed clearly and properly.

I thought about the magic of this place and how, originally, it had unnerved me. Now it seemed that it unfolded naturally in answer to my every question. I remembered the former emptiness of my loveless existence, and how with the company of the priest and his daughter it had been transformed. I measured my journey, no longer with my eyes, but with my heart. Love is a powerful force.

Finally my mouth opened for speech, and as they watched and listened, nothing came from my lips to fill the room but silence.

I did not know why I was unable to speak, or by what power I had lost my voice. I felt deeply foolish for being unable to express myself and braced for their laughter. Instead they looked knowingly to each other and reassured me with their kind expressions. Finally Mah Lin spoke and I was relieved that at least one of us had not fallen dumb.

"Arkthar, the one that knows it cannot speak it, and the one that speaks it does not know it. Such is the power of the Way. Sleep now for your next season will be full, you will learn to properly wield the hammer and stoke the flame. You will learn the Art of the Five Elements."

Both Mah Lin and Selah rose at the same time, I remained sitting still thinking about what the monk had said. As Selah passed me she touched my flushed cheek with her hand, leaned down and kissed my lips gently. Before her father I was once again unable to speak, once again like a man with no tongue.

This time however, his laughter did quickly and loudly come and continued with him as he left the room.

SELAH

The next morning as the men awakened, Selah prepared their packaged lunch and readied their breakfast. She sang sweetly, at peace with herself, her world, and these two men. She often thought about her mother, and missed her deeply. Selah had always been thankful for what that woman had shown her of traditional medicine. Lately, however, she was increasingly grateful for what her mother had taught her about love.

Her father and Arkthar ate well that morning, and spoke about the technique of forge and the working of fire, air, and metal. There would not be the usual academic study for the next moon's passing. Her student's lessons would for now come directly in the cavern from the warrior priest, and his classroom would be where the hammer meets the anvil.

As Mah Lin and Arkthar made ready for the forge, Selah noticed the wear in his robes, but the blue was still vivid and true. She thought to herself that new garments should soon be made. Her reflections lingered on this barbarian that had entered their lives so broken and yet had grown in time so strong. Through these many seasons he had, as a student, surpassed her highest standards, and as a man he had fulfilled her deepest dreams. Now as she handed him the food for two, she smiled as the raven called the name spoken by her heart.

She watched the only two men she had ever loved walk away as brothers, secure in their stride and moving as a force united. Selah's love for Arkthar was as a growing plant. Small at its beginning, her memory of his first sight being only sorrow, her feeling of her first touch being only compassion. Sorrow and pity had blossomed to become joy; compassion had been transformed into passion. Duty had given rise to fulfillment, and time had given birth to love.

She watched the raven steal some of the oats that she scattered for the laying hens, and checked the weather against the ants. After the cows were milked and the ripest of the garden produce harvested, she walked into the great hall and strolled among the weapons. Most were picked from her father's monastery, others already here from a time long gone and places unnamed.

This day she looked carefully at the various pieces of armor, and thought how they would fit on Arkthar's muscled frame. She felt like the mother that selects the warmest of clothing for her child who may be taken by a winter's storm. From first touch she wanted to protect and keep him safe. Now, as a woman, she understood her mother's anguish and joy on that night long ago, when she had healed a near dead monk, and her child had met her father for the very first time.

She felt pulled to a corner of the hall that she had not often explored, and her hand guided by instinct touched the armor that would soon become his. She lifted it with only one arm, surprised by its lightness. She did not think it was from their world, for it seemed a better fit to his. It was not like anything she had seen before, it was not rigid or stiff, but like silk it took the shape of what it covered.

Selah placed the armor on the floor where she could see and examine it better. It was shorter than his robe, but longer than a shirt length. Its fluid draping allowed swift and unhindered movement. This was no ordinary mantle of silk or wool, this was a shirt of steel. Created link by link, it seemed knit by the hands of angels. She remembered well how her mother's silken weave had protected her father from the many arrows so long ago, and prayed that for her man this would do the same.

She smiled openly for another reason; this chainmail armor had grown in its power to protect, the same way that Arkthar's power had grown—ring by ring.

THE BOW

Satisfied that she had chosen well for Arkthar, Selah tried to concentrate on the household duties, but for most of the afternoon she felt drawn once more to the great hall, although she could not think of any reason why this was so. When her work was finished, she returned and stood at the doorway of the huge chamber and peered in. Echoes of lives lived and lost seemed to reach out to her, eventually she gave in to their seductive song, and entered.

She wandered about the hall. She had no purpose and so she meandered through it like a slow river. She looked with all senses feeling for what had brought her back. Selah remembered her father's search upon the ruined mountain, and she realized she was doing just the same. Back now to the area she had least explored, she stopped near a long shield that leaned heavily against the stone wall. She reached for it tentatively, sure that it was too heavy to be moved. It crashed to the floor at her lightest touch, revealing the treasure hidden behind it.

Truly she did not know if she had chosen this bow, or if it had chosen her, but it was a good fit. It was made of layered horn and wood, glued together with precision. Its fierce recurve was tamed by ancient cord, its wooden arrows tipped by metal, and steadied in flight by the tail feathers of a bird of prey. These were the elements of her world.

Although she had never before held a bow, the one now firmly in her grip felt natural, almost familiar. She knew that it had come from the plains of the Huns, well beyond the great wall that the First Emperor had built to keep them out. She had heard stories of their speed and precision in battlefield maneuvers. It was said that a Hun warrior could fire ten arrows within the space of three breaths. The bowstring was gut, and even though it was old and dry the arrows beside it seemed to beg for flight. Unable to resist, she placed one on the ancient sinew and drew it back slowly.

The feathered end brushed her cheek with a gentle touch, as she held with her eye a helmet at the hall's far end. The arrow freed itself with a powerful whisper, and flew easily through the metal, sending the feathers that steadied its flight scattering in all directions. Simultaneously the ancient string of gut snapped violently and dangled uselessly from both tips. Ruining an arrow and a string was a small price she thought for touching the power that would become hers. She was satisfied now that this was what had called to her, and she thanked the Hun that had made it and said a prayer for the soul of the warrior that had lost it.

She looked steadily at the weapon still gripped in her hand. Its draw had been formidable but not overwhelming, and its short stature was perfect for firing from horseback. She walked slowly to retrieve the arrow that she had ruined. With a careful examination she was pleased that it was not beyond repair, but she knew there was still much work to do.

She knew the sword called the Five Elements would claim the warrior Arkthar as its wielder, and that her father's rhythm fit well the long metal staff. In her left hand she felt the unstrung potential of the splendid bow and knew that it was hers. Three weapons, three people, and three ranges, her instincts rang true.

She would once again draw from the worms, this time not to weave garments that shield the wearer from the elements. Protection would come from the bowstring she would weave to harness and tame the power of the northern plains.

With the men working on her father's new blade, she would have all the time needed to master this nomadic skill.

THE BLADE OF MAH LIN

For the next moon's passing, my days were spent with Mah Lin within the cavern's forge. I was like the midwife's assistant aiding the birth of living steel.

The embryo began as a small, cold square conglomeration of steel. Its origin was both old and distant, for this was the last remnants of the ore the monk called *wootz*. This was the last offering of this temple, miserly saved from the sands of time and brought from the homeland of the Bodhidharma. It was a layered and twisted mixture of properties that yielded weapons without rival. It was refined to liquid in a cauldron of living flame the priest called "crucible steel." As if replying to my superstitions he said, "Not the tool of witches, Arkthar, think of this ancient cauldron simply as your Holy Grail."

As the bellows pumped with the action of the water, liquid poured from my body. Mah Lin laughed and told me that I was fortunate not to be pumping the bellows by hand.

"Save your sweat for the hammer, Arkthar, for when your body dances to the rhythm of this monastery's ageless song."

From the coals Mah Lin drew out the white-hot cube of metal with the tongs held in his left hand and placed it on the anvil. With a small hammer in his right hand he struck, and sparks flew. His blows were my guide as I hovered over the steel with the heavy long-handled sledge. When he struck, I struck. Where he struck, I struck. I followed his rhythm and his direction, and we hammered until the color of the metal dulled and was reburied among the white glowing coals.

Again and again we heated and struck, and when it lengthened he held the chisel for me to pound. Cut now and bent down, he folded it back upon itself, back to the beginning, back to cube, back to the fire, and back to the anvil. When he was satisfied that our day's work was complete, he would set the lengthening steel back to the coals to wait for our morning return, and then the work would begin anew. This was the snail speed progress of our first week.

Over time the shape of Mah Lin's blade took form. It was shorter by half then the Five Element Sword, and its edge was two sided. Running down the middle and tapering into the sharp tip was a groove. With monastic knowledge as his foundation, the hammering and shaping continued.

With the final hammerings, the shape and nature of the flying sparks also changed. They were smaller and brighter, and when the hammer struck they flew a greater distance, they became more animated themselves with the anticipation of the birth of blade. The shadowed darkness of the cavern forge was as a womb, the rhythmic clang of hammer and anvil was like the body's rhythm of birth, stopping only while the steel was in the heat and starting up again when it was drawn out, like the primal work of contraction.

One more quench when it glowed with the precise color, and it was formed enough for the grinding of edge to begin. Looking from the bottom where the steel was thick, he showed me its two shades. The hard wrapped by the soft was clearly visible in the cross section, as were the folds that layered the blade several thousand strong.

As I was honing the blade with the fine black sand, Mah Lin spoke.

"For a blade to live it must be as life, a circle. We are born toothless, bald, wrinkled, muttering, incontinent, and helpless. If we are lucky to live long enough, old age brings us back to where we started. The metal of the blade started in the black sands with which you now polish, and soon it will meet the clay from where all life began."

I set the shining blade where Mah Lin took it and coated it painstakingly with the reddened clay he had been mixing. Thicker in the middle and hair thin at its edge, he explained that the clay controls the cooling rate of the final and most important quench.

When it had hardened it was put once more to coal and drawn forth in the darkness of the cavern. It glowed white red and then disappeared sputtering into the water trough, leaving in its wake only sound, steam, and darkness. The clay flaked off in the water that boiled violently, and with the final and finest polishing it was an instrument to behold. Its haft was given a rounded oaken handle, simple at first glance, but it was crafted to fit perfectly into the hollow steel staff forged to become its permanent home.

In the light of late afternoon we walked home, filthy once more from our day's exertion. What we had created was a spear, a horse cutter, and a walking staff all in one. Near the end of its first hollowed chamber, I noticed a small round hole, and Mah Lin smiled when I asked him about this feature. He replied only, "I like to hear the music of my movement, and when two must fight as one, my position will be heard."

It had been an arduous but productive time, and I had learned much from the hard lessons of the forge. We saw Selah running to us from a distance, and she reached us before we were halfway home. She begged to see it, like a child wanting to see a new toy. She felt its weight and cast an educated eye along the length of its blade, passing it back to the monk she said, "Show me."

He sprinted toward a grove of the bamboo whose structure had inspired the shaft. The metal was in full spin as he approached them, and as the wind passed over the hole, his weapon sung with his movements like a flute. The blade severed the thickest, and before the trunk could reach the ground, the butt of the shaft had sent it skyward. From there to the next he moved without stopping, leaving in his wake only hollow stumps protruding from the rich black earth.

We continued onward to our home. I looked to see him walking with his child, and he seemed like a man as old as time, his walking aided by the staff that carried him. But the decimated stand of severed hollow trunks spoke otherwise.

When we entered the house to the smell of our dinner, Selah quickly removed something from her tunic. She placed the perfectly fitted leather sheath that she had made over her father's naked blade. She seemed like an aunt that wraps a woven bonnet around the head of a new baby and welcomes the newest family member home.

The priest and I saw the strung bow on the table beside a quiver of arrows. Mah Lin smiled at his daughter and said, "I see we have all been busy."

He smiled again when he saw the black feathered fletch of the arrow she had repaired and whispered, "It seems even your bird has something of value to contribute. Give him a special morsel to express my deepest gratitude."

LOTUS AND SWORD

Mah Lin was well pleased with the weapon he had created. He seemed tireless now in practice and peerless in the execution of its technique. We trained side by side in the shadow of the wooden cross, and vigorously sparred at the closing of the day. My shortened wooden sword was no match for the long blade of Mah Lin, but when I bridged the gap I could do some damage at close quarters. I discovered that the sound of the monk's bladed staff gave me insight into its movements and intentions. I was learning to listen within the heat of battle, learning to listen from within.

In the softened light of dusk as the three of us walked towards our home, Mah Lin asked, "What speaks to your soul from these sacred grounds?" I looked around and thought of many things, for every living thing upon the earth now seemed to have a voice.

I cast the food upon the surface of the pond at the entrance, and listened as the fish responded. I thought of ant, hen, and bird, of briar, and of oak, and I heard once more the raven call my name. The liyu were gone now, retreated gently to the solace of the depths. I followed the approaching wind as it descended like the coal black bird. From the rustle of distant leaves it swooped toward me along the ground. I felt it dance around me briefly, its parting touch rippled quickly across the water, and then like the fish, it too had vanished.

In the silence of its wake, I heard the flower of the pond speak clearly of my journey. I had arrived here broken, covered by the dark mire of my own ignorance. Knowing neither purpose nor destiny, I was drawn up by the sun. Now finally I am unfolding upon the surface, opening myself to the light of universal creation.

Selah and Mah Lin watched me quietly from the doorway as I listened to the world around me. I wanted to tell them all that I had heard, and so reached down and plucked the lotus from the cold pond waters. I held it gently between my fingers and let its splendor be my voice.

Time was lost in the peaceful silence of my answer, and, in truth, I do not know how long we lingered there. Perhaps a moment or perhaps a lifetime's passage, and it mattered not at all. I did eventually return the blossom to the pond, and the monk spoke gently to his daughter. "Bring it, Selah, its time has arrived." With that his daughter went into the house and on return carried with her the Sword of Five Elements.

Mah Lin spoke as Selah strapped the sword and sheath upon my back. "Arkthar, you are not the first to speak the sermon of the lotus. The Five Elements has chosen you, and you, in turn, have chosen it. Wear it well, for now you belong to each other."

I knew the significance of this presentation. Simultaneously I drew the long sword from my back and the short wooden one from my waist. I held them before me as a Celtic cross and bowed to the priest and to Selah. As my weapons separated I saw the blade of my old world in my left, and the blade of my new one in my right, and I began to move.

In the twilight my body traced the rhythms of wood and steel, and a song of old and new united rang out over the ancient grounds. I flowed freely in the ways of Celtic warrior and warrior monk. Mah Lin pulled his daughter closer as I moved. At times I followed and at times I led the edges of oak and metal, and in time I was spent, and drew breath deeply form the world around me.

The short weapon slipped easily into my waist, but the Five Elements was a different story. The atmosphere was still charged with the heavy tone of the honor that Mah Lin had just bestowed upon me. The problem was twofold, I had never worn a sword upon my back, and nobody had shown me how to return it to its sheath. For the next long minute I began a spastic dance of twist reach bend and fumble, all in a frantic effort to get the blade back into its scabbard.

Finally, Selah stepped behind me, guiding the metal tip deftly into the opening. The blade glided smoothly down into the sheath, disappeared, and clicked home, but not before their laughter had shattered the solemn occasion. Selah with eyes dancing whispered gently in my ear, "Since this sword has now become your wife, you should strongly consider improving the quality and smoothness of this operation," and her meaning did not escape me.

For me the Way of Two Swords had been born, and I with diligence would work to master it.

FULL CIRCLE

The commander's passage home was as rapid as the siege was lingering. All stops were brief, made only to resupply and keep moving. His mounted bear-clad frame had become an ever present incentive for his men to hasten an end to this campaign. At all times now he remained distant and detached, and for this blessing there were no complaints. His descent from the frigid highlands mirrored his downward journey into the cold and solitary world of madness.

He had lost over one thousand soldiers, few of whom he could call by name. Such was war. The loss of the siege weapons lightened their return march, and for this too, his men were guardedly grateful. He was no longer concerned about what the emperor might think, in part, because he thought him weak and in part because he brought a gift of epic proportions. It was a gift that would enshrine both their places in history.

His troops were now ruled only by fear, both his and theirs. At night when the weary soldiers slept or guarded the tent that sheltered the rolled up carpet of siege, he hid within his own tent and conversed with the head of his vanquished enemy. Volume and intensity rose with each jar of liquor consumed. Clutching the rebel's hair with his left hand, he thirsted to hold the head of the monk in his right. Until that end was met, there would be no rest.

The men were not in good spirits even though their mission was nearing its end, tempers flared and fists flew. They had nothing to show for their work except the imagined glory that their commander seemed to wallow in. Even his young page, formerly innocent and good-natured, had grown bitter and cynical over the past year. It seemed that despair hovered over them and followed their return like some monstrous black bird.

They passed quickly over sights that were appreciated on their trek to battle. Now the lush beauty of the lowlands was barely noticed; more testimony that siege warfare steals humanity from the soul of its executioners. The men that returned to the capital after so long away now resembled those that had left in outward appearance only. As fast as their homeward journey was, news of their return traveled even faster.

The citizens of the city lined the streets as they entered the main gates. The bear-clad commander rode at the forefront. His horse was still skittish to the bear's touch, terrified still of claw on equine flanks. The commander seemed to infect any that stared too long, with dread and desolation. All eyes were respectfully averted, save for two. The commander's horse was struck by them, and rose in fear at their icy black touch. Its oblivious rider simply grappled to regain the animal's composure and once balance was restored, moved on.

The long awaited acclamation of the grateful throng was sadly lacking. What their returning ears did receive were hushed whispers and halfhearted cheers. What their eyes received was the sight of families seeking among their corps those that had not returned. It was the timeless search for lives forever lost.

As the returning military procession reached the main square they disbanded, their mayhem had run its course. Only in dispersal did their spirits lift as families long apart were now reunited. Before revelry could completely overwhelm military discipline, the commander barked a final order, "The Northerner's carpet to my quarters."

While others joined their wives and much grown children, he proceeded to his room within the palace walls to keep company with the head of the rebel, to drink, prepare his report, and to await the emperor's summons.

The wait would not be a long one.

THE IMPERIAL COURT

The commander was interrupted mid rant in the privacy of his quarters by a knock from his young page. "What?" he slurred angrily.

The page wondered if the commander was already drunk or if his ruined face could no longer speak clearly even the simplest of words. "Sir," he began, "the Emperor wishes to see you." The boy retreated down the hallway without even waiting for a reply.

The court was already crammed with high officials and shuffling bureaucrats. Their whispered conversations ended as the commander strode in. He was clad in his standard polished armor, over which he boldly wore his robe of bear. As the putrid hide trailed behind him, the claws could be heard clearly, dragging across the smooth stone floor. The commander seemed more animal than the bear whose dead shell cloaked him, his face more savage than the ursine skull that framed it.

He walked disrespectfully tall and dangerously close to the Son of Heaven before dropping to his knees and bowing head to floor three times. The court was silent, the bodyguards were on edge, and the emperor was both displeased and disturbed. It was clear that the imperial arm of civilization had somewhere turned feral, and the emperor knew well that once an animal turns, it will never again turn back.

The commander rose to one knee and sounding hollow through the bear skull visor began to give his report. Stunned silence met its delivery, for it was spoken with the harshness and severity of a snarling animal, sometimes in a low growl and sometimes rising to a heavy roar. It was not the voice of a man, but some dark beast dressed in flesh and kneeling in the form of one who had once been human.

"The siege was long and hard fought; the rebels gave no quarter, and flatly rejected my emperor's benevolent hand. They were well prepared, and it is with great sorrow that I must report the loss of one thousand one hundred and eleven men. All died valiantly in the service of The Son of Heaven. Casualties on the enemy side numbered in excess of thirty-two thousand. Although minor compared to the brave lives lost, the machines of war were lost during their routine deployment in the early assault. Notwithstanding, I am pleased to report a successful completion of mission, and the total annihilation of northern pestilence and rebellion. By the might and wisdom of the emperor, peace has been restored."

The emperor weighed the commander's report silently against the periodic sources of information gleaned during the year of the campaign. Without delving into the obvious contradictions, the emperor pushed on.

"Is there anything else?"

"Yes, Your Eminence," growled the commander. "I bring two treasures from the rebel stronghold worthy of your reception." With a dramatic flair he pulled himself to full height and shouted, "Now!" On cue, ten of his most trusted men carried in on their shoulders the rolled northern carpet and unfurled it as practiced, on the cavernous palace floor.

All present including the emperor were stunned at its unearthly beauty. The two dragons of north and south faced each other in a dance of celestial majesty. Truly it was a treasure worthy of an emperor. It was a living symbol of the unification of the northern and southern regions, two dragons now dancing as one. From the age of the First Emperor, it spoke in rich colors of the heavenly origin of imperial power and the unstoppable cycle of dynastic rule.

The emperor had the ten men that had carried it in, hang it in its rightful place of honor on the wall directly behind his celestial throne. The whispers of appreciation and admiration that swirled around the court like a sycophantic storm were cut short when the emperor began to speak.

"You have done well, Commander, you may ask one favor."

Without hesitation the commander rose to eye level and addressed the Son of Heaven face to mangled face.

"More than fifteen years ago I embarked on a vital mission of imperial decree. It has been accurately reported to me that although I was successful in the emperor's glorious cause, one criminal escaped and still lives, and I am told that his power grows. I suspect that it was he that stole the monastic library, and it may yet be recovered. Let me assemble a force of five hundred hand-picked men to complete your mission with the finality that it deserves."

All including the emperor knew the mission to which he referred. There was a long silence as the Son of Heaven studied the animal before him and carefully measured the permutations of possibilities.

Finally the words, "Permission granted," issued from the Imperial Seat.

As the commander prepared to take his immediate leave, he was halted by a question from the throne of power.

"You spoke of two treasures, what is the second one?"

The commander stopped his hasty exit and almost as a

casual afterthought reached under the cloak of hair and hide. Smiling in his damaged way, he drew forth and held up the severed head of the rebel insurgent.

A collective shudder of revulsion passed over and through the imperial court like the icy touch of a northern wind. The few that did not quickly avert their eyes beheld a face that smiled at death and one that decay had strangely not molested. They looked upon a man whose features, even though bodiless, were much more human than those of the man that held it. In the void of shock and silence, the commander tucked it away, pivoted awkwardly, and marched out.

Ministers jostled to move rapidly out of his way, as unhindered, untouched, and unhurried, he left the shaken hall.

THE POX

Death has his time and perspective, and men have theirs. They are flightless creatures and so can see only the ground before them. Death soars in effortless circles sometimes gently and sometimes ferociously riding the winds. This higher view often leads to deeper understanding, or more accurately, overstanding, and does not fall easily within man's grasp.

If it did, they would have seen death flow steadily from north to south like a mighty river, a river that fills the channel where men once marched. They would have seen it branching off like tributaries. They would have seen it stop at the imperial palace and radiate out from the wall behind the throne to the far reaches of the kingdom like the spokes of some great wheel. Instead they knew only that Death came, and for a flightless earthbound creature, perhaps this was enough.

Like the first rain drops of a gathering tempest, reports began to trickle in from the far reaches of the empire. A sickness had struck with the suddenness of a summer storm. Even the earthbound could now discern its rapid progression.

The soldiers had returned free of plunder, but not free of disease, and this is what entered their homes and embraced their families. The plague infiltrated like a spy and lay dormant like a sleeper cell. It incubated within the carrier unnoticed, it gave away nothing of its presence; it hid, it grew, it traveled, and then it struck. Innocent and quiet at first, it began as a minor irritation of the skin, a few red spots. Like brook to stream and stream to raging river, its symptoms grew to rage in torrents.

The red welts swelled to ugly sores which spread and festered. Hard and painful to the touch they soon covered the body and lined even the mouths of those infected. Even through the highest fever, the itch could drive men mad. The angry boils puckered and broke like volcanic craters. The strong survived and the weak perished. Scabs eventually formed and dropped off. Some of the lucky were left blind, all of the lucky were left pock scared and disfigured.

This was Death slashing from horseback upon the stallion known as War. It struck with the unpredictability of battle, a scythe that knows not wheat from weed. Young or old, man or woman, rich or poor, any could fall before it. Some survived while many perished, and others it left alone.

There were no walls high enough to keep it out, or thick enough to keep it in. Not even the walls of the imperial palace. For the emperor, the death of his people was only one consideration. With a great dying the economy grinds to a halt, and before plagues of great magnitude, even empires crumble. As trickle became flood, the seriousness of the situation weighed upon his shoulders, and with every passing day that weight increased.

The commander spoke to the dead young rebel often, sometimes about this accursed pox, and often about killing the smelly boy. He remembered little of the bargain that the rebel had offered and that he had refused, for overstanding was not his strength, and delusion was now his overlord.

All the commander knew was that the ranks of the military were decimated, and that he and those that still stood were pressed to bury the dead. It was a curse upon his head, not because of death or suffering, but because it had delayed his revenge. The monk would live, at least until the plague had run its course.

Within the imperial walls the emperor's minister was also ravaged by the plague. Not directly, for that would have been a blessing, but indirectly like so many others. This man of wealth and power could do nothing to ease the suffering of his beloved eldest son. This minister, in spite of rank or wealth, could do nothing when Death came and took his boy. As the funeral fire burned, and the blackened smoke that was once his boy rose up, the anguished cries of a grieving father mingled with the winds that blew across the land.

This was the reaping of the lesser pox, the smallpox, and it was this black carpet that now rolled out to cover the empire.

Fathers and Sons

This Chancellor, once the emperor's most trusted minister, ambled throughout the palace grounds like a wraith. He had always borne the responsibility of his post well, but now it paled by comparison to the weight that pulled him down and slowed his every step. He was without purpose, a man who knew that in reality his life had amounted to nothing. Sorrow was a heavy burden, and the fact that he would never really know his son added to it greatly.

His regrets were many. Their time spent together was as an official with his heir, he wished now it had been much more as a father with his son. There was no comfort and no solution, and for all his worldly influence, he was now utterly powerless. He had steered his boy away from all things frivolous, but would now give anything just to hear that childish laugh once more.

With no real way to escape his pain, he wandered vacantly to the only place that gave him small respite. As he approached this private spot, he froze when he saw another in his place. He stood quietly and watched carefully to see what the boy had come to steal. Instead he saw the page light an offering before the urn that held the ashes of his son. The smoke rose and circled as the boy bowed three times and thrust the incense into the bowl of alter sand.

An image of chopsticks stuck in a rice bowl came to mind. He walked forward, and at the sound of his closing footsteps, the page's tear-wet face turned suddenly in his direction. The frightened boy stood clumsily and prepared to flee. "Stay," the minister bid, and reluctantly but without choice the boy sat once more. "Why are you here?" the chancellor asked, and when the page answered, "I came to visit my friend," his eyes could not hide their surprise.

He raked through memory for anything his son may have told him about this friendship, but there was nothing. He did remember the distain his boy had of the rough commander, and what once he thought irrational now began to make more sense. Their status was as opposite as night and day, but their ages were similar. In the adult realm of the palace, the minister was starting to believe that his son may have had a secret friend. The Chancellor asked bluntly, "What besides your years could you two possibly have had in common?"

The page responded with an unwavering stare, and with an answer that took the emperor's highest official completely off guard, "Horses, Sir. Your son loved horses." There was a time his boy walked into the palace smelling like the stable, and the memory of how he had rebuked his child now scalded him like bitter tears.

Over the course of the afternoon he gleaned many details from the page about a boy that he didn't know. The minister heard about his son's dreams of one day joining the military. Proudly he heard that his son was kind to the page and the animals that he tended. In a short time the minister realized that this boy knew his son much better than he did, and he took delight in every hidden detail.

The page eventually apologized but explained that he had his duties to attend to, and that any slip would bring harsh retribution. The minister did not want him to go but understood the workings of the palace. He felt much lighter as he stood to face the page whose position now grew more desperate with every passing moment.

"Sir," the page intoned with one final recollection, "It was your son's strongest desire to rid the land of the sickness that came in time to claim him." With an awkward and uncustomary embrace the minister said, "Goodbye."

The minister walked with new direction, grateful for the gift the young page had given him. He was clearer in thought and lighter in spirit than he had been since his son's departure. Once inside his private chamber, he took his position behind his desk. He sat straight and breathed deeply as he looked at the blank silk paper that lay before him. Gathering in mind the spirit of his boy, he dipped the brush and began to write in his beautiful cursive script.

Before assigning his seal, he examined carefully his first official decree since the death of his son, and was well satisfied. The minister had written a summons to physicians, wise men, and magicians from all over the empire, to come to the capital and try to find some remedy.

The official proclamation was sent out across the entire kingdom. It went out over the land like the smoke of the many funeral pyres and touched the furthest corners of the realm.

THE GUEST

Guided patiently by Mah Lin, over time and through great effort, I grew more skilled with the handling of two blades. Under the discerning eye of his loving daughter, I made headway unraveling the mysteries of the written word. Step by step, proceeding in an orderly fashion, my body and my education flourished. I grew by leaps and bounds, for no man eats like one who has known starvation.

Selah and Mah Lin told me of monks who traveled to far off places, and yet in body never left the quietness of cave or cloister. For these masters, time and distance were not an obstacle nor were they now for me. While my flesh sat at the oaken table, my mind walked with healers and holy men, with warriors and wise men, with scientists and philosophers. For me this was the true magic of the written word.

To read is a wondrous gift. It is an invitation into the mind of others, to be a guest at their table. Even more extraordinary is that this visit transcends both time and mortality. Here within the library walls I heard with my eyes the words of great teachers that lived and died centuries before I was born. In the quietness of this stone cut room, and upon its thick oak table, I dined with greatness.

It was true that the long staff we created was a work of art, but to see Mah Lin train with it was the real wonder. Selah, too, had continued to hone her martial skills. On horseback she rode in the ways of Hunnish warriors; arrows flying in rapid succession from the string of her ancient bow. At full gallop she could fell an acorn cluster from the highest branches of my oak.

Her legs controlled her horse, the bow and a fistful of arrows clutched in her left hand, the right plucking, drawing, and releasing her deadly projectiles. With a girl's delight she would charge at her father unleashing fierce volley while he practiced. Mah Lin would parry each missile with the bladed staff as easily as a mantis impales a cricket.

When not within my hands, the Five Element Sword and its shorter wooden ally were always on my back and at my waist. The intensity of all our physical training continued to increase, spurred by an urgency the monk chose not to reveal.

Until, "Arkthar," he said on a cool fall day. He gazed northward with a serious expression, like the poorest farmer checks the weather. "Sickness in the body is the expression of an imbalance; Selah has taught you much about this theory."

"Yes, Mah Lin, that is true," I replied.

"I sense imbalance of another sort. I feel it gathering like a storm, ready to move from north to south."

I was disturbed by the tone and demeanor of the monk. I looked at his bright eyes to see their focus.

"Protect and love my daughter for all time," he said solemnly.

A silent "Yes," was the answer of my eyes and soul.

Selah joined us now from across the field, her dark hair moved freely in the autumn breeze. She scanned our masked faces, which gave no clues of our private conversation, and yet, without so much as a question, she added, "I feel it too."

The three of us walked toward the house. We knew that our time of peace here in the eye of the storm was coming to an end. I spread the remaining bat manure onto our hungry garden. It had served us well over the last three years, as I looked at it I realized its time too, was coming to an end. It would produce little more, and most of its food had been harvested. Selah had preserved what would keep us through the mild winter months, and I wondered what the next spring would yield.

I entered the house as the monk and his daughter finished the spicing of the evening meal. They shared a laugh at my smell, for I had spread the guano with my hands. Selah handed me the small garden shovel that I could not find, together with the soap and water. When I was clean and ready to sit, the priest said casually to his daughter, "Set another place for our guest." At the prompting of the monk, Selah used the finest porcelain. Beside the matching cup and bowl, she carefully laid a beautiful pair of rosewood eating sticks. We had never had company, and there was comfort in seclusion. We wolfed down our good meal in the powerful presence of the formal but vacant setting.

Mah Lin refilled the nearly empty teapot from the boiling kettle above the central hearth. As he set it back upon the table, there was a loud cry outside from Selah's raven. The bird's harsh call was followed by three weak knocks at the wooden door. Before I could move to answer it, our guest was inside and sitting before the empty bowl. Without hesitation Selah had filled it to the stranger's polite protests of, "It is enough."

I said nothing but stared at the old one as he happily ate. I saw the tattered black robes and the purple veins of his boney hands. They branched and twisted like the boughs and roots of the oak, or the streams that feed a river viewed from a great height, or the flash of lightning across the night sky. His glance in my direction pulled me back to the present.

He was enjoying every mouthful and savored morsels between swallows like each was a new experience.

Only when his bowl was emptied and his cup refilled did

he and Mah Lin begin to freely speak. He was comfortable within our ancient walls, not like one who visited, but like an animal that after a life of wandering had finally returned home. I felt drawn to this beggar, but continued to study him from a respectful distance. His pale white skin was stretched to wrap his skeletal frame, and I saw that it was covered in ugly scars. Only those round black eyes spoke of his youth and vigor, those coal black eyes that spoke so loudly of life.

"Thank you," he said to Selah through his toothless mouth, and turning to me like a proud grandfather, he added, "Arkthar, you have grown well."

We four sat by hearth fire until the blackness melted from the eastern sky, and it began to glow red from the bellows of the coming day.

THE PATTERN IN
THE THREADS

The beggar spoke of many things. He told Mah Lin the terrible details of the Northern siege and of a bear-cloaked commander who Mah Lin seemed to know. He talked with admiration of a young rebel, and he spoke of death. He looked at me often, to see if I was following the conversation, and kindly he spoke slowly and clearly. I had almost forgotten the horrors of war, for that was another life, but now the rhythm of his words joined my past with the present, and it was not a welcome guest. I felt the barren coldness of the northland blow across my soul.

As quickly as the account of siege ended, the story of the plague began. The dark stranger wove words with the power of a carpet maker, their crossing threads and fibers bound me to my place, and I listened deeply. There was a great dying over the entire land. It seemed that there were few places still untouched.

Selah also sat quietly, and listened with the open mind of the healer. When silence settled, she began the questioning of a skilled physician. "There is no pattern to this plague?"

"None that I have seen," was the beggar's empty answer.

"You have walked in its shadow from its beginning, comforting the dying and burying the dead?"

"I have."

"How is it that you did not fall?"

"Selah," he ventured, "I do not know. I know only that I was young when the fever took me, and I have worn the scars of this illness ever since. I knew its touch, but not its embrace. Death did not claim me, for my fate it seems was with the living." There was silence, as now we listened and she continued.

"Do you have any symptoms?" she asked.

"Only these," he said as he rolled up a tattered sleeve to reveal two small boils on his skinny upper arm. "Usually there is nothing, but sometimes after I have been near the dying, I will get a small blemish on arm or leg. No fever, no pain, and no illness, just a small boil that bothers nothing and heals quickly."

Selah was lost in deep concentration. Her mind examined all that she had ever learned about illness and affliction. She retraced and reviewed the process of healing, and the progression of disease. She chased after the solution but it remained hidden, cloaked in swirling mists at the farthest reaches of her mind. She strained at the work of drawing solid answers from miasmic thoughts. Mah Lin placed a concerned arm around his daughter's tired shoulders and soothed her worried mind. "Sleep my daughter," he said. With a faraway look in her eyes she bid us goodnight.

In her dreams she continued to thrash about. Beside her mother once again, she saw the healing of her near dead father, and watched from shadow a woman's love wrestling life from the boney hands of Death. She struggled to pull clarity from the grip of chaos.

The truth arrived like a clap of thunder descending from the clouds of experience and intellect. The bolt on which it rode lit the darkness of her dreams. Awakened by this brightness, she opened her eyes and smiled the same calm smile as her beautiful mother, and said with certainty, "This is the pattern of the plague."

The next morning as we sat for breakfast, Selah spoke her thoughts aloud. "It strikes with the random force of a storm's lightning, and like the bolt it never strikes the same place twice. Once hit, your body knows the enemy and has built its permanent defense. It cannot ravish those who already know its touch."

Guided by a healer's wisdom and without any hesitation, she drew forth the needles that I had once feared so long ago. She held the tiny sword deftly between her fingers and scratched the surface of the beggar's lesion. Without fear she passed its small sharp tip to her forearm and moved it back and forth until the blood came.

In horror I was frozen even as she moved close and did the same to me, and then smoothly to her father who had already rolled up the sleeve of his saffron robe and revealed his mighty arm.

He looked to our guest, and amid the terror of war and disease, he smiled peacefully at Death.

Departure

The following day we slept late, well past the roosters morning call, for we were not quite well. The beggar ministered to us with care, the scratches on our arms had grown to a hard and angry abscess, and we three shared a fever and discomfort. The boil puckered and took on the look of a navel; it scabbed as the fevers passed. They healed as a pocked scar within a half-moon's passage. Selah carefully collected the fallen scabs, and we were sound once more.

When I awoke with the new dawn, I could not find my threadbare scholar's robes. With bare chest I entered the main room. The scars of my warrior past were now my only clothing. On the table before me was the chain mail armor that Selah had selected for me from the great hall. It was the armor of my country, but through its interlocking links she had woven the silken strips of my scholar robe into an artful pattern of love, power, and protection. The deepest of blues shone from between the metal rings. On top of this she had carefully placed my sword of Five Elements.

Our appetites had returned, and our tattered guest served us a beggar's breakfast. It was small, it was good, and it was enough. On the table before us he placed the open proclamation of the high chancellor. Its deep folds told of the time and distance over which it had been carried. There was no doubt, no hesitation, and no debate. We had our purpose and our direction. Mah Lin once again tucked the dragon's compass beneath his shimmering robes.

By the morning light we outfitted four horses for our journey to the capital. Provisions were packed by Selah and equally distributed among us. Mah Lin's freshly shaven head and many colored robe brought me back to the time of our first meeting. He adjusted his steel staff on the side of his mount. Selah was dressed in the simple brown robes of the desert's caress, the same ones from that time so long ago, the only visible difference was the bow and full quiver she now carried.

I expected nothing. I was in deportment closer to the nature of our horses. They were pleased to be worked and ridden, and indeed seemed happy to share in each other's company. The armored shirt was in itself a work of skill and wonder, and with the weavings of my silken robes it slid comfortably over my soldier's frame. I was not sure of our mission's duration, and focused instead on our task's noble purpose.

The beggar by contrast seemed almost jovial. A traveler by nature, he was happy not to be walking, and pleased to indulge in the ease and luxury of horseback. He smiled as he stroked the pale grey stallion and quoted an ancient proverb, "If wishes were horses, than beggars would ride." The simple wisdom of these words amused the priest and instantly lightened our load. With a movement that belied his great age, he was up in the saddle and steadied his horse with an easy redistribution of his weight and a gentle tug on its bridle.

Selah watched from atop her white horse as I strapped my blade to my back and secured my wooden sword beneath my waistband. I swung my leg over the red charger and we were off. The horses moved without command along the river that was theirs. I surveyed our land from the height of my mount and was once more impressed by its rugged beauty. Onward we rode, past my sacred oak, past the roaring falls, and once again out into the world of the wild and the unfamiliar. The creatures of this place cast a glance at our departure, perhaps their gesture of respect.

I smiled inwardly, for I saw this now as profound but natural, far removed from former thoughts of witchcraft and sorcery. With our journey begun I felt at peace and comfortably energized. We four now moved as one. I saw the raven flash overhead as we left these ancient grounds.

With a subtle tipping of its outstretched wings it rose much higher, and looking downward a faded cry spoke its blessing.

FROM THE EYE

We rode in single file, and for most of our journey the pale horse and its black rider led the way. Steadily by the monk's compass and the beggar's memory, we moved northward and to the west. Through villages and towns we rode, and there was no joy at the sight of us. In fact, there was no joy anywhere along our route. It was a path paved instead by suspicion, fear, and misery. We saw crops rotting in their fields. The pox was still a bigger problem than the hunger that had not yet arrived. Everywhere we saw the new markers of the recently dug and the freshly buried.

In contrast to the dying, I saw wonders of engineering; smooth straight roads and immense stone bridges that by great design hung suspended over wide rivers. On occasion, majestic pagodas of wood and brick towered higher than any building of my world amid the untamed beauty of forest and meadow. I knew that by these standards the world from which I came was primitive, but in the face of a plague, these wonders meant nothing.

I did not know that it was possible for the earth to mourn, but as we rode farther, I heard its wails and saw its many tears. We had left our peaceful home less than a week before, and now we were much farther than a world away.

We stopped briefly at an inn when we were perhaps one full moon into our journey. What used to be a place of shelter and hospitality was now cold and foreboding. At the prompting of his shy but stubborn wife, its keeper brought us into its dark back room. A child lay wet and red on damp and dirty sheets. It cried softly, weak from fever and listless in appearance. Selah approached it as we watched, and cradled the child lovingly in her arms. The innkeeper looked lost for words, and I saw the eyes of its mother, red and swollen from tears already spent.

Selah was in her realm as she sang the ancient songs of healing to the baby girl. They were songs that she had heard her mother sing on the full moon of winter's longest night. I watched her put a trace of powder into the small nostrils, and with warm breath blow it gently into the weakened infant. The baby stopped crying and drifted into comfortable sleep. She spoke to the child's mother in the hushed tones that only women know.

"The sores have not yet come, and she will live if she can fight the fever for three more days."

Selah made a brew of herb and set it out before the mother as she explained its dose and schedule. There are not words to explain well the reaction of the innkeeper's wife, so it must suffice to say that the sorrow we had felt follow us for so long, was at least here laid to rest.

The couple pleaded with us to stay the night, and I was greatly relieved when the monk accepted. Both we and our horses were road weary, and the chance to eat well and bed warmly was a blessing. We would soon enter the capital, and it would be well to do so refreshed and alert. The room they led us to was humble by most standards but was a palace spa by ours.

I lay my head upon its soft pillow and remembered little else.

THE AWAKENING

Here there is no memory, and yet here there is all memory. Here memory is not merely a past event echoing through the mind of the living. It is a noise that rumbles from distant origin and fades only at time's far end. From the dead through the living and to the not yet born, and it is a resonance that echoes not within the mind, but within the soul. It is a sound heard not faintly with my ears but loudly with my spirit.

I am not alone, the priest and the woman are with me. Like the snow, the river, and the mist, we are three as one, and we are not alone. Death is here, and Life is also here. I know now that Death and Life are not two separate beings but two separate parts of one whole. As long as Life remains, Death can only wait. It can touch but it cannot yet hold. I listen with all my senses, for Death does not always speak with the words of men.

From familiar ground, we look upon what was once a mountain. Time has whittled it to just a hill. I stand comfortably on a lush green highland. I see a solitary oak and a river's falls, and in the great distance, a lion; a sentinel of standing metal.

From the north, the light cirrus clouds move over and past the peaceful highlands. The sky thickens. Their formations turn from wispy white to serious grey, and these move over me like the march of a great army. The dark northern sky lights up with flashes, and its low pitched growl reaches my ears in the time of three deep breaths. The rumblings move steadily closer, like the heavy weapons of siege drawn by the relentless cavalry of the advancing campaign.

I see in the ever-darkening sky that the approaching lightning cracks ever more destructive, and that it is no longer held by bonds of altitude but shoots down violently from the heavens to wound and scorch the earth. They flash like the jagged shapes of oaken roots, and I am afraid. I look for shelter, but the presence of Death steadies me, and in silent kindness, he bids me watch.

This I do, and as the celestial flashes descend around me, I feel the rain. Gentle refreshment at first, it builds quickly to a driving lash. Through my legs I hear the earth tremble, not from within like the mountain of fire, but from the surface and down. I see, with open-mouthed wonder, the ancient being that brings the rains.

It moves slowly in the measured steps of time. The sun-bleached bones that I once touched are now wrapped in the living flesh of muscle, sinew, and blood. Bones wrapped in the miracle of life.

The earth quakes with its every methodical step, and it comes to rest above the sheltered cavern, its size the measure of the shrinking landscape. The dragon rests upon its hollow nest and casts an eternal eye in my direction, it seems to implore me to release it unto Death and release it unto Life, so that it, too, can flow out to join the world and shape the destiny of all mankind. It wants only in death, to live once more.

I look away from its cold, all-knowing gaze, but am sternly guided back by Death who bids me once again to watch. One last flash in the blinding rain and my whole world goes white and rumbles. The noise obliterates all my senses. It expands within me, and in fear I fight my way to consciousness.

The explosion faded to an echo, and I woke safely within the comforting walls of this inn's simple room. Shaken to my core, I trembled as I drew on my armor and flew to meet the others. Mah Lin, Selah, and the beggar sit relaxed and smiling before their warm morning meal.

They had chosen not to wake me, and decided instead, to leave me to my dreams.

THE CAPITAL CITY

In my world, towns and cities are a cluster of shelters that grow haphazardly around ports of commerce. They are a random assortment of stone and wooden hovels. Man and livestock all thrown together to survive as best they can. There is no order to the laying of road or walkway, and the population of their people is far outnumbered by pest and vermin. My capital is merely a wooden-walled fortress built upon the banks of a mighty river. While it is true that in my homeland there are great stone castles that impose their presence upon the landscape, all would pale compared to the vision that was now before me.

I strained both sight and imagination to take in properly all that I was seeing. I beheld a city that seemed impossible to be the work of mortal men. Its surrounding landscape dotted with thatched huts and hamlets and well-tended fields and canals gradually merged toward the mighty stone foundation. They provided scale for the vista, as did the measure of time needed to ride from first sight to final destination. I studied carefully the details of this splendor. The white walls of the city formed a rectangular shape and were higher by far than even my mighty oak. By my estimation, they spanned an enclosed length of seven thousand and a width of six thousand long paces.

As we drew closer I saw that each of the three walls held four gates, and that the south facing wall, the one that we now approached, had only three. Around the entire structure was a moat wider than a strong man could cast a stone, and the banks of both sides were lined with willow trees. Although I could not begin to guess its depth, I could see that its surface reflected the turrets that sat atop every wall, evenly spaced at a distance of about one hundred paces.

The gate before us was an amazing structure. Its roof floated like a ship upon a ship, and its elaborate elegance hid well its defensive purpose. Before we had reached the bridge that spanned the moat, we were met by this capital's military arm. For an instant their general seemed thinking to attack; I felt the sword speaking from my back, and wisely he decided not to. The beggar held up the tattered proclamation, and this secured our escorted passage through a humble passage in the monstrous gate and toward the heart of the palace.

We were not delayed or even questioned, this spoke of the power of the written word upon the beggar's paper. We were accompanied at a steady pace through the outer city along an avenue of immense width and proportion. This street was lined by water furrows filled with the ephemeral beauty of the floating lotus. We were escorted through the gate of a second great wall and through the inner city. The size and expanse of the inner city was breathtaking. Our horses in single file did follow the beggar's grey stallion. Its rider knew the streets like the raven knew our homestead.

We rode by lakes and fountains, parks and squares. Everywhere the air seemed full of fragrance, some the sweetness of flower and tree, some of pungent spice, and some just the normal stench of daily human life. We crossed canals on beautiful bridges, and rode on level streets and wide avenues laid in orderly fashion.

To my eyes and ears the population was thicker than any I had ever seen, but the grave faces of those I rode with spoke a different story. To them the city bustle seemed eerily muted.

Any that looked in our direction quickly looked away and scurried behind a closing wooden door or window shade. Even the screams and laughter of the wild urban children had been dramatically stifled. Like the bones of the rain bringer, my imagination brought this city back to life, back to the vitality of normal times. If this capital was a mighty dragon, it was one who trembled in the throes of death. It was a beast that now faced and understood its own mortality.

Finally we arrived at the blood red outer walls of the imperial palace they called the 'grand inner.' It lay nestled and protected in the center of this great urban expanse. After passing through yet another gate, we were herded like animals through the corridors of stone by our military escort. Their sideways glances told us that we were not the first that had responded to the minister's proclamation, and that none had been successful. It was also clear that although we were not the first, we were perhaps the strangest.

As we spilled into the large nine-pillared hall, dignitaries were already in their places. The large throne, with carved dragons on each arm, was empty, and our eyes focused on a carpet of exquisite beauty that hung behind it.

My eyes were pulled briefly from the image of its two dragons, as a grey-caped commander hurriedly brushed by to find the darker corners of the hall. His face was kept low as if trying to be invisible, but the mangled features could not hide their contempt and hatred no matter how his head was held. I looked to Mah Lin for a sign of explanation, but could read nothing but serenity upon his strong features.

I turned back now to the direction of the carpet as the emperor entered and took his place upon the throne. A man of quiet dignity stood by his side.

THE GRAND INNER

Understand that the position of the imperial chroniclers is a serious one, but sometimes accuracy is deemed less important than the need to engage future generations. Often a more riveting tale will usurp the mundane details of stark event. History would record us as a Taoist hermit from Omei Shan, a holy physician, a 'numinous old woman' (in this case a nun), and a 'Ouija board immortal.' In any event, we had arrived, and it was recorded correctly that we would introduce inoculation to the empire.

The emperor recognized the robes of Mah Lin's order, but his voice betrayed nothing as he bade us speak. Selah calmly spoke for us. "While we cannot cure those already ill, we can prevent the pox from taking hold of those untouched." In this land, a great physician is not one that heals the sick; a great physician is one that prevents the healthy from contracting the disease.

The minister stooped and whispered to the emperor's ear. The ruler wore his mask well, but it could not hide an incredulous glance in our direction. His features quickly regained their composure and he spoke for all to hear.

"None so far have been successful, and none have looked more unlikely to succeed than you. Even the greatest of rulers must bow sometimes to the advice of his most trusted. You may stay, and I will pray for your success." We obviously had powerful allies within the court, but clearly we also had powerful enemies.

Spurred on perhaps by the emperor's derision, it was the beggar who initially poked at the festering boil of hatred and venom and brought it quickly to a head. With the support of Selah and Mah Lin he instructed, no, commanded the emperor to destroy the carpet, before our work would begin.

He was direct, "That is the trophy that holds the seeds of pestilence and must be burned."

Everyone within the court drew breath at the same time. It held the tension of a drawn bowstring. The imperial guards were steadied by an almost imperceptible wave of the monarch's hand. The first minister feared his life was forfeit for this brazen affront. It was clear to the Son of Heaven that these strangers knew nothing of palace protocol. Still, he wondered whether they were monumentally foolhardy, or heroically courageous. Time, he surmised, would tell.

I felt once more the sword on my back as I turned and saw him. This one sought the shadows, but his hatred found the light. I saw evil wrapped in the flesh of a man and skin of beast. He glared with wrathful eye at the monk's back.

His unmasked loathing blew through me like a strong wind. The fires of my warrior mind flared. I heard Death whisper unknown words to the heat that seared my soul, but the drawing of a single breath brought it once again to peace.

EVIL GROWS

The commander had heard the news of their arrival even before the emperor, and dressed quickly to see if it were true. He was too slow even in his great haste, for the strangers had already been escorted to the safety of the palace. From the shadows of the court he tracked his prey.

The monk he easily recognized; older now and much more powerful. His face ached as his eyes and memory focused. He was shocked and unnerved by the presence of the tattered beggar, and he now wished that he had killed him in the street when he had had the chance. And then his eyes took in Selah. Even to the commander, Selah was remarkably beautiful, and he had quickly incinerated this thought with fantasies of her rape and murder.

The pale one wore the chain mail shirt of foreign lands, and the silken blue, between the rings, shimmered even in the dull light of the court. His hair was the color of the mountain deer and his eyes the color of the deepest sea. The commander knew by visceral instinct the sword that nestled on this warrior's back, but dismissed the lowly wooden toy carried under the warrior's waistband. His face throbbed with rising intensity.

The carpet behind the throne was the source of his pride, the visible testimony to what was his life's greatest accomplishment. These were the twin dragons of north and south that had gained his favor from the Son of Heaven. What world is this, where a beggar directs an emperor? This is surely too much to swallow. Control was a virtue that did not come easy for the commander. Yet here in the imperial court he knew that he must harness himself, for if he were to attack now, he would be cut down like a dog by the emperor's bodyguards, and the victory of sweet revenge would at best be short-lived.

He tried to calm himself as he stood, recalling the long cold passage of the day he had waited to kill the bear, and the long cold passage of siege before he killed the rebel. Time would drag on like the suffering of disease, but eventually it would end, and he would be ready. Yes, he must be both patient and controlled, for the time was not yet, and the place was not here.

Most likely their mission would be fruitless, their time and effort wasted. To stop this sickness was only the pitiful dream of a broken man, a minister who had lost everything and now clung only to hope. Although the commander had lived life unburdened by any spiritual creed, he would now pray for their downfall, and he would wait for his time. Fail or succeed, the work of his enemies would inevitably conclude, and they would return from where they came. The power of the emperor could not always protect them, and in distant place Death would do his bidding.

He had already secured permission for their destruction, and an emperor's word cannot easily be undone. Still, in light of present circumstance, stealth seemed a prudent strategy, for he had at least learned the value of a coward's patience. Within his mind, soothing thoughts crooned that in the long run it mattered not that revenge must wait a little longer, as long as the outcome would remain unchanged.

From the shadowed comfort of the imperial court, he plotted. The commander need wait only until the time was right. He would endure the slow and agonizing passing of the heavens and stay away from the revealing light.

THE TASK AT HAND

None of us ate lavishly or availed ourselves of the palace luxuries that were ours for the asking, instead, we centered ourselves for the battle that was before us. Palace protocol was broken for us, and we were allowed to keep our weapons within arm's reach, even in the company of The Son of Heaven. This was a title that contrasted strongly with the concept that I had been raised with, but I said nothing, for this was not my place, it was theirs.

In their place, in this palace, I felt the cruel eyes of the one called Supreme Commander follow our every move. They watched from the shadows. His hatred was tangible, and I felt like one who walks through a forest of northern wolves. The Sword of Five Elements on my back gave me comfort, and I was not negligent in my practice. Every day I would find time to trace the five cuts and sit with hands in the position of the vajra mudra. In my solace I prayed for peace, and in my movement I prepared for war.

Ironically, with the scale of the task before us, it was crucial that we have the cooperation and partnership of the commander's military forces. Selah would turn these military forces from the purpose of killing to the duty of healing. This, too, must have greatly irritated the Supreme Commander like the painful sores of the lesser pox. But within the red palace walls, only the will and the wishes of the emperor had power.

We four were set up within days. The method of scratching and infecting was not the best for such a large scale project, and the implanting of the sprouts of a virus still very viable was dangerous. She had from the beginning chosen to work with the fallen scabs. The dead ones she called them.

"Like the crows of siege, the dead must now feed the living."

As was sometimes the case, I didn't understand her fully, but I served her as well as I could. Sometimes I was her protector, sometimes her helper, and always I was her lover. Over time and the course of multiple inoculations, she could harvest the scabs of the ones who had been inoculated with the scabs of someone who had been inoculated. They were weaker and less virulent but still triggered the body's defense.

We were a strange healing factory. The black-robed beggar used his brass begging bowl as a pestle and ground scabs to a fine dark powder all day long. This powder was placed in the nostrils upon cotton. The body heard the attack, sounded the alarm, and responded with intrinsic wisdom. It quickly built inner walls to stop its unseen foe.

This is the technique that we passed to the military. They, in turn, brought it from the palace to the far reaches of the empire. The cure flowed out like the minister's proclamation.

THE MANTIS KING

He was socially awkward in the world of people, but within the world of nature he was in his element. Animals liked him, and he in turn enjoyed their friendship and company. In the wordless presence of those entrusted to his care he was confident and guileless. It was a gift, and it had secured his job as page. Like many gifts though, under the cruel eyes of his commander, he often felt it more a curse.

Rest and recreation was a privilege that seldom came the boy's way, but now that it had, he would use it wisely. The commander's page searched happily in a wilder region of the sprawling metropolis called Kaifeng. Along urban ditches he walked, happy to be away from the rigors of his day and the oppressive presence of the Supreme Commander. A small grove of fresh green bamboo rose up from the sewage trenches like a small oasis in an urban desert. It was beauty rising tall and majestic from raw filth, strengthened by the squalor that fed its root.

It was in these small groves that he searched with well-trained eye. He was a hunter and this was his domain. Finally he saw it. The bright green insect flew ineptly from one grove to the next, with the young page in hot pursuit. It was clumsy in flight, but on ground it was a skillful warrior. He held his breath while moving towards his quarry from behind and downwind, and with a single pounce he seized his prize.

The young man felt the flutter of wings within his cupped palms. He carefully slipped the fresh captive into its new home made of discarded eating sticks and fine silk mesh. The insect secured, he studied the preying mantis as it reared up like a horse, its green eyes scanning and its arms held strike-ready across its chest. It was prepared to defend and protect, in an instant, poised to kill. "Surely," the lad said to himself, as he walked back to the stables, "This is a champion."

At night the soldiers gathered within the confines of the barracks to talk, to drink, and most importantly to wager. Mantis fights drew a raucous crowd, and serious money often changed hands. He had a good eye for mantid gladiators, and this one was an amazing specimen. He saw heroism in its stance, perhaps it would make him wealthy.

His happy musings were sharply cut by the sight of the approaching commander. The commander, too, had been hunting, and the look on his damaged face told the boy that he was the prey. The page had felt the commander's rage many times; he knew the beating was inevitable, and his only thoughts were for security of his tiny warrior. He managed to place the cage down safely, just before he was sent sprawling by a closed fist.

It was always a gamble, and he wondered if he should try to stand or stay down. It mattered not, for the bet was fixed. Whichever course he chose, it would be the wrong one. A heavy kick landed on his ribs, and he rolled in pain. The commander seemed more angry than usual this day, and the beating was relentless. The commander had caught up to the rolling figure of the page and was about to launch another blow.

He was frozen mid-strike by the commanding voice of Mah Lin.

"Stop," was all he said, but with a force that could halt a charging horse.

The commander turned in full fury towards the monk, who stared coldly back into the dark eyes and mangled face. "You dare to order me?" he asked, as he moved menacingly closer to the priest. He was used to seeing those he addressed tremble, but there was no fear upon the robed one's face.

"It is not me that speaks it. The request comes from high imperial circles. Your young page will be working closely with us while we fight this plague, and this is ordered by the Son of Heaven."

Not even the Supreme Commander would think of going against an Imperial request, and he spat his anger at the man in robes. Bile oozed from his lacerated face, and he quickly wiped it with his arm. Looking with open hatred first to the page who sat bleeding, and then to the monk, the commander stormed away. His last long look, so close that the priest could smell the alcohol on his breath, held a promise.

The monk picked up the broken boy who cried like the lost and bloodied child he was. As they began the walk back to the palace, he reached down and scooped up the insect that the page had forgotten. "Gambling is a risky business," he said to the sobbing boy by his side. A reluctant smile burst from the face stained with blood and tears.

"Teach me how to fight him," the young man asked. "I will kill him if you show me how."

The monk smiled the gentle smile of a loving parent, "That will not be necessary."

They walked on in silence, and the page felt the pain of the beating begin to fade like the waking memories of a bad dream. When the two had arrived back to the stables, Mah Lin said quietly to the boy, "If you want to learn the art of defense, you must learn it from a great Master." A hopeful spark shone from young eyes. "I will study by night and day," the boy replied. Hope was replaced by confusion as the monk held the cage with the captured insect carefully up to the page's face and said, "Here is your Master. Study well all the lessons that he will teach you."

The page sat in silence long after the monk had left. Idle and thoughtless, he took a blade of straw from the stable floor and slipped it through the mesh. His prisoner was ready, and impaled it with the speed of lightning. That evening while the rough soldiers gambled and drank, the page studied the skills of his mantis in the privacy of his small cold room.

As he watched the graceful parries and deadly strikes coming from within the small mesh cage, the thought settled that he had found his teacher, and that their journey would be life-long.

A Challenge in
the Sand

The priest, his daughter, the beggar, and I continued to work steadily at our task. The young page was often by our side helping with the vigor of youth and learning steadily the healing ways of the ancients. He had also found unexpected favor within the court. The emperor's trusted high minister had bonded with the boy, for indeed the youth had many qualities of his buried son. On this day, Mah Lin turned to me and said, "All is well here, Arkthar, why don't you go and train."

He was right. He knew that I had become like the guardian lion of our homestead, and that I could use a small respite. The sword kept my body whole and the meditation of the vajra mudra kept my mind sound. With his blessing I walked from the inner palace to the sanctity of the outdoor training grounds.

Although all thoughts of war were for me a distant memory, I still enjoyed watching the young soldiers training upon the open military fields. I walked past the large archery fields and smiled inwardly, for Selah's skill with an arrow was already better than the best of what I saw. The sound of arrows flight was replaced by the steady knock of wooden swords, this changed to steel on steel as I walked on towards a far more private area of this field. I drew the sword from my back, and in lone tranquility began to meld my mind and body.

The first hour I spent in basic exercises. The Viken pirates of the North had taught me a valuable lesson, one which I would never forget, and the Iron Palm that Mah Lin had taught me in the cavern merged perfectly with the Viken wisdom of training equally the left and right. I began with palming. Not the iron filled bags, however, now I palmed the handle of my beloved Five Element Sword. From left hand to right hand, at first nothing more than a simple catching in midair. If the fist was the hardest weapon of the hand, then the catch was the softest, and I would neglect neither.

Within the passage of half my hour, the intensity and rhythm of my catches had increased and both my palms had begun to ache accordingly. With the time of hour approaching, my steel did ring out from the battering of my hands. I would break both rhythm and speed for the last ten minutes, until even holding her became a task to push right through.

Finished now, I sat as sweat ran, and massaged the healing jow into my throbbing palms. I enjoyed the smell of the medicine that Selah had prepared, and my hands cried in thirst for more. I ignored the stares from the caped commander in the distance, but took note that he and the three strong men with him meant me no good.

After this brief rest I picked up my sword again and began the pattern of the five cuts. In solitary practice I continued this training gradually increasing speed until my arm began to slow from fatigue and the nagging of my old wound. I was tired but not fully spent as the commander and his three men drew closer. With changing weather my arm throbbed, and I knew that I must not provoke it with overzealous movement, so I sat and massaged limb and shoulder with Selah's healing liniment.

In a voice thick with alcohol, the commander addressed me roughly. "You will never be skilled if you only practice alone, allow my men to help you improve." I saw immediately that this was to be no training session. His men attacked with full speed, full power, and bad intentions. The sounds of battle rang out across the open space. In their defense, they did not all attack at the same time, but took turns, first one, and then the next. I was in heart, glad to cross swords again, and although I was outnumbered, I was not outmatched.

Every attack was met and thwarted efficiently, for my wounded arm had taught me the wisdom of economy. Their movements were large, and as I maintained my distance I could foresee their every motion. The intensity of their blows increased, and I could feel my energy beginning to wane. I knew that danger flowed around me like the torrent of our river's falls, and I felt my body being pummeled once again by its cold and fierce cascade. I was awake and alive as I sprang now upon each in turn, but fatigue was gaining ground.

I did not know how this would be resolved, and felt as one who leaves his body. From a height I saw our clash evolving and saw the commander looking for the weakness in my style. He did not need to look far, for my left arm ached now, and The Sword of Five Elements was becoming a heavy burden. Finally the biggest and the freshest of the three moved fast and broke my careful distance. Close enough to smell the sweat of his effort, he slipped from my parry and drove the hilt of his sword heavily into my old wound. I felt the pain like a bolt travel from shoulder to mind, and I heard a cry that I thought must have come from me.

But it had not; it was an order to stop.

The Face of the Enemy

I was surprised that he had ended the fight, and was surprised as well to see that I was on my knees and that my weapon now sat lifeless within my aching left palm. He shed the hide of the great moon bear and passed it to one of his men. He motioned them back and stepped forward to face me. One look told me all. He was now confident in his assessment of my skills, and he wanted to be the one to finish me. Here in this open field, whether by accident or purpose, my death would not demand harsh retribution.

Slowly he took his position before me, and in hand held a sword of fine monk steel. My chest heaved to draw in air, and the look upon his twisted features was already one of gloating victory. I thought it strange that this man, fully grown, was no more than a playground bully who torments only the smaller and weaker children, and underneath the façade of gilded military might, I saw and knew that he was just a coward. I saw his world through his eyes. I stayed on my knees struggling for breath. I was weak, tired, and in pain. I must have seemed a very easy kill.

I felt no fear, and met the hatred in his eyes with peaceful countenance. All senses woke and time slowed. My hands scooped the wet clay, and the commander watched as I rubbed it evenly between my palms. I heard my raspy breathing settle, and smelled the familiar comfort of the sandy grit. I felt the welcome traction added to my grip. I watched his world change in a heartbeat as he saw me switch my weapon from my weary and wounded left arm into the untouched strength of my powerful right.

Fear is the mind killer, and the commander now wore his openly upon his twisted features. His brash advance became a stutter and a hesitation. Finally he attacked. It was not much more than a confused step forward and a downward cut with his steel monk blade. I met him easily. With ear and arm I felt and heard steel crash against steel. He did not withdraw and pressed forward angrily with slash and thrust. He was skilled, but he was not fully committed to any course of action, and because there was no commitment, he was easy to handle.

The men that are the hardest to subdue are the ones that hold on to nothing. They have no expectation of win or lose, and no expectation of living or dying. In short they are free, and it is this freedom that makes their movements truly dangerous. This man held on to everything. I was perfectly positioned to release him from his burden and more than willing to set him free.

The commander attacked at least five times and I did not respond in kind. I had settled comfortably into the rhythms of breathing and combat, and I was moving backwards at each volley of his vicious blows just to keep my distance. I saw the demeanor of his men, the ones that he had used to soften me for the kill. Their action would influence mine, but I read easily that they wanted no further involvement and that they were well content to let the commander fall into the trap that he had created.

He moved forward quickly but clumsily as he felt the nature of our bladed conversation change. He seemed to glance for help in the direction of the others, but as I suspected no help came his way. He was alone, and he was increasingly frightened by this stark reality. He began to circle as if trying to reach my back, hoping I think to find my weaker side. Again and again he attacked; each time more savagely than before. His assault was not launched from solid ground, its foundation lay somewhere on the shifting sands of panic.

The commander's sweating grimace could not mask his fear, and I felt the mood of skirmish change once more. It moved past fear to preservation. Few men knew better than me how powerful the instinct of survival is. It is a place of strength beyond body or mind, and within the distance of one step and the time of one heartbeat, the commander had arrived there.

He now attacked with a new fury, pushing off from the brink of madness and destruction. The hammering of steel on steel deafened me momentarily, and in truth, I was caught off guard. Had I kept my distance I could have struck a limb, but I had not, and he pressed this advantage with murderous resolution. I felt my shoulder bitten by the snake of diagonal downstroke but kept my focus upon the ruined face of my foe.

He had found the place of my old wound, and I felt my blood flow once again from my shoulder. Had I buckled I would be dead, instead I slid my sharpened blade down along his sword. This I did in reflex, hoping only to intercept the force of the potential backstroke and prevent a killing blow. Luck was with me, however, for my sword slid further and sliced the meat along the forearm. The pain flew up his arm and froze the working of his frenzy. For an instant, all time stopped, and in this place the beast of my distant past was once again set free.

I harnessed not the power of survival but of bloodlust. I had thought it tamed by the training of monk and maiden, but now it sprang through me and through my Five Elements more fiercely than ever before. I remembered the cave that held the corpses of my people and the Viken raiders that had left them there to turn to bone.

My attack was smooth and precise, faster than the commander could follow with eyes or sword, and I struck with all my being. Like the child with the lossough, I slipped the wooden short sword of my world from my waist, and it descended like a bird of prey. I was surprised as I watched without thought, for I did not strike to kill my enemy, I struck only to bring the conflict to its end. The sound of wood on steel resounded in the afternoon heat. I stood still now, eyes riveted on a visibly shaken commander, who held only the handle of his shattered weapon in his grip, and I released him.

I tucked the shortened oar into its place upon my waist and sheathed my weapon across my back. The four stood back as I moved past them. The commander's pain and terror had morphed once more to spewing malice, and the look from his men was of barely hidden disrespect. I left at an even pace to join my family within the palace, as I breathed in the fresh air of the open training fields. I was grateful that the bite was not too deep but would be thankful for Selah's skill with needle and with silk.

As I walked back toward palace safety, I felt the sun upon my wounded shoulder and saw my blood drip once more onto thirsty sands.

A DARK VISITATION

I lay quietly in my room within the palace grounds. Selah slept serenely at my side breathing deeply and gently like a child. The rooms of the sleeping quarters were large and opulent by my standards, but simple compared to most others within these imperial walls. The passing of the months prior had been fruitful. We had moved steadily forward in the work of stemming the plague, and my feelings for Selah had continued to deepen.

My thoughts froze and my breathing ceased. I reached quickly and quietly for the comfort of the wooden handle and listened to the lightest of footsteps approaching our room. They seemed to linger outside our doorway; they backed off, approached, and hovered in the hallway once again. I waited and watched the bolt to see if it would begin to gently slide, but it did not. Instead a gentle knock, and even in this sound I heard the echoes of indecision. My Five Elements was beside me now hidden by the cover of fur and blanket. I felt Selah stir as I answered the muffled wooden thud, "Enter."

The page entered apologetic and unsure, and glanced from Selah, whose eyes now struggled open. His darted around unsure of any target before finally settling on the floor before him. I said nothing, preferring instead to give the gentle boy a chance to find his comfort and his tongue. Finally and with some difficulty he began to speak the purpose of his visit. He was a good lad that was clear, far less clear were the words that he delivered. He meandered and stammered, backed off and backed up, regrouped and pushed forward, until at last, embarrassed and unsure he stood open mouthed and refreshingly silent.

"What do you want," I said trying not to push or intimidate. "Arkthar," he said, "I want... that is could you... I mean would you—teach me how to kill." This request seemed out of place from one so fresh and young, something vile and tainted pouring from the mouth of innocence. I knew without explanation the target of his intention, and I saw the look of disbelief on Selah's gentle features and watched it turn to angry shock as I gave my answer. "I can and I will."

"But, you could study the blade from now until old age and you would not acquire the skill you need for your purpose. You will need an assassin's heart and a mind that has no conscience." The youth nodded, and I was sure he had pondered this dark possibility many times. He looked at me with hope renewed, alive again if even for just the moment.

I rose bare chested from beneath my coverings, and the young page paled either from the sight of sword already in hand or the scars of war etched across my arm, chest, and torso. I saw that it was the newest one upon my shoulder, still pulled shut by worm thread that held his attention. He shrank back quickly as I drew myself to full height. Wide eyed he had the look of one who was already rethinking his course of action, but he gathered courage and stood his ground.

I began quietly, "To achieve what you want, you must wait. For you, killing must be a crime of opportunity. When chance presents itself, it must be seized with all your heart. Any less and you will fail." The boy looked sheepishly in my direction, and while his eyes were weak, Selah's burned into me with a fire that I had never before seen in her. I continued evenly, "You have seen enough of war to know the working of death upon the body, sometimes it is slow, but for your needs it must come fast," and I reached with finger to push upon his soft neck and drew down lower to show the entrance to the heart.

The boy was pallid and unnerved as I drove home his final lesson like a blade, "Patience and control are the skills you need to cultivate. It must be done away from this place, away from the eyes of all others. Be strong and your chance will come, and when it does you must be stronger. At that time you must think nothing and feel nothing, for only then you will gain your freedom. This I tell you as one slave to another."

With a stumble and a sideward second look the page was out the door, and I turned to Selah whose eyes now screamed with rage. "How could you, Arkthar?" she seethed, "He's just a boy. He knows nothing of killing and hatred; he is still a child, a lamb among the wolves." She paused between sobbing breaths only long enough to finish with, "He is pure." I reached out to embrace her but she wanted none of me.

I tried to explain myself, "Selah," I said firmly, "I have seen many like him die at the hands of others, the soft crushed by the hard." She would not be consoled even though I used a milder tone, "I gave him only hope and choice, and without those gifts life is hard in its living." She did not answer, but her eyes darted frantically like a small animal in a hunter's trap.

Her tears now streamed down like bitter rain, choosing escape she pushed past me, running quickly from the room. Her footsteps faded down the hallway, and as I lay upon the cold, empty bed of my darkened room, I knew that on this night I would sleep alone.

The room was quieter than I had ever remembered, and I wished silently that I had told her that 'only the free have choice.'

THE SUNG

I remember vividly the wonder I had felt from distance when I had first seen her outer walls. It had increased steadily as on horseback we drew near. It grew continuously as we passed under and through those mighty gates, through outer and inner city, and finally through the gates of the imperial palace itself. Time within its earthen walls had done nothing to lessen the impact of this place.

This was an age of great philosophy. One people unified by three doctrines. Its modern thinkers reorganized the ancient cannons of a seeker, sage, and nature itself, into what they termed, 'the Learning of the Way.' This held much appeal for me, for Buddha, Confucius, and the Tao, spoke directly to my soul of spirit, mind, and body.

Here the arts flourished. Within the Grand Inner I had heard music and watched the dancers. I saw paintings of landscape so beautiful and so real that they appeared alive; vistas created to be walked upon rather than looked at. Portraits of past rulers hung on walls capturing their likeness perfectly, preserving forever their moment in time. Poets and calligraphers spun works with word and brush. Literature was everywhere in the form of printed books. Scholars and philosophers congregated ubiquitously; ever locked in noble debate.

My imagination had been captured by this age of mechanization. In the Grand Inner I had pondered the workings of the 'cosmic engine.' Driven by water, this great machine harmonized space and time. This huge clock told the exact hour and related it by celestial globe to the movements of the stars and heavenly bodies. Perched upon its tower it was a moving model of the universe. The sun, the moon, and five planets rotated accurately to provide calendric verifications. By contrast, in the world from which I had come, the earth was still quite flat.

As time passed and the scourge of pox lessened, life returned to this mighty capital. I had always been feared as a life taker, but here my life had changed. For our healing work in the service of this empire, we held a position of respect. I enjoyed my time within the palace walls, but on this late evening my soldier's heart bid me roam the streets and be free. The guards moved briskly aside as I left the inner grounds.

From an outlying gazebo the plucking of strings and the sweet voice of a courtesan were carried to me upon the stillness of the evening air. I heard the boisterous laughter and rowdy applause of the man come quickly and loudly in appreciation of the performance. I knew him even before I saw him, for his gregarious spirit stood out among a court full of serious mandarins. The famous poet waved me over as he called my name. His voice and manner were warm and eloquent, and his large hand pulled me down beside him.

I suspected that he was a man of great appetites, his girth, the many empty wine cups in front of him, and the admiring looks of the beautifully painted courtesan now confirmed it. Instantly, two beakers of hot cinnamon wine were brought for us, and just as quickly the serving girl receded back into the night, but the sweetness of her perfume lingered long after she had gone. The musician began again, this time she chose a softer melody that allowed for friendly conversation.

I saw the brushes scattered before him, and the poems written quickly on wine-splashed pages. His easy manner allayed my fears that I was disturbing his work, and laughing he waved a thick hand toward the thinnest sliver of a moon, the empty cups, and the beautiful musician. I understood that inspiration would remain long after I had left, and that his night was only just beginning.

"Arkthar," he said softly, "I thank you for the gift you bring my people. A man that gives freely is rare in dangerous times." I was starting to understand something of the careful way words were chosen within the court. Wrapped within his compliment, the word "dangerous" held a subtle warning. I wanted to protest his gratitude, for I did not act alone and was easily the least important member of our troupe, but he would have none of it. With another easy wave of his hand more wine was brought. By the end of my second cup, I was feeling the effects and enjoying his company and the music thoroughly.

Before long the moon had risen to full height, and he would have to move to observe it further. I decided to continue exploring the city around me, and we gulped more wine in a farewell toast. As I stood and turned, the poet said, "Your deeds here will be remembered long after my verses have turned to dust." I chose my words with as much precision as my vocabulary would allow, and made strong effort in the accuracy of tone, "I strongly disagree."

His heavy laughter erupted quickly, and then the serious words that too much wine can bring. "Warrior, on this night the manner of a man has touched me more than the beauty of the waxing moon. Please check on my progress when you return from your excursion."

With that I was on the move again, leaving the poet Li Bia, and the wine and laughter of the rosewood pavilion to the moonlight.

URBAN NIGHT

This was a city that never slept. I crossed the Dragon Ford Bridge on the imperial walkway, which formed the central north-south axis running through the old and new cities. Both sides of the walkway were lined with commoners' quarters and aristocrat mansions, shopping galleries, and merchant stalls of all description. Everywhere the staccato call of the hawkers cried their wares. The resplendent red lanterns of the night market caught my eye, and I quickly disappeared into the bustling vitality of the pulsing urban night.

I crossed the canal that passed through the city and was its life line. It fed the moat around the outer walls and floated barges of goods and food to and from the surrounding warehouses. It joined the city to the Grand Canal in the south and the Yellow River to the north.

This city was tumultuously cosmopolitan, filled with multitudes from every place in every manner of attire. Gymnasts soared and tumbled in the streets while riches also climbed and fell in financial acrobatics. Fortune tellers read the lines etched on outstretched hands. Money flashed auspiciously through countless fingers, fortunes truly held within the palm. I walked on past temple gardens and restaurants, but soon the number of people and the regular grid of the wards stifled me, and I chose instead to follow the quieter wandering banks of the canal with no thoughts in mind of destination or purpose.

They led me gently past the booths that featured everything from shoes and clothing to the shops of traditional healers and their herbal medicine. The dank coolness of the green water flowed on, and I flowed with it. The grunting and squealing of the pigs reached my ears just before the smell of the abattoirs reached my nostrils. Strangely, it was a refreshing respite from the perfumed courtesans of the palace.

I continued to walk, and as the cry of the pigs diminished with the growing distance, the high- pitched sound of female voices grew to take its place. Many comments and proposals came my way as I strode through the neighborhood brothel like any other soldier. However, I was not inclined toward tryst or dalliance and so kept pace with the moving waterway.

Before too long, something of interest did again catch my ear. It was the steady pounding sound of machinery and industry. I had arrived in the fabric district. Once more I left the serenity of the banks, and taking to the narrow laneways, I meandered happily through silk and garment, carpets and weavings, but it was the sound of constant rhythm that drew me onward. I felt the wooden cadence of the engine pull me through the darkness to the open door of the run-down shop.

What I heard with ear was the click clack tempo of unknown machine, but what I heard with heart was the ghostly echo of marching soldiers.

The Morning Looms

She and many of her people had settled within the protective walls of the very capital that had made them refugees. She worked the great loom by day and by night, driven by survival rather than artistic calling, guided by necessity rather than inspiration. Although she was always vigilant, she could not have heard his approach above the clatter of the loom, and yet she looked toward the open doorway even before his tall frame had filled it.

Hope reared up with the memory of her husband, and in the less time than the beat of a bird's wing, reality had banished it. It could not be him. At a glance she knew the stranger that entered was not a drunken castoff from the brothel region, but a warrior from a far distant land, and she froze before the threads. He was embarrassed and apologetic for his clumsy interruption, and in an accent bordering on incomprehensible, he managed to make it clear that his interest lay in the wonders of the machine before her and implored her to "Work on."

This she did, and although initially self-conscious, she soon relaxed back into the symphony of color and strand. The noisy beat and measure marched within the room once more, as the warrior sat with sword on back. While he quietly watched and listened, her powerful legs worked the treadles as her fingers moved like lightning over and between the delicate fibers of her craft.

In the cold comfort of this hovel, he marveled at how she controlled the loom. The cosmic engine of the palatial courtyard harmonized time and space, but she transcended it. He looked at the finished rugs hung haphazardly upon the walls, and his eye was drawn to the room's shadowed corner. There he saw her two small boys safely covered by warm layers of wool and silk. They lay in the deep and peaceful sleep of childhood, entwined together like an animal's litter. Both were red-faced and plump, healthy, and happily alive.

The shadow of her husband's memory returned now with every glimpse of the man before her. She knew who he must be, for in the crowded quarters of the poor, stories are told and retold flowing downward from palatial heights. She worked steadily on, beckoning him closer to catch a subtle movement of her hand or finger, or showing without words the intricate movement and design of her instrument, and time flew by for both.

Unwelcomed came the sound of distant drumming that marked the end of commerce and revelry, and signaled that it was now his time to return to his family within the palace. He stood and strode to the children's corner and without thought placed all his paper money down beside them. He saw the look of protest on her face, and she saw the resolve on his.

By lamps soft light she had seen the color shimmer through his armor and searched briefly among the shadowed piles that sat upon the floor. Like her movements at the loom, her actions were deliberate, and she soon stood before him, now holding the woad blue weaving from her former life. She did not question the course she chose, but pressed the woven fragment into the strong hands of this warrior. He humbly accepted her gift. He saw clearly the skill of its weaver locked within its fabric, and knew that its small size and single color spoke that this was not a carpet.

She explained gently that, "this is the last and unfinished work of a master weaver from the northlands. I thought I would keep it forever, but now I see its purpose. It will fit perfectly between your saddle and your charger. It is the color within your armor and will show you well upon your stallion."

Arkthar looked from it to her and understood that real beauty is woven on the looms of strength and forbearance. She released her hold upon the textile and felt a great weight lift from her tired shoulders. In that instant she knew that life would go on.

Her hands reached up and pulled him quickly down to her. Their lips met in the impassioned kiss of encounter and farewell. In this embrace time ceased, and began anew only after they had released their hold. He looked briefly to her resting cubs, and then stared deeply into eyes that overflowed with the waters of deep emotion. In a heartbeat he had turned and disappeared into the growing brightness of the coming dawn, as though he had never been at all.

She would never wonder why she had handed her loving husband's last work to a foreign stranger on a slim moon's night, for like the man she loved; she could now read well the changing patterns of the threads.

THE POEM OF LI BAI

I moved quickly back along the way that I had come. The city of night folded swiftly with practiced precision. Revelers and merchants alike evaporated in the rays of the coming day. To be caught out after the drumming had ended brought retribution, for here order was the law.

As I approached the palace, the growing light revealed details hidden by the veil of night. I stopped at the poet's nest and saw that it lay within a garden of great tranquility. Water flowed over rock, while leaf and blossoms of a solitary tree lent shelter to the empty bench beneath it. The singing and music long ended, the echoed smell of perfume, wine, and rosewood still danced beneath its roof. Li Bia slumped and snored where I had left him. The pretty courtesan had covered him from the morning dampness, and gathered carefully his papered verses, all but one. "This verse," she said, "he called 'Crows Calling at Night,'" and added softly, "For you."

Looking down I saw the flowing splendor of his script and read the fluid beauty of his words.

> *Yellow clouds beside the walls; crows near the tower.*
>
> *Flying back, they caw, caw; calling in the boughs.*
>
> *In the loom she weaves brocade, the Qin river girl,*
>
> *made of sapphire yarn like mist.*

The window hides her words.

She stops the shuttle, sorrowful, and thinks of the distant man.

She stays alone in the lonely room, her tears just like the rain.

THE EMPEROR

The movement of time does not flow like the straight and level roads of the empire, but revolves like a great wheel that turns upon them. More than a thousand years have passed since the First Emperor held the throne, and yet his power is still felt throughout this realm. It is reflected in the very infrastructure of this kingdom, monetary and military, financial and filial, and all had nearly come crashing down. Under the watchful eye of his trusted minister, the current ruler stared out at the Sacred Peaks of Longevity in the distance, then swallowed his potent and bitter elixir of immortality. Standing tall and still, he paused for introspection. He pondered his legacy and wondered how history would portray him.

He held his arms straight out to the sides as his minions dressed him in the imperial robes of yellow. His mind settled as his thoughts fell into their process. The meaning of his title is "celestial magnificence," the mediator between heaven and his people. The Mandate of Heaven was slipping, and the signs of its impending loss were everywhere. The disorder and destruction that marks the end of every dynasty had certainly begun. He knew that when an emperor's power is rescinded by heaven, it is seized by men. As he thought about the northern battle and the plague that followed it, he realized that the siege had not ended with the insurgent's death, it had escalated.

The speech he had been handed had been reviewed, but he would not use it, choosing instead to speak from his heart.

Words for him came easily when spoken to those that had to listen, a short two hours would be enough for him to express his gratitude and say goodbye.

The First Emperor's great wall had done its work well. The Middle Kingdom had existed in isolation for a millennium, and yet a warrior from a world away now graced his court. This wild one had a power that came from within, all the makings of a great King. If the scars he carried were honest, this man had survived where many others had perished. Arkthar had given freely to a people not even his own, and the emperor knew that all this great warrior had offered was driven by a force called love.

The beautiful young woman was wise beyond her years. The emperor's own royal physicians had wilted before her knowledge and insight, and they had been reeducated in the traditions of this girl. The Son of Heaven looked forward to lavishly rewarding her.

He studied Mah Lin and had almost come to regret the monastic genocide he had ordered so many years ago. The duties of an emperor weigh heavy sometimes, but as he had watched this monk's deadly artistry with the cutting staff, he knew it had been a necessary one. He was pleased that this priest harbored no grudge.

As the Imperial robes of authority and power were secured, his outstretched arms began to grow weary and thoughts turned to the one in rags. The Son of Heaven liked neither his blackened tatters nor his lingering smell, but he too, had been instrumental in the plague's eradication. The disease that had come so close to finishing this present dynasty had been conquered, the march toward chaos, slowed. Only the wisest of rulers would have known to let him live. The emperor wondered what favors a beggar would ask to be bestowed.

Fully dressed, he was ready to deliver his speech of departure. It was a farewell to these strange guests, and perhaps the last oration of an aging emperor. He was indeed grateful, not just for the vanquishing of the pox, but for his involvement in it. He smiled inwardly; before they came he would never have been remembered as a great emperor, but because of them, he will, at the very least, be remembered as a good one.

As his outstretched limbs thankfully began to lower, his litter was prepared and waiting. With his High Minister respectfully in place behind the carriage, the emperor's journey to the Great Hall began.

THE TIME DRAWS NEAR

In the months that followed that initial meeting within the palace court, he had watched the four concentrate on their task. Putting the scabs of disease in the nostrils of the healthy was more madness than he could fathom. It was witchcraft, and it stank of occult malevolence.

The commander took no joy from the stemming of the smallpox or the role that his men had in it. His young page led the forefront of its organized treatment, and for this open betrayal, the boy would be made to suffer. He had been advised to stop the beatings. He would comply, not because of respect, but because he had a much crueler punishment in store for him.

Time had slowed for the commander, now the passage of a single week seemed more the passage of an entire year. Waiting without acting had been difficult for this man who saw himself a man of action. Gradually, however, painful weeks had piled to months and the time of their departure drew closer. Finally, he had on this day received the summons to report to the palace. The day of their exodus and subsequent demise had arrived. He would endure the pitiful speech of a grateful ruler, and wait.

Over the passing of half a year he had not exacted direct revenge, yet he had not been idle. Back in his quarters, alone but for the severed head of the rebel, iniquity had continued to feast. He relied heavily on strong spirits to numb his raging pain, and within his mind built silken scaffolds of scheme and plot. These webs he tore down and constructed anew and grew in confidence at their refining. Now that the time had arrived, he felt himself ready to strike once more from the safety of distance and the hidden shadows of dark and solitary inspiration. He had tasted humiliating defeat upon the training field, and it was a flavor that he would be loath to experience again.

The page was shocked at the appearance of his overlord, who strode proudly toward the palace court for the assembly. He was in stride almost jubilant as if the cloak of hide and hair held no weight upon his shoulders. The wound on the forearm of his commander had healed well, and the boy still wished that it had been fatal. With this thought the lad realized he had been looking at his master's face and turned his gaze away fearing another beating. It did not come, however, for on this day the imperial might of military command was, in fact, elated.

It was known by all within the palace grounds that the four who had stemmed the sickness of the kingdom would be leaving very soon. This saddened the page greatly. They had brought about many changes within the empire and within him. He had been diligent in his lessons from his masters. Every night he struck as they struck and parried as they parried. The boy had even begun to plunge his fingers through sand and stones to make them strong and durable. He had taken Arkthar's dark advice to heart, and life was easier in the wait. One day he knew that he would get his chance.

Still, he was unnerved by the good mood of his tormentor, for this was an unusual development.

As the heavy steps of the man faded into the direction of the palace court, a boy's intuitive wisdom sounded that something sinister was now afoot.

Two Favors

Within seven full moons the deadly march of the great epidemic had been halted, and my time in palace opulence was, in the word of the beggar, "Enough." I longed for my home on the ancient temple grounds and wanted only to get back to the life I had with Mah Lin and Selah. In truth, the sword had spoken to me from its place upon my back often and loudly. This was not a place of safety and not a place of peace. The harmony that had settled here was brought by us, and I was sure it would vanish with our leaving.

Selah was initially cold toward me after my night meeting with the page, but in the weeks that followed that icy demeanor warmed like the changing of the seasons. The page, too, was less friendly, he seemed afraid, as if it were me who had stirred his hidden thoughts. Only the monk and the beggar had cast no judgment. In time, however, things returned to their natural place, and our job here was almost complete, we had conquered an enemy that was smaller by far than the eye could see. It was my smallest foe but perhaps my greatest victory, and finally it was time to return from where we had come.

I was in good spirits when the summons from the emperor had arrived. Like all conquests this one also demanded all the pomp and ceremony that imperial protocol dictated, and a long-winded speech would be a small price to pay for freedom. It is true that freedom rules the heart of every slave, and soon I would be free once more to be love's captive, and ruled by the bonds of family.

We four gathered and assembled in front of the great throne and awaited the emperor's entrance. Even upon bended knee and with eyes cast down, my sword whispered to me the location of the commander within the large hall, and the heavy drifting smell of fetid bear hide confirmed it.

The murmurs of gratitude and admiration ceased as the emperor was carried in and took his place upon the Dragon Throne. He smiled graciously to our party and seemed in every way a divine ruler. He did not slow his words for me, but occasionally for my benefit he spoke them louder. Words turned to a drone as my mind and eyes chose to occupy themselves elsewhere. Indeed, his robe offered them a feast. It, too, was made by the worms, and although more ornate than my attire, I doubted that it was spun with love.

It was yellow in background and dazzling in execution. The bottom hem was lined with the overlapping waves of the sea, blue and white, water and foam. Across the chest of The Son of Heaven was emblazoned the five-clawed beast of dreams. It seemed to frolic amid clouds of drifting silk embroidery, this beast that brings the rains.

With a change in tone, I came back to the room in which we stood and made effort to follow the speech. It had moved on to farewells and eternal gratitude. It seemed this man had grown fond of our unique clan, and it seemed we would be missed but never forgotten.

The usually stoic priest was clearly proud of his daughter, and the beggar, still in blackened tatters, was unmoving beneath his shabby attire.

The accursed spoils of war that once hung behind the seat

of power had long since gone, as had the heavy dread that had once filled the city. Indeed initially, the feel within this court seemed unusually warm and light.

My mind and ears now floated up and outside these red brick walls and towers. I could hear the laughter and joy of children once again running wild. Trade and commerce had begun to pulse, and the many open sores of plague had begun to heal. Life had now returned after the long winter of pestilence and annihilation. Spring had come once more.

Our horses were well looked after thanks mostly to the commander's awkward page, and in my mind I was already riding. They, too, would enjoy the work and the journey ahead. They were fit and fed and I looked forward to their company.

My mind soon returned to the large court, and again I could feel the disturbing presence of the cloaked commander far behind me and to my left. I knew his hatred had not tempered, and to me he seemed more mad dog than man. The speech from the throne was coming to an end, but had seemed almost as long as our entire stay.

Finally the emperor was finished, and now no longer speaking to all assembled, he looked to us and said, "Ask of me any favor and it will promptly be granted."

Mah Lin spoke first, "I want for nothing, my lord."

Selah was the next and she looked with love to her father and to me, "I want for nothing, my lord." was all she said as she smiled shyly.

The emperor then turned to me, "speak warrior," he urged.

"I, too, want for nothing, my lord."

He nodded in silent understanding. Lastly he addressed the beggar. "You who have never had anything may ask any favor."

The beggar removed his hood, and although old and frail,

his powerful presence now controlled the heart of imperial power.

"I ask two favors, my lord."

The emperor was pleased that at least for one of us he could be of service. "Speak them," he implored.

The beggar did not hesitate, "I need a bag of fine silk to carry my treasure to its northern home."

The emperor was amused by the thought of a beggar's treasure, and moved quickly to strip a fine bag from his high-standing minister, and slung it with ceremony across the black rags that half hid the skinny shoulders. The emperor had been expecting a far more opulent request.

The ruler bid him, "Ask again."

The beggar now paused and looked around the whispering court. His black eyes returned and held the emperor in their fearless grip, as he drew forth from beneath his rags his brass begging bowl. He spun with the power and grace of an untamed animal and sent the large heavy bowl skittering loudly across the cold stone floor.

It came to rest in the darkest and farthest corner by the feet of the shocked Supreme Commander. As everyone stared in disbelief, the loud voice of the beggar echoed through the silence of the hall. To the emperor and for all to hear he implored, "Bring me the head of the northern rebel, it is time that he find rest."

As the shocked and empty voice from the throne spoke the words, "It shall be done," the unearthly cry of a human animal rose up from the shadows and resonated in the caverns of the beggar's bowl.

THE HOMEWARD JOURNEY

Within the hour we were ready, for like our horses we wanted to quickly leave. Selah's white mare nuzzled and snorted happily at the reunion. Her horse danced and played as the young page brought the other three. He had centered my saddle upon the blue square weaving, and on the back of my charger its quality and color came to life in the sunlight. All three noticed and nodded in appreciation. The page stroked our mounts farewell, and to us he whispered, "Be careful."

By saying little he had said much, but it was really nothing we did not already feel. The beggar had his favors tucked beneath his rags. It was understood that he would return with us before traveling to the cold northern lands, where the rebel would find his final place of peace.

The complexion of the land over which we returned was much healthier, although many of its people now bore the lifelong scars. We moved smoothly by daylight compass and nighttime star. This was not a carefree journey, although it was not completely joyless either. We stopped briefly at the same inn, and Selah held her former patient and once more crooned the songs of her childhood.

The blade of Mah Lin's staff was now always unsheathed. We would move fast, stay vigilant, and deal with anything that may come our way. There was little doubt, however, that in some form it would come, and we would not be taken by surprise.

I have had this feeling many times before a fight. It is a burning of the senses that the instinct to survive ignites. Mah Lin was ever more a warrior priest, and as I watched the beggar I knew that despite his tattered exterior, he would not wilt in battle. I rode close to Selah, on the promise made to a loving father; even though she was far from helpless, I sought to always protect her.

We were nearing the end of our journey and approached the safety of our homeland. Silently I tracked the distant cloud of rising dust for more than an hour.

"What do you see, Arkthar," Mah Lin asked.

"Light infantry, no horses, no heavy weapons, fifty perhaps sixty in number, moving fast, no way around, and we are too close to home not to give up our location," was my terse report.

"What would you advise?"

"We must cut through them like steel through iron. We are lost without horses. Selah and the beggar must push ahead with all four and protect them. When safe she can shield us from a distance with arrow cover; we will break through and be past them. They will limp home, and we will ride."

With curt nods from his daughter and the beggar, Mah Lin looked at me. "We agree."

So it was upon this road that we met imperial troops but gave no signal of our concern. At two hundred yards their archers released first volley. We charged under and towards with the speed of demons. The beggar held four reigns, and Selah at the forefront released arrows with machine precision. Many fell well before we had reached them, and many more fell under the hooves of our mounts.

At full gallop Mah Lin and I dismounted as the four horses and two riders were past and safe. Selah sat backwards now, and with the beggar in control of the flight, she fired arrow after arrow, most biting deeply into their mark. For Mah Lin and me striking at a full sprint was second nature. These soldiers knew only how to stand and fight. It was as the carnage of the bamboo grove, but now men fell instead of wood.

As wind moved over his weapon, the sound of the monk's bladed staff sang to me of his location, and the damage of long and short-range steel was as brutally thorough as it was final. Panic soon gripped the soldiers, and Selah and the beggar charged back to us again. All the while her arrows flew and men perished.

Mounted in an instant we flew for the protection that distance would afford. Behind us any that were not dead were stumbling, and the few that were not lying or stumbling, were running in the opposite direction. We were so close to safety when I heard the whisper of the feathered flight, and the thud of flesh struck well.

She cried out briefly and fell forward onto the red-stained neck of her white mare. The beggar grabbed her reins, and we flew home as quickly as the wind before the storm.

THE TRUSTED MINISTER

His life within the palace had changed much and he had changed with it. For his family, past and future, he would continue as he always had, giving advice to be accepted or rejected by the Son of Heaven. His one solace was the company of the page, a boy not unlike his son, and like his son, a boy he could no longer protect. Duty bound, he gathered his thoughts and prepared to advise his tired ruler.

The events of recent days had unfolded quickly, and would ignite a course of action that he could influence very little. Perhaps this was the biggest change. His life before had revolved around Imperial power, but now it revolved around a world of limitations and shortcomings, both his and those of his beloved emperor. Loyalty was his only constant.

The minister must lay the facts before the feet of power. Soldiers of the Imperial army had been killed. The emperor listened to his report without emotion. In these times no weakness, real or perceived, could be shown.

The job of advisor was often a balancing act of delicate proportions. As a trusted official his job was to inform, but sometimes in the delivery of information lies the ability to sway. "My Lord," he began, "there has been an occurrence close to the homeland of our recent guests. It is an incident of a serious nature and one requiring your immediate attention." In the somber quiet of the private chamber, he pressed on with the details. Twenty-three of our soldiers are dead, twelve wounded.

Although his report covered only the imperial perspective, he would try to shed light on the truth.

Thankfully after a long silence his ruler asked, "Who fired the first volley?" He measured his reply, "Official reports state that first blood was drawn by the four, but it seems unlikely..." A wave of the emperor's hand cut short his interjection. The ruler again fell back into contemplation, and the minister knew that only official reports carry weight. After a moment that seemed longer than eternity did the power of the throne speak again, "Mercy is a virtue extended only by the weak."

"My Lord, it is obvious that these events were spawned by the one that has always challenged..." Once again the minister was cut silent. "I already know the truth."

The minister watched now as the emperor stared blankly, his mind moving and measuring before he spoke again. "I thank you for your report and your loyalty, but there is nothing left to say." The minister stood speechless as tears welled up and spoke above his ordered silence.

Uncharacteristically, the emperor placed a hand upon his servant's shoulder and in a gesture both kind and unexpected, explained gently, "They saved my people and I owe them much, but they are not more important than the future of my kingdom. In each I perceived a light of destiny, a power perhaps equal only to my own. These are strange times, and events must now unfold by their own course."

Through a lens of tears the minister looked proudly upon his emperor, as the voice of all power continued. "What is meant to happen is already written. The motion of the heavens will not be stopped. It may be that the bear has bitten more than he can chew. Have faith in the ever-expanding universe, that chaos will rule only briefly, before balance is restored. Take comfort in my words, for although I struggle to cling to the power of this dynasty, am I not still… The Son of Heaven?"

With that the emperor took his leave, and in his wake the minister stood in shock. The high official once so bound up the workings of the material world of power and politics had now caught a glimpse of the ethereal and the spiritual. As the words of the emperor faded like a distant echo, he bowed his head and prayed once more. He did not pray for the death of the commander however, for he was beginning to understand that evil carries the seeds of its own destruction.

Instead he prayed for the four that had answered his official proclamation, and for the life of the page that had become his son.

THE PREY

For once the commander had suppressed his irritation and planned his maneuvers well. He had not left the palace for three full weeks. Instead, he had remained under the watchful eyes of the entire court and sent his orders quietly from afar. He had calculated accurately that fifty infantry would not be enough, and he had reasoned perfectly that there would be survivors to tell the tale of an unprovoked attack. Now he would be able to attend personally to the butchering of the monk and all his family.

The commander missed the company of the northern rebel, and he looked forward to bringing him back. He received the expected summons for a private audience and smiled his damaged smile as he weighed his prospects. He swung the heavy cloak over his polished-armored shoulders and marched into a small, secured anteroom to hear the Son of Heaven tell him what he already knew.

The emperor was grim and serious as he reported the news. On bended knees and with his head to the floor, there was no real need for the commander to listen. He heard the important parts. An unprovoked attack on an unsuspecting Imperial squadron could not go unpunished. He was to assemble with all haste and proceed south and to the east in the service of the empire.

The five hundred men that he selected were the most ruthless that had ever served under him. Good soldiers are ones who have a sense of duty, but the men selected were loyal only to the pleasure of the kill. They enjoyed rape, child murder, and the senseless slaughter of civilians. In short, the people that the commander hand-picked were all men very much like himself.

There was, however, one exception, and the commander called roughly to his page, "Polish my armor but don't touch my cloak. I'll take my meal in my quarters tonight, and you leave with me tomorrow." He waited cruelly for the boy's confused look before he added, "We go to kill your new friends." The page was silent and looked down toward the mantis held secretly in his hand so that the commander could read nothing on his young features.

By evening the final preparations were finished, and the well-satisfied commander retired to his quarters. They would leave early in the morning, and the march would be set double time to reach the quarry quickly. He had gotten the reports of the incident from his own sources and was mildly surprised by how well the staff and sword had functioned together. No matter, he thought, against this five hundred there would be only one outcome.

He took no alcohol that evening, preferring to be fresh when they left. He looked at the bearskin that was draped across his bed, and he thought proudly of the trap that he had set. Free from drink he had trouble falling asleep, but would not risk the company of another whore, and when sleep finally did come, it brought no rest.

Alone and eerily content, he found tracks in the new fallen snow. He followed the large, fresh paw prints of a moon bear. He was careful not to be taken by surprise and paid close attention to the nervousness of his battle-tested horse. The tracks led eventually to the mouth of a cave.

Tethering his steed to a leafless stunted tree not far from the cave opening, he climbed quietly to a rocky outcrop twenty-five feet high and directly above it. The plan was a simple one, and one that he had seen executed many times as a boy. He sat in patient silence and watched his exhaled breath fog in steady bursts, as it mixed with the cold, crisp air.

The image of the blackened beggar and his bowl filled his mind. He sat quietly like him, but instead of a bowl he cradled the rebel's severed head in his frost-covered lap, and to his left he laid carefully his war bow and quiver. The wait would not be a long one.

Already his horse whimpered and tugged skittishly at reins that secured him like a lamb tethered for slaughter. The commander could feel the heat rise from the opening as the large grey head appeared below him and sniffed the air cautiously. Hunger has a powerful pull, and his wild-eyed horse as if on cue began to panic. As the huge grey shag shoulders cleared the entrance, he lost his grip on the rebel's head, and his reflex to save it caused him to lose balance and fall forward from the ledge. He fell from his height and landed square upon the shoulders of the raging bear.

From flat upon the ground he saw that the lunar crescent on the animal's chest restored and whole once more. He felt the powerful claws rip flesh from muscle and tendon from sinew. The pain was excruciating; he could hear and feel the cracking and breaking of his bones. The massive jaws gnawed his face, while the weight of the beast crushed out his empty life.

He heard the crunching of his skull, shattered by the bear as easily as an egg cracks. The nightmare sound was drowned out only by the pain. The bear tightened its vise-like bite, and he felt his body lifted from the ground. With a mighty shake of its thick neck, the commander felt his head ripped from his body, and he screamed himself awake.

Drenched in cold sweat, he rose on weak legs. The rising sun had turned the morning clouds blood red, like a crimson blanket spread upon the powdered snow. The commander shuttered.

A red morning sky would mean bad weather.

THE CAVERN'S BOUNTY

Her father and I carried Selah's blood-soaked body from her horse into the main room, with the beggar following closely behind. Carefully we laid her upon the table taking care not to disturb the arrow that protruded from her back. The blood was dark and her breathing was shallow and irregular. I had seen wounds like this before, it was mortal. I stood numbly, I had not protected her.

The beggar moved me aside, and quickly he and Mah Lin had loosened her tunic to examine the wound. Their faces were stern and grave as they conferred. They looked at the torn flesh around the shaft for clues about the shape of the arrowhead. The beggar noted the feathered flights were not spiraled so at least there was no rotation, but he was not pleased that the bleeding no longer flowed outwardly.

He did not like her ashen features or the coldness of her skin. He did not like the darkened color of her blood. He did not like the whisper of the pulse he heard with fingers gently placed upon the arrow's wooden shaft.

The look on his face spoke everything to her father and to me, and yet inevitably his words still came.

"Selah is dying," he said. His voice was hollow and detached from all emotion. It seemed to float above our heads as it continued, "If there is any hope, it rests with Dragon Fire."

The word hope reached down through my despair and touched my soul. The word Dragon shook it to the core, and fully woke it.

The two men were already in motion and ignored my question, "What is Dragon Fire?"

Mah Lin was searching through Selah's sewing box, and the tattered beggar was writing what looked like a prescription. They finished their tasks at the same time and approached me. Mah Lin was the first to speak, as he pressed Selah's thimble into my waistband. "Ride quickly to the cave," he said, as the beggar pushed both bowl and parchment into my idle hands. The blackened beggar had given me his written list and carrying vessel, the priest had given me the measure. I was like a child being sent to the market.

The beggar spoke in tones of life and death, and held my eye.

"Arkthar, do not stray from my formula. With her thimble measure carefully and accurately into my bowl six of the white snow that lies near the bat manure, four of the willow charcoal of the cavern forge, and two of yellow brimstone that cling to the walls like the bats."

This man was indeed, more than he did seem. My mind wandered in the midst of my sorrow, but his sharp voice brought me back to center.

"Bring back the one-arm hammer and a mix of moss and clay as well. Is it clear? Do you understand?"

"Yes," I said, although I did not understand at all. I understood well though how to follow orders, and I left for the cavern riding with the fear fed speed of the truly desperate.

I had never been in the cavern forge at night, and on this night the moon and stars hid mournfully behind the dark veil of cloud. I entered through the dry back tunnel, and I set about finding and lighting the torches on the walls. The bellows were silent but the water still rushed, and the wind sang sorrowfully of our circumstance. Within this great cathedral it howled like the Banshee of my homeland. It cried for my fallen people and it cried for those who were soon to die.

I quickly plucked the green moss that covers the entrance rocks and scooped some red clay that we used in the tempering of the blade. This done, I retrieved Mah Lin's small hammer. Then carefully I attended to the beggar's written order.

I fought with the desolation and focused on the task set for me. I held the formula and the bowl, and I thought of Selah happily sewing my scholar's robes as she wore the thimble that I now held. It seemed such a small measure for medicine that I prayed was magically potent. I read twice and measured once each of the ingredients and poured them into the old brass bowl. Strong in unwavering purpose I left the darkness to join the others.

I had not been gone long in the measure of living time, but it was more than long enough to see that Selah's beautiful spirit had continued to slip away.

DRAGON FIRE

The beggar anxiously took his bowl, and with a spice mortar began to grind the carefully measured ingredients into a fine dark powder. It called to mind his work within the palace, but Selah was cut down by wound not sickness. He had me mix moss, clay, and water into thickened paste upon the table where she lay unmoving. Mah Lin now turned the attention of his sharp knife to the arrow shaft buried deeply in her back.

As I mixed, I watched him cut the wooden shaft by two thirds, so that it now protruded out the exact thickness of her chest. Into the fletchless remnant of the arrow, he began to carve a hollow trough. He was careful not to move it, and the work was painstaking. When he had finished, he was covered with the sweat of his endeavor.

An incense stick burned mid table. The heady aroma of sandalwood centered me and brought me strength.

We all were finished with each of our tasks, and Mah Lin propped up his lifeless daughter as we three gathered around her dimming frame. The beggar filled the shaft's deep groove with the black powder. It seemed like the loading of a small canoe with the provisions of a dangerous journey. He looked to me to have ready the clay moss paste, and he looked to the monk as if to borrow some of the priest's deep inner power.

Mah Lin's voice cracked the shell of dread.

"Arkthar, take the hammer. Set fear aside and bind your mind with courage. Look not directly at the shaft. On the command, and with one blow to arrow's end, you must drive it through her chest but not strike past her gentle back. You must aim the arrow between the ribs. May your God direct your hand."

I readied my weapon as I was told, while Mah Lin placed his hand at Selah's chest to catch the arrow's tip. The beggar took the burning stick and held its glow just above the well-packed groove. He counted clearly and at three touched it to the dark powder held within the carved and severed shaft. Instantly the room blazed white.

There was no time for horror as I struck with all my being to the beat of the blinding flash. Both the dazzling white light and the arrow were gone, and from the front Mah Lin caught and pulled it fully through. She cried out as her wound drew in the heat and brightness with a sputter, and the smell of her burning flesh joined the acrid stench of the powder's rising smoke. In darkness and by feel, we immediately pushed the clay and moss into the blackened holes of chest and back, her body stiffened and collapsed, and in less than a heartbeat it was over.

The two men bound her wound quickly and tightly with silken strips. The monk laid his daughter back down upon the table as I stood by, blind and open mouthed.

My vision began to recover from the great burst of light, and I soon saw the arrows shortened length upon the table. Its ugly metal broad-head and the charred and hollowed shaft dripped with black red blood. Mah Lin's put his ear close and listened to the rhythms of his daughter chest.

He straightened slowly as the dawn's light began to fill the room. Mah Lin turned to the beggar and myself and announced, "The Dragon Fire has sealed her well. She will live."

There were no words for what I felt. We had not lost her.

I lay down peacefully beside her on the table and listened to her breathing.

With eyes closed I still saw the dragon's fire. It had painted its image inside my eyelids, and its power blazed within my soul.

SAGES AND KINGS

Sleep took me until early evening. I felt nothing of the table's hardness, and knew nothing until I woke to the touch of Selah's hand upon my cheek.

"Arkthar," she said, "I had dreams."

"Rest love," I said quietly, and was happy to see that color had come back to her face.

Mah Lin and the beggar were preparing a meal, and the monk handed me a cup of bitter herb to ease past his daughters lips. For the moment there was peace in our home, but we knew our situation was precarious. We had at most only a full moon's cycle before the hounds of war would be fully unleashed upon us. Until then we would live in quiet resolution.

I still practiced the standing exercise daily, drawing on the strength and tenacity of my ancient oak. On a windy afternoon, I finished and turned, thinking I had felt the arrival of the raven, but instead was greeted by the ragged black beggar who had been quietly watching.

His face smiled, but in a serious tone he said, "Arkthar, it is by their stillness that men become sages, and it is by their actions that they become Kings."

I had come to like the beggar, and he for his part seemed fond of me, but in truth I did not always understand the meaning of his words.

Selah was recovering well, and by our third day back she was on her feet, although it would be a long time before she would be able to launch an arrow. After the evening meal we four sat in front of the hearth, and I stared relaxed and alert at the pictures within the glowing coals. When a loud crack rang out that sent sparks swirling into the heights, I remembered as a boy an old soldier telling me that these were the fairies coming from their world into ours. I held Selah gently in my arms and I touched the elements.

I watched the fire play and roll along the soot-covered bottom of the large kettle, and listened to the steady clanging of its lid, as the water within it boiled and bubbled. I scanned the hearth from bottom to top. I saw the hearth's earthen floor, its burning wood, the nimble flames, its silver kettle, and its bubbling water, and I wondered once again what would happen if the lid could not rise up to release the pressure.

The beggar drew me from these thoughts, "Young King, you have shown me much about life and its great purpose. You have reminded me about the power of love. This is an experience for which I will always be grateful. I bid you good night."

"Good night," I replied, and as I went to my sleeping place, I added for his amusement, "Is it enough?" He laughed happily and was gone.

The dreams came upon me strongly that night.

THE HORDE APPROACHES

The commander marched with all possible haste. He flew over land with the strength and speed of one possessed. The end was but days away and he was emboldened by the smell of blood, a creature starved for flesh. Many times along the way he beat his page who would often slow to a mere trot. Indeed, even the hardiest of his killing brood were hard pressed to meet his pace but kept on in fear of retribution.

The night's repose was no longer for rest, it was used to sharpen instruments of killing and whet the appetite of destruction. The thought of their deaths consumed him. He craved it. The commander wondered if the beautiful witch was dead, and reveled in the thought that the monk may now be suffering as he had suffered. Part of him hoped that she still clung painfully to life, so the monk would see him take it from her. He knew almost their exact location, and he would with might and steel crush them between the stones of their ancient temple site.

Often the commander thought about the beggar and wondered why he had dared to steal his prize and destroy his rightful spoils of war. Was it because he had nothing that he must take so much? Soon he would have something. Soon he would have a slow and lingering death, and his screams of anguish would voice his payment. His thoughts pleased him and drove him forward.

The warrior was also large within his mind. At the palace, that man had dared to look upon his face and disgraced him on the training field. The slave called Arkthar will regret his loyalty. Like the vile beggar, he, too, will cry and plead for mercy, but there will be none. When all are dead the library will be gathered and packed. His emperor will be humbly grateful at its presentation. The commander smiled, vengeance and redemption were almost close enough to touch.

The bear skin weighed heavy upon his shoulders, and he thought of throwing it aside so that he would not be slowed. But he could not, for this, too, was the rightful spoils of an attack gone well, a plan followed and a plan carried out. He thought briefly of his nightmare and of the red dawn. Over his shoulder he watched the skies darken.

He cast the dreams away.

ANSWERS

The dreams came like the flashing images of a violent thunderstorm. I saw the eyes of the dragon and knew that I would release it, and I knew that once released it would never again be contained. I rode through the blackness and I spoke freely with Death. I felt the earth cool and saw life grow from the ashes upon the mountain of fire. I saw metal harden and I heard thunder upon the time worn hills.

I flew with the monk and the healer clothed in the tapestry of life's emergence. We spun like the needle of the compass, and we drank the sweet water of creations beginnings.

I saw the machines of war and malice, and I saw them grow throughout the ages. I saw Death and I embraced him. For without death there is no life, and without struggle there is nothing to overcome. My heart sang with the joy of victory. I was again a man upon the earth and looked up into the beauty of the starry heavens. I was incinerated by a mighty flash and then rose up in the smoke of all humanity.

Rising as a cloud I saw the desert growing smaller beneath me, and I cried tears of joy. My tears gathered like a single voice, joined one by one by a choir of great number, until I cried the tears of all humanity, and they fell as rain. From high above the desert I saw life in multitude and myriad begin to blossom from the desolate sands below me, and as celestial cloud I reached out gently and touched the timeless creature. Lightning flashed through me with the intensity of Dragon Fire.

I remembered all, and I over stood.

GATHERING POWER

I awoke early, my dream fresh upon my mind. I moved with the precision and economy of a man with a mission. I gorged my breakfast, for I did not know when I would eat again. I wore no top, the armor would slow me down, and I preferred to see the many battle scars that had helped to make me who I was. I was clear in mind and free in spirit, but to my three companions, I must have seemed a man unbalanced. I saddled my horse and rode, driven and directed by the visions of my night.

We galloped full charge to the large clearing, where from horseback I reached up and touched the inscription from the time of the First Emperor. I spoke his words aloud, "Forever may this temple guardian protect the righteous and crush all evil that may choose to come against it," and felt my heart beat faster. It beat with hope renewed.

I continued on far past the great lion. I thought of the ancient prophets of my time and place. I thought of the Conquering Lion from the Book of Revelations and the final battle of good against evil, while I rode onward. Over the crest of distant hill, I found what I was seeking.

It lay covered by vines and overgrowth long hidden from the world of men. These I put to flame. The fire burned and the smoke rose up until the ancient section was revealed. It was made of large hewn stone, skillfully laid, filled between with earth and rubble. It measured three men high and two in width. It was intact and strong for a length of four horses, and the ground dropped away from it steeply on the far side.

This was once a wall and moat, built to shelter and protect. This hidden remnant that had stood so long, would serve my purpose well. Its charred façade cooled gradually as I marked it within my mind so strongly that I could find it blind. I rode in haste back past the iron guardian to the cavern of the forge. Through the coldness of the beating falls, I entered the dragon's nest and pushed my body to its limits and beyond.

The water driven bellows I quickly disengaged, and I harnessed its power to drive an ancient millstone instead. This time I measured the formula for dragon fire not by thimble but by the bucket. For two days and two nights I ground not with a bowl and pestle, but with the large stone that had once crushed grain and rice for this monastery monks' daily sustenance.

I slept short periods within the heart of the cavern, ignoring the cold rock beneath my bare back. On the morning of the third day, I began to work as hard as any slave, a slave that works toward freedom, and as I toiled I prayed for the deliverance of all that I had ever loved.

By the barrel with the wheel, I carried a load of the black powder to the guardian, and I emptied it by funnel through a cracked seam atop its regal head. Load after load I wheeled and carefully poured the grainy contents into the ancient guardian. Through that day and entire night, I labored. I worked like the mighty ant that piles one by one the sand grains high and narrow around the entrance of its home when it feels the coming of a great storm. I am the ant that builds to protect its family and its tribe, and tell all who look from above the nature of the approaching weather.

As the sun rose on the fourth day it was almost fully packed, and I remembered the voice of Death in dream telling me "that to unleash the dragon you must imprison it." Through aching muscle and with tired mind, I poured the last bucket and I heard the voice of the beggar whisper gently within my mind, "It is enough," and in my exhaustion I thought their voices sounded much alike.

My return home was greeted by shocked expressions and Selah's laughter. I laughed also, for I was blacker by far than the beggar had ever been. Mah Lin nodded when I asked if he had seen the smoke, and I said, "Remember where." He nodded also when I suggested gravely that, "It may be time to pack the library into the saddle bags."

"Spoken like a true scholar," Selah added as she laughed behind me.

As the morning sky darkened, I washed in the battle blue dye of my homeland, put on my armor, and honed the cutting edge of my Five Element Sword.

THE DIE IS CAST

I stood among them, indigo colored from head to toe, my nakedness covered only with rough leggings and my chain mail armor. They stared at my face and blue-dyed hands and then to each other, but no words passed between them. The beggar had finished packing and loading the library manuscripts into the saddlebags. Our horses were ready and waiting. Selah had gathered everything that was important, and although she could still work only slowly, she was methodical and efficient. A week's provisions were what would be carried. The dragon compass of the imperial army was slung across the priest's saddle.

We all gathered at the pond of fish and flower by the entrance of our home, and fed them one last time. Life had somehow become as clear as the water and as colorful as the liyu themselves. The smallest and simplest of details seemed breathtakingly beautiful. We four watched quietly as they devoured the treats we offered. We saw the ancient, weathered rock cradle the freshest lotus blossoms. A dragonfly hovered over the surface and settled momentarily on the flower's round green leaf.

The brilliant colors of the fish were like the red and white coals of the forge, and as they broke the water's surface they brightened as if touched by the action of the bellows breath. The dragonfly quickly fled, gone now as though it never was. Passed the churning surface we peered deeply at the foreign world of life below. The shell of a painted turtle moved smoothly through its underworld like the casting of an oracle's vision, and then it, too, was gone.

From above us the raven's urgent cry broke our peaceful spell, and we looked to its sound, up into the menacing clouds. The bringer of the rains approached us, and distant flashes in the northern sky drew ever closer.

I saw the high flight of the sea birds move passed us, and we knew that the jackals were also closing quickly on our scent. With the jostling of a restless steed, a sacred painting fell from the stowage and unfurled upon the ground. It was Vajrapani, patron saint of the monastery called Shaolin, the oldest bohdisattvas of Mahayana Buddhism, and the guide and protector of the Buddha. His fearsome visage stared up at us, adorned with the trappings of war. He stood atop a lotus blossom in front of a wall of flame and smoke. He was clad in the orange skin of a strange striped lion, and in his hand he delicately held the vajra thunderbolt.

It was his color, however, that caused the three to look at me once more, for his skin was as blue as mine, and I understood their previous glances. My soul passed through this awareness with the sound of thunder, and quickly my mind and body moved on. Mah Lin's silence was the voice of trust. They could see that I now walked in two worlds. For me the dominion of dream had awakened into day, and I moved without doubt or hesitation.

The woad blue weaving from the capital lay in place beneath my saddle, and I was upon it before any could ask a question. Bending from my mount, I kissed Selah one last time and turned in the direction of the approaching battalion. Mah Lin was by my side, and to his protests I said easily, "You and the beggar know what must be done. Your path is priesthood. You must protect the treasures of this land. I have always ridden the winds of war, and that will never change. Ride now, out past the smoke you saw and into the journey that lies beyond it."

Mah Lin strapped his cutting staff to my beast as I tugged the reigns, kicked my heels, and galloped toward the approaching storm.

Away

They rode at a quickened pace, and although Selah did not complain, the monk and beggar knew that she could feel every placing of her horse's hooves. Together they reached the oak tree. It was as leafless as when her warrior had first seen it, and it spoke to Selah of courage and endurance. She remembered when it had reached into the heavens to take what it needed, she remembered how it drank so deeply on that late summer's day so long ago, and she remembered that first long kiss. Selah smiled, but only briefly, for present reality quickly overpowered reverie.

The three traveled along the river that had graciously shared its rainbow fish and moved up beside the roaring falls of forge and cavern. The horses paused to drink as lightning arced across the sky and threatened to lash down upon what was once a mountain of fire. A quiet cry emerged from Selah's lips. The priest and beggar didn't know if it was a sudden pain or the thought of Arkthar alone and embattled. It mattered not, and to the sound of the raven overhead they pushed onward.

They spoke with no words, moving upon a sea of destruction together in one small boat. The three looked upon everything as they passed it and touched everything with all their senses. They tried to savor every moment and cherish every memory, but the pain of Arkthar's absence sliced through every peaceful recollection like a vengeful sword. The rains dripped freely now from horse and rider. It was a cold downpour and drove sideways, pushed by wind or perhaps by wings.

Within the hour they were huddled in the clearing. The lion looked down at them from its great height. Selah thought once more about the warrior as she reached up and touched the inscription as she had before, but now those words of protection only mocked her loneliness and misery. Black was both the color of her sorrow and the powder on her palm. Unlike the powder, however, it would not be washed away by the driving rain.

Her father and the beggar pulled her forcefully from her desolation. Arkthar's actions would not be in vain. Mah Lin knew that in the warrior's world a pure sacrifice is offered to seek the favor of his god, perhaps it is not so different here. The horses carried them through the expanse of that clearing and onward to where the warrior's fire had liberated the fractured ruins of the protecting wall.

They rode through the forgotten stones onto the side of the dry moat's trench; they passed through Death's cold gateway and into exile.

THE MEASURE TAKEN

Mah Lin once told me that my horse's breed is of the desert land from whence they claimed me. A heavenly horse he had called it. At full speed the rhythm of its beating hooves sounded like the drums of battle. I wondered if it would truly sweat blood like the priest had said. Before the animal had broken into a full and furious lather, I came upon a party of twelve advancing scouts. Although the rhythmic pounding of our approach was far from stealthy, they stood shocked and frozen by our sudden appearance. It was the costly moment of indecision that often comes before defeat, and it was through this moment that my steel did cut.

I drew first blood. My weapon moved so swiftly that the eye could not see it, and with the beginnings of a scream the first man fell and writhed upon the damp dark ground. My sword found the next closest, and he made not sound nor movement from where he lay. Fear and confusion gripped them tightly, as they encircled us as best they could. I descended from my perch and sliced cleanly through the next as I landed. Without command my steed held firmly to my back, and with eyes battle wild, rose and flayed as men fell before him. Back to flank we held fast and met each new attack with steel and hoof.

I saw the largest of the soldiers draw the knife from his leather belt. He hurled it with all his power towards my chest, but with a turn of waist the missile flew past and lodged with a thud in the heart of its launcher's compatriot. The man's eyes widened and he fell without word. My blade flew low to cleave the leg of the next man standing and flashed once more to end the scream.

Their compliance mirrored their relief when I shouted, "Drop your weapons."

With these four men who now held nothing but their fear, I pressed onward to meet the main body. From horseback I could see the one in bear cloak from a great distance as he paced among and yet apart from his men. He stopped in his tracks when we were spotted, and in his long moment of hesitation a voice from deep inside me rang out for all to hear.

"My name is Arkthar. In the language of my people, its meaning is Bear."

The Supreme Commander felt these words fly like a black fletched arrow to the heart of his nightmare, and although the blood drained instantly from his twisted face, his fear was hidden behind the moon bear's fierce visage. He saw the remnants of his elite scouting party standing downcast before me, and he raged openly at their incompetence.

My voice continued.

"Know now that all evil that chooses to come against us shall be crushed, and know that here, by command of the First Emperor, the righteous are protected for all time."

I watched for the response and it came swiftly. A signal from the commander released the arrows, and as the scouts fell before me, my sword cut through the shower of falling arrows like child's play, and within its mist I retreated. At the end of this great volley, the commander strained his vision through the distance to assess the damage inflicted. The commander saw neither horse nor rider. We had disappeared as if by magic, and the memory of the temple mount stung him once again. But on this day he vowed the prey would not elude him, and he screamed the order to advance.

By the time he and his troops had reached the twisted pile of his own dead men, my steed and I had reached our empty home.

THE HARE AND
THE HOUNDS

I had seen 'The Hare and the Hounds' played many times as a child. The rabbit was released into a large flat field and ran terrified toward the safety of the forest. At the count of sixty, the dogs were set free and flew barking after the prey. The bets were made, and we as children laughed and cheered the sport. Seldom did the hare lose, because while the dogs ran only for their dinner, the hare was running for its life.

I had given my family a good head start, and now I would ensure their safe escape. I could hear the horde, as their distance began to close. The din sounded like the snapping and snarling of the winter wolves hunting in a hungry pack, moving on the scent of blood and life. I patted the side of my great steed to calm him for our task. As I drew away my hand I was astonished. The priest was right, they do sweat blood. My amazement vanished when a closer inspection revealed the wound upon his back. It was not mortal, but it would slow us down. I bound it quickly, as best I could, and reassessed the chances of the hare.

When I mounted, the steed reared in painful protest. As I fought to steady him, a long branch of lightning streaked across the blackened sky, and the shimmering rains fell. I took measure of the position of the ever-closing evil and felt the eternal eye of the long dead beast look down from its great height. It begged from clouds for its release. "The Dragon is here," I said to no one.

As I entered the clearing of the great iron guardian, I reached down and drew Mah Lin's steel staff from its place on my charger's flank. I vaulted from my steed up upon the lion's cold wet back. Ignoring the treacherous footing, I climbed high upon its unflinching head and stared up into the char black skies. I raised the bladed tip to salute the maelstrom and drove it down and through the enormous iron mane. From my height I saw the distant forms of men and weapons and waited patiently for the hunters to see me too.

The chase began. I was down in a flash, and upon my wounded horse I rode desperately for the shelter of the wall. Although the distance was not a great one, I could not push my horse beyond a canter. Time slowed painfully. At last the protecting stones appeared before me, and I drove my mount the final lengths to the safety of their far side. I scrambled with sword in hand to the highest peak of the massive blocks and looked back upon the clearing. It filled and swelled with the commander and his murderous troops.

On mass they poured into the clearing like a mindless hunter entering the cave of the great moon bear, and the winds howled with the plaintive cries of her orphaned cubs.

Lightning now overflowed from its heavenly confines and spilt down around me. I raised the Sword of Five Elements and called out to the dragon in the language of my dreams. I saw without thought that I now gripped its handle with my left index finger along its shaft and cradled it with the fist of my right, the position of the vajra mudra.

The elements lay before me. Surrounded by forest wood, the metal effigy stood proud and unrepentant upon the earth while the water of the falling rain washed over all. High above me, fire, the giver and taker of life, lacerated the crow black clouds. I felt Death by my side, as I shouted up through the winds.

I spoke the language from before the time of men.

THE APOCALYPSE

With one great crack the massive bolt of lightning split the heavens and descended with all the force of Thor's great hammer. It flew straight and true, piercing both rain and darkness. Drawn to Mah Lin's steel staff embedded high upon the head of the guardian, it struck, and in that moment linked the earth with the heavens.

My eyes burned with the blinding white flash, and my dark world was lit with the power of a thousand suns. A heartbeat later my ears were deafened by the unleashing of the dragon, another beat within my chest, and I was blown back and off the wall and fell lifeless to the bottom of the deep, damp trench. I did not see the skies rain blood and flesh of those that were once men.

I tumbled backwards through the world of dreams and sensed nothing but the beating of a single drum. Empty silence soon took its place as I sank deeper through a great abyss. In the blackness I heard the old one call my name. I saw the woman dressed in white and listened to her song. Like a fish I swam upwards to the powerful sound of her gentle voice, and at the surface I awoke within her arms. My eyes opened but it was not an ancient face I saw, it was Selah's.

Tears flowed down her cheeks and I watched their forms mingle with the drops of driving rain. The monk and the beggar knelt beside me, their lips moved but I still heard only the rushing winds of my dreams. They had come back for me.

Mah Lin held my sword, and as they helped me to my feet, the sound of the gentling rains returned.

I climbed back to my perch upon the wall and looked to the clearing to see if it had been only a dream. Leafless trees still held their ground. The broken, twisted branches of the blackened trunks held rags and strips that were now the leaves of nightmare. The guardian lion of the First Emperor was gone. A round and blackened scar marked its place upon the earth where it had for so long proudly stood.

The complexion of war had been forever changed, and Death would reap like never before. I heard beneath the silence of a solitary hill, the stirring of the terra cotta soldiers and the waking of an Emperor.

We on four horses, one red, one white, one black, and one pale grey, moved silently beyond the devastation, onward.

THE VALLEY OF DECISION

Most within the fertile glen were dead. The boy had thrown himself upon the ground to call on his god's help. He prayed not for himself, but for his friends, the quarry that he had been forced to chase. Fate had protected him. His selfless and penitent action had secured his salvation. Prostrated upon the ground, the gentle page had felt the unleashing of the dragon. It had emerged from the clouds and stepped from the world of dreams down into the world of men.

In its aftermath he struggled to stand, in tatters and in shock. He stumbled forward, driven only by the primal urge to escape this nightmare. Staggering through the anguish, he thought that he was free. Relief washed over him like the steady downpour, and tears of joy carved channels down his muddied cheeks. Outside the glen he collapsed upon the blood red dirt.

The boy had no idea how long he had lain unconscious, but the coldness of his body spoke of hours. He looked nervously into the glen to see if all remembered might just have been imagined, but it had not. Weapons of war and the broken remnants of life littered the field like the oak leaves of autumn. The odor burned within his nostrils. It was brimstone and fire; it was the smell of death. The page wandered aimless and unsteady, back into the open field unsure of purpose or direction.

The cry of a wounded animal drew his attention, yet he saw no scavengers here to feast upon the dead. Watching and listening, he saw a movement that chilled his soul. Not twenty paces from where he stood, the blackened hide rose and fell and tried once more to come alive. Ironically, it was the moon bear's own hide that shielded and protected the man who had taken her from life and family.

The page moved through the fog of war with only the thought, 'the time is now' to drive him on. Like the walking wounded the page advanced upon the animal, unaware of the muddied boulder he carried between his hands. He drew alongside the commander, paused, and drew new breath. Arkthar's lessons were fresh again upon his mind, 'think nothing, feel nothing.' His arms strained and trembled as the large rock was hoisted high above his head.

The commander collapsed again and rolled over, so that now they met eye to eye, one supine and one stretched tall. All thoughts of murder had compressed into this one defining moment, in an instant he would at last be free. The boy hovered between heaven and earth as he looked upon the man that had menaced him for so long. The commander gazed up at the heavy stone and back to the page that held it. The cruel eyes begged him now, not for life but for freedom from it, and in an instant it was over.

The rock was hurled down landing beside the commander's twisted face with a loud but harmless thud.

SOUTHERN WINDS

She came like the southern winds, unseen by all until she was upon them. She stood before the page, who rubbed his eyes as if waking from a dream. She had changed much since their last encounter, yet he knew her well. Amid the ruins of the mangled grove, she was resplendent. Her silver hair was neatly pinned, and white was the color she now wore. He stared at the leather amulet around her neck from which coins and jade hung like the cascade of a gentle waterfall. She filled his silence with a graceful bow, "I am here to serve, young Lord," she said in a voice much younger than her many years.

She had journeyed far. Over many *li* she had trudged through changing landscapes, and like them, she, too, had been transformed. Since her night with the beggar, the madness no longer came to plague her mind. Her gift of divination faded, new sounds called her from beyond. They began quietly at first, a rustling of dry leaves in a surging breeze. She listened as she walked, and their voices grew clearer. In place and time the dead can speak loudly to the living, and they led the broken oracle along a different path. From her chrysalis of desolation, the sacred shaman had emerged.

She spun slowly, but with balanced precision, taking survey of the destruction that surrounded them. The screams of the wounded filled the air, but far louder to her were the cries of men already dead. Her voice felt to the page like a potent balm on an open wound, "We have much work to do." The young man nodded and drew strength from her presence. The boy felt the winds of change swirling around him. He straightened, collected, and began.

Not trained to the military way, he never the less intuitively brought order. He organized the slightly wounded and the merely terrified into a cohesive working unit. They were responsible for stopping the flow of blood and the binding of broken limbs. In time the moans of the wounded subsided, and many others too damaged to continue, died where the lion had thrown them. He borrowed power from the shaman, who chanted and danced in ceremony to free the spirits of the dead.

Salvage was order, and anything that could be used to carry the wounded home was crafted for its new purpose. When he was satisfied with the progress made on these fronts, he began his dreadful task. From the anguish of men, he moved to address the suffering of the horses. Some were shaken but unscathed, some wounded but not beyond function, and some he dispatched quickly to end their agony. When he had finished this, he turned to reassess the changing needs of the destroyed battalion.

The commander was laid and bound on a level section of the glen. The page assigned an older soldier to tend his wounds and give him water should he ask. None questioned how it was that a mere youth of no rank or stature had taken command. When all is undone, respect is earned by competence and ability, and the boy had both of these. The cart he had seen near the ancient homestead was drawn by hand to the glen. The page looked toward the shaman, who still danced upon the bridge between two worlds. Her gaze directed his attention to the crater where once a lion had stood, and he understood exactly what the next task would be, for the hole was wide and deep.

The needs of the living taken care of, the needs of the dead now followed. Into the pit they were respectfully placed, some whole, most broken, and others just a limb, or head. By late afternoon the field had been cleared. The bodies overflowed the depths of the earthen bowl and formed a mountain, not unlike the one she had climbed before. At the end of her song she spoke the name, "Qin Shi Huang Di."

She bid the page look up at the colorful promise that spanned the sky. In silence the mound was covered with the shattered boughs and branches of what had once been living trees. The fire would burn long into the night, and the woman in white would tend it reverently.

The commander was placed into the horseless cart, the bear hide used to form a harness for the boy to do the pulling. With a grip of iron, he pulled the boy close so that his words would not be lost. "The library," was all he said. The page struggled for a more comfortable distance, and looking down into the eyes of the man, he replied, "yes, lord, do not worry, it is safe."

In all, one hundred and fifty men, made up of both the wounded and the able, returned to the capital. They emerged slowly from this valley, a broken man bound by rags, pulled by a boy now bound by duty.

The page had chosen, and in his choices he had found his freedom.

THE BEGINNING

Selah cleaned and dressed again the wound upon my horse's back. We rode on in the contemplative silence of life's uneasy embrace. The storm had passed and rays of sunlight reached down to touch and warm the earth. The voice of the songbird and the gentle rustle of leaves kissed by the changing winds wove an enchanting melody, but its lightness only added to the burden of our hearts, for our survival had come at a heavy price.

In the distance ahead we saw the glint of silver light reflected through the heavy foliage, like sunset's diamonds upon a now calm sea. We rode towards it at a leisurely pace, drawn by its call. Mah Lin dismounted to investigate further and returned without a word. In his hand he held the length of steel bamboo. The shaft was blackened but not bent, and its blade was even brighter than before. With a graceful spin he tucked it back in place along his stallion's flank.

We were painfully aware that we would soon lose the company of the beggar; his favors bulged beneath his rags. In a way it seemed that he had always been with us, and we with him. As we ate lunch he bid us look back at the sky from where we had come. The promise of the distant rainbow faded only when our meal was done.

The old beggar turned to me and quoted the ancient scholars:

"When human beings interfere with the Way,
the sky becomes as mud,

the earth becomes exhausted,
the balance crumbles,
and a myriad of living creatures become extinct."

As I chewed and swallowed the last of my meal, I tasted these words from the Book of the Way, and thought deeply about the beggar. When we had drained the last of our tea and prepared to ride, he bid us each farewell and blessed us with his grace.

"Our paths now change," he said, and when he tried to return Mah Lin's horse, the monk would not take it. "If wishes were horses then beggars would ride." The monk said, as the beggar flashed his toothless smile and swung his body upward. Mounted, the beggar sat tall and straight in the saddle and looked not old at all. He turned his pale steed towards me and said, "Young King, we will meet again." Turning away he set out in a northern direction.

I called to him as he began to leave, "Beggar, I don't even know your name." To which he laughed, and even the monk seemed amused. The black rider paused, steadied his mount, and caught my eye.

"Arkthar, I have had many names through many times, but I assure you, you do indeed know well my name. Remember me kindly in your writing, Arkthar, for in the world of men I am already much maligned."

With that he turned and was on his way, and we were once more three in number. To the piercing call of Selah's black-eyed pet we moved on, for there was no longer a place in this land for us. When what remains of the battalion finally staggers back to the capital, the full fury of imperial power will be released against us. As ominous as this truth was, it could not detract from our joy to have each other.

By evening's muted light, Mah Lin laid out our new direction, "We return to the western frontier not far from where we claimed you. There is a thriving community of monks there, men who know the value of the sacred word. The hot, dry climate here suits well the task of preservation. In the high cliffs that guard them, we will hide the wisdom of the ages, to be resurrected only when all truth in the outside world is lost in war and greed."

He paused to let his words sink in, and then continued, "It is a place called Dunhuang. The brothers there will supply us with all we need for the long and perilous journey ahead." His eyes held us, "I suggest we might find refuge in the land of Arkthar's birth."

Despite the seriousness of the monk's tone and the danger that it conveyed, the thought of returning to my homeland pleased me. I had under my armor the broad-point that had almost taken Selah's life. In the land from which I had been stolen, I will fire up a forge and hammer it into a ring of Celtic knots. Under oak and in the presence of the monk, I will ease it on her finger, for in truth, she is the stone that will forever sharpen the edge of steel. In each of our minds the spark of hope rekindled. For now, however, we rode on and did not even cast a glance at Mah Lin's dragon compass.

So it was that as quickly as one life together had ended another one had begun; one journey finished and another started. It has been this way since before the time of men. Beginnings and endings eternally bound together like the great dragon holding the tip of its long tail between its powerful teeth as it rests within its lair.

EPILOGUE

They made their way westward. As sunset approached, the warrior, the witch, and the wizard made camp beside a tranquil lake. Its waters spanned the horizon, and gave them a dinner of fresh pulled greens and fresh caught fish. These were bigger by far than the rainbow species of their land and held an earthy taste. The blue smoke of the cooking fire descended gently and hovered closely over the surface of the lake. They sat quietly as the sun painted warm colors on cloud, smoke, and water, before disappearing over the earth's far edge.

His children were tired and fell asleep together even before all the stars had made their appearance. The monk, however, was not. He took his bladed steel and slung a traveling bag across his shoulder. He began to climb up towards a high rocky outcrop. His upward journey leveled off, and soon he passed through a clearing and emerged upon the flat granite cliff top.

Here between heaven and earth he began to move by full moon's light. The blackened hollow staff whirled and sang as the night air rushed over the tiny hole. Within an hour he was drenched in sweat, his silk robe clung to his muscular frame, and he pushed himself onward. Fully spent, he lay with his back against the granite floor and stared up into the clear night sky. From his lone vantage, it seemed as if the heavens revolved around him. Here he lay, watching from its center.

The monk contemplated the weapon of Thor. The lightning issues with blinding light, and eventually the thunder sounds to mark its passing. Mah Lin saw the mighty bolt descend within the glade. He suspected now that the ensuing thunder was held within his hands. It had taken form months before. It had arrived quietly, and until now gone unnoticed and unrecognized. The staff created as a basic weapon had not changed in appearance, but in purpose. He saw a new invention, one that held a dreadful promise.

Sitting upright, he looked out over moonlit lake from his high vantage on the cliffs, and prayed.

The dawn arrived quickly, and night stars yielded to the growing brightness of the sky. Mah Lin stood and briefly stretched, he felt refreshed even though his night had been sleepless. Like the wizened oracle, he sat cross-legged and opened the satchel he had brought with him. From within he removed an arrow, a stick of temple incense, and a small leather pouch. The thin smoke trail rose as the stick burned, mingling with the fragrances of the new day. His weapon rested across his lap as he loosened the pouch strings.

He held the arrow and ran his finger gently over its black raven feathers. His strong hands moved to its iron tip and snapped it off with an ease that belied the strength of the wooden shaft. Discarding the deadly tip, he poured the black powder from the pouch through the small singing hole of his metal staff. From beneath his robe, he took the silver thunderbolt and swathed its lower end in sphagnum pulled from his granite base. Into the hollow end of his weapon, he placed the moss-wrapped vajra, and with the headless wooden arrow, plunged it down to meet the powder.

The priest stood and drew fresh breath and stuck his blade into a crack in the rocks so that it angled toward the lake. Mah Lin gazed sadly out over the horizon. "It is time," he said to himself as he held the burning incense in his hand.

The priest pushed the burning ember tip into the hole. With

a mighty crack and a flash of smoke and flame, the barrel emptied and the world forever changed. The wondrous symphony of morning songbird was instantly silenced, as the echoes of the explosion dimmed and faded. The cloud of blue grey smoke momentarily wrapped the priest, then drifted and disappeared. Mah Lin's features remained stern and unshakeable. In his hand he held a new weapon, and he felt the need for haste.

More than a mile away the sharp-eyed raven saw the small splash far below him. Swooping low it watched the rings spread concentrically over the polished surface, as the silver steel thunderbolt sank quietly beneath the dark lake waters.

HISTORICAL NOTE

After a time of wandering the countryside during a period of great famine a young Daoist priest settled at the sacred Mogao grotto complex in Dunhuang. Wang Yuan-lu (1849-1931), was determined to restore the site which had fallen into disrepair. In 1900 his accidental discovery of a sealed up cave (Cave 17, presently known as the Library Cave) revealed the priceless treasure of an ancient library perfectly preserved by the dry desert climate.

Most of the manuscripts dated between the 4th and the 11th centuries are Buddhist, as well as Daoist, Manichean, and Nestorian Christians. The manuscripts, on paper, silk, wood, and other materials are paintings, printings, and writings in many languages, including Sanskrit, Tibetan, Tangut, and even Hebrew in addition to Chinese. Their contents cover religion, history, literature, astronomy, and astrology.

Dunhuang, once a thriving outpost, lies at the gateway to the Silk Road, which in ancient times was the primary entrance and exit to all of China. Scholars still speculate as to why the Library came to be hidden there, and by whom.

Acknowledgements

When I was a young man I lived with my Aunt Evelyn on her small farm in Ireland's rugged County Mayo. By the hearth's turf fire she spoke of Irish culture and history. She talked often of the Storytellers, "mighty men who once walked the whole width and breadth of Ireland for a buttered slice of thick soda bread, a drop of whiskey, and an audience."

"They are rare now," she said, "disappearing like the Old Ways, replaced by this modern age." It was her opinion that "stories surround them like the air, and the dying art of the teller is rooted simply in their ability to inhale and remember the language of their dreams."

Many years have passed, and I am forever grateful for that time, hopeful that now I may finally have learned to listen, to breathe, and to remember.

The journey from story to book has been a wonderful one, and I owe a debt to many along the way. I would thank my friend Jody Amblard who told me I can write well, for belief is the beginning of magic. My children also had an important role. My son Umojah sat spellbound while I read aloud to him chapter by chapter, and at the end of each would kindly share his thoughts and feelings. My daughter Naomi who loves to read said only that she will wait until it is a real book. If magic is kindled by belief, it is fueled by faith, and hers was unwavering.

Finally, I want to acknowledge the people of YMAA publishing, for without them there would be no book. In this time of economic uncertainty, David Ripianzi was brave enough to publish the first novel of a relatively new writer. David Silver generously shared his wealth of martial arts knowledge with me; it was his insight that added depth and dimension to the bones of my tale.

My editor Leslie Takao's work on this project will never receive the full recognition that it truly deserves. If the reader enjoys a turn of phrase or the clear expression of a complex thought, there is a great chance that she is behind it. Without her unwearied and prolonged effort, this work would be like armor that is dull in the bright sunlight, or a sword that has not been well sharpened for the battle ahead.

From my heart I thank you all.

About the Author

Vincent Pratchett was born to an Irish mother and English father. The Irish tradition of storytellers on one side, and accomplished writers on the other. He is related by blood to renowned fantasy novelist Terry Pratchett. Vincent's writing includes novels, screenplays, children's storybooks, and numerous magazine articles.

He began training in the martial arts at age ten. He has taught martial arts at the University of Guelph, and Qigong at the Ontario College of Traditional Chinese Medicine.

As a young man Vincent traveled across Asia, walking in the footsteps of Alexander the Great, Marco Polo, and Genghis Khan. He settled eventually in Hong Kong where he worked as a bouncer for a prominent nightclub until breaking into the Hong Kong film industry as an actor and stuntman.

Returning to Canada, Vincent became a professional firefighter and continues to teach and train in martial arts. He resides in Toronto, with his two children.